DESERT BASE STRIKE

GUSTAVO BONDONI

SEVERED PRESS
HOBART TASMANIA

DESERT BASE STRIKE

CHAPTER 1

"That's stupid," Johanna said, as they walked through the mall in the general direction of the food court, where the rest of the sophomores waited. "No way they're bringing back the *Outside* series for another season. They got off the planet and rescued the girl in the last episode. What else can they do?"

Rita seethed. She was a much bigger fan of science fiction series—*any* science fiction series—than Johanna was. "But don't you want to know how it goes between them? Aren't you curious to see how Emily adapts to real life on Tau Ceti? Or, for that matter, how they're going to download her onto a real body so she can actually live there?"

"Not really," Johanna replied.

"But…" Rita never finished her sentence.

Glass broke behind them and they turned to see some kind of huge grey animal—at least seven feet high—tear away the metal frames of the outside doors that had gotten wrapped around its neck.

At first, Johanna thought it was a rhino. It looked that way in the distance, but when it finally got clear of the frames and stretched, she realized it was some kind of huge, bipedal reptile.

Rita's scream spurred Johanna into action. With a shouted "Come on!" Johanna ran across the mall and dove under a steel sculpture of a horse. She'd never understood why the mall insisted on having an art exhibit in the main hall—no one ever noticed the art, unless it was to vandalize it—but she was grateful for it now. These sculptures looked like they could take a pounding.

She wedged herself under the brown-painted iron and turned to look for Rita.

Rita hadn't followed. She was still standing paralyzed in the middle of the main hall.

"No! Rita, get out of there. Run!"

Rita turned toward Johanna's voice, a dumb expression on her face. Before she could react, however, the massive grey form bowled her over and her skull slammed into the ground. Johanna wanted to scream, but she held it back. That thing would hear her and…

And it would do what it was doing to Rita. It sniffed the prone girl and poked it with an exploratory foot claw. Apparently convinced that its prey wouldn't fight back, it opened a mouth full of sharp teeth an inch long, and it bit down on the exposed skin of Rita's neck.

Johanna did scream this time.

Her anguish attracted more of the things. They must have entered the mall when she wasn't looking, and now she could hear them scratching against the metal around her. A claw raked her arm, but the monsters weren't strong enough to move the sculpture, and they weren't heavy enough to push them.

A grey snub-nose with red markings snuffled inches from her face, but it couldn't get far enough to grab her. A yellow eye with a vertical slit gazed evilly at her, the naked hunger obvious in it.

Johanna heard yells from somewhere else in the mall and the head and eye disappeared. She saw the creature pad away, occasionally slipping on the polished floor of the mall.

Clickety-clack, went the claws on the cement.

Johanna realized that there were several of the monsters in the mall. Anyone coming towards this exit would find their way blocked.

And they would die.

But that wasn't Johanna's problem right now. Her interest in other people's well-being had ended when Rita had her throat ripped out. She tore her eyes away from the bloody pile of rags that had once been the best friend anyone could ever have and turned towards the exit door.

There was nothing between her and the mangled entrance. The monsters had gone further inside.

She slipped off her boots—the heels always made a lot of noise—and carefully edged out of her hiding place. Once out she cast one last look behind her. The monsters were twenty yards away, so she ran.

A squeak behind told her she'd been spotted. The clacking told her the monster was gaining.

She was nearly out the door, but what difference would it make? The thing could tear her to pieces just as easily outside as inside. Johanna imagined she could feel its breath on her back.

She screamed. Not in terror, but from pain. For a second she thought the thing had grabbed her foot... but then she realized that it was just the glass from the mangled door cutting into her soles.

Fighting back the pain, she forced herself to go on. Even if she could only survive a few more seconds, it would be worth it. She didn't want to die.

But it looked inevitable. She was barely five yards out of the mall when she saw the monster emerge. It was gaining fast.

Johanna could barely stay on her feet. The glass had cut her to ribbons and, judging by the way she felt, a lot of it was still in her feet. She stumbled at the curb and hit the street hard, shoulder-first.

The monster behind her crouched and tensed to leap.

Then it staggered and fell to the ground beside her, a round hole as thick as her thumb oozing blood onto the blacktop.

Arms grabbed her and Rita found herself hauled onto the broad shoulders of a man in the light brown uniform of the Sheriff's Office. The man ran as well as he could under the burden, past a barricade of police cars, and deposited her in the arms of a paramedic.

"You're safe," the man said. "It's all right."

Now, she sobbed. "No, it isn't. It will never be all right again."

She hugged him hard, but it didn't seem to help. All Johanna could think of was how casually the monster had killed her best friend. Like the vibrant young woman from June High was just a prey animal, so much meat to satisfy the hunger of a larger animal with big teeth.

Johanna cried.

***

Abdou sweated profusely.

Night shouldn't be this hot. Night was the time given to man to rest from the heat. His people knew all about heat, and trying to escape its clutches... but they also knew that heat was fair, sent by God to test the men of the desert, but not to bow them over. Strong men would wait out the day and recover their strength at night.

But the way of his homeland didn't work here, in the tropical forests of central Nigeria. Here, the heat was wet and sticky. It wasn't the clean, dry heat of his beloved desert. And it didn't stop draining your energy merely because the sun had gone down.

But he had his orders. Bringing the butchers of Boko Haram under control was a joint effort between the Nigerian Army and that of Niger. He was honored to represent his country. A lot of people forgot that Niger existed, and that what created problems for their larger neighbor to the south was also a problem for them.

Of course, a lot of it had to do with the fact that he spoke English better than most of his peers.

He crouched next to a man named Samuel, a Captain in the Nigerian Army. The third man with them was called Porter and, though he professed to be descended from Nigerians, he was a huge man—perhaps not much taller than the rest of the soldiers, but broader in every dimension... and every gram of his body was muscle.

The huge man was American, and he was the reason the task force had come here, so far from the Boko Haram's usual haunts in northeast Nigeria. The man had intelligence that spoke of a new base of operations here in the center of the country, another step towards ensuring that no Nigerian would ever feel safe from the group's campaign of terror.

Unfortunately, it was in a dense, humid forest full of insects and mud. An awful, unclean place.

On the bright side, Porter was even more uncomfortable than the Africans. He swatted some bug that got into his face, and spoke in a whisper: "Are your teams in position?"

"Yes," Samuel replied. "They're waiting for our signal."

Porter looked into the handheld screen he was carrying. "The drone is showing a big heat signature. We should go now while they're all packed together."

"So I can send my men in?"

"Yes."

Technically, they weren't all Samuel's men. At least a third of them reported to Abdou, but for the purposes of the operation, they'd decided to put everyone under Nigerian command.

Samuel spoke into the mike on his headset. "Go, go, go!"

They were perched on a slight rise overlooking the wooded hollow where the enemy had set up their base. Abdou had been surprised at how close they'd been able to approach. They'd expected sentries, tripwires, something... but nothing had impeded their progress. The drone's infrared and UV had shown that nothing bigger than a rat was moving outside of that clump of trees.

Except for their little group and the twenty men they'd brought with them.

A hundred meters away, shooting started. The unmistakable clatter of Ak-47s cut through the humid air. Unfortunately, there was no way to tell whose weapons they were. Everyone in Africa used the same basic rifle.

"Report," Samuel said, no longer bothering to be silent. "Have you made contact with the enemy?"

Static came in over the radio, punctuated by words Abdou couldn't catch, a shouted warning and then... nothing.

"We need to get down there," Abdou said.

"Stay here," the American replied, looking into his screen. "There's no need to run in that direction: they're coming this way. Look."

He showed them the screen. Orange dots moved across a green background. Abdou had no idea what he was supposed to be looking at. He had the basic knowledge that any soldier would of night vision and heat detection, but it was impossible to tell which way was which on that screen.

"If you say so," he replied.

"Your men must be pushing them this way. They'll walk right into us," Porter replied. He checked the safety on his own rifle, some American thing that looked too modern—and too fragile—to work in the primeval African night. "They should have posted sentries. Now, they're gonna pay the price."

They could see the trees—short, wispy things—moving on the slope beneath them. But it wasn't really necessary to watch the entire slope: the only way a man could get up the hill without hacking through fifty meters of brush was along the well-worn path. If anyone tried to come up that way, they'd have plenty of time to react and to cut them apart with the machine guns.

"Here they come," Samuel said. Abdou rolled his eyes: the man was a talker. No competent soldier would have risked giving away their ambush just to make an inane—and obvious—comment.

A figure—a darker shadow in the night—burst out of the path and came towards them. Abdou would have waited for more of the enemy to show themselves, but Samuel was having none of it. With a shout of "Nigeria!" he stood up and opened fire.

The figure dropped to the ground and all three of them waited in silence for his compatriots to return fire.

Nothing happened.

"Let's go see who we bagged," Porter said.

"Wait," Abdou replied. "What's your screen saying?"

"The drone was low on batteries and landed back at the original site. But they've got to be coming. Just keep an eye on the path," Porter said. "I'll see if our friend over there is breathing. Would be nice to grab one or two alive."

The American advanced towards the fallen enemy and Abdou stopped to admire it. The man was well-trained and moved through the night like a wraith. Even knowing where he was, it was difficult to find the man in the night. Only when he had to cross an open area did Abdou see him clearly. Then he was gone again, kneeling beside the enemy.

"What the fuck?"

The voice carried through the night and Abdou jumped, not so much at the exclamation itself but at the fact that this soldier who'd seemed to be the embodiment of modern warfare could possibly forget himself to the point where he'd speak openly like that. What had happened?

Abdou started to advance towards the American's position.

But then, the forest came alive. From out of the growth around the path, a dozen dark forms emerged. They were much too big to be soldiers, unless they were wearing some exotic kind of body armor.

Samuel's gun began to fire. The man screamed curses, challenges and threats at the figures before him. He might be undisciplined, but you couldn't fault his bravery.

Abdou's own courage failed him, however. He wasn't equipped to fight a dozen or more soldiers in suits. He turned to run.

Something grabbed his ankle and pain shot through him as he fell to the ground. He looked down to see what he'd caught his leg on, only to find that his leg was nothing more than a bloody stump that ended halfway down his shin. Had they shot his leg off? What were they using?

A dark figure loomed over him and, he tried to crawl away, backwards, showing his hands to display the fact that he'd dropped his rifle and was unarmed.

The figure emerged from the shadows and, for a fleeting moment it was visible in the moonlight.

That was when Abdou understood he was a dead man. The dragon towering over him didn't care if he was armed or not. It wasn't there to accept his surrender.

The last thing he saw was the moonlight glinting off teeth in the largest open mouth he'd ever seen.

***

Wao Tang smiled as the motors strained against the weight of the fully-laden nets and a sharp wind blew out from the leaden sky of the deep south.

He loved fishing the waters just off the Patagonian coast. The combination of bountiful fisheries, the incompetence of the Argentine Coast Guard to keep unauthorized ships like his from their activities and the fact that not many people came all the way from overcrowded Asia to the underpopulated tip of South America made the pickings rich ones indeed. And with his factory on board, he didn't need to rush to port to get the catch processed. He could fish at his leisure.

The only thing you needed to be careful of was not to go too close to the Falklands… the British got touchy about that.

The weather helped as well. The overcast would keep him hidden in case the Argentine Navy decided to do any aerial patrols. That was the one thing that could put a damper on the afternoon: the Argentines couldn't cover the entire coast with the equipment they had, but if one did have the misfortune to get spotted, they could be trigger-happy. There had been several instances of the Argentine Coast Guard opening fire on Chinese-flag vessels over the past decade, even the sinking of a factory ship just like his own.

But that would never happen to Wao Tang. He was much too smart for such a primitive military.

He shouted orders to his crew, even though they were perfectly capable of operating without his guidance. The way to keep his crew working well was for the captain to assert his authority.

"Hu! Slow the winch down. We're in no hurry," he shouted down to his first mate. The man remained expressionless and obeyed the order. That was how it should be.

Tang smiled to himself. In fact, Hu had probably known what he was going to ask for and merely pretended to follow the order. You couldn't hear anything with the howling wind.

At least the seas hadn't gotten really rough yet. They'd have time to secure the catch before it got too choppy.

A man in a red jacket was waving to him from the stern of the ship. Tang recognized the jacket: it was Li. But he couldn't hear a word the man was saying. He motioned for the sailor to come up onto the bridge.

The man shook his head and pointed into the water behind the ship.

For a panicked moment, Tang thought there might be something wrong with a cable. A frayed line could cost them the day's work.

But no one else seemed to be concerned, not even the men whose job it was to monitor such things.

Besides, even if a problem existed, Li had to obey orders without question. There could be no exceptions.

Tang motioned for the sailor to approach, and the man did so, reluctantly.

When Li arrived, he bowed deeply. "I'm sorry, but…"

"But nothing," Tang retorted. "You cannot disobey my commands, even under the most dire of circumstances. Is that understood?"

Li bowed deeper. "Yes."

"Good. Now tell me what was so important that you had to make me look a fool in front of my entire crew."

"There's… there's something following us. Black. Big. I think it might be a submarine."

With those words, Tang forgot about discipline. The forms had been followed, and now it was time for drastic action.

"Come with me."

They sprinted towards the back of the ship.

Li was right. There was a huge dark shadow visible beneath the surface about a hundred meters behind them.

Tang looked up. Those dark forms were usually shadows, but the weak grey light coming through the overcast wouldn't give such sharply defined shade.

There was definitely something down there.

"Ask Hu how far the net is."

Li sprinted towards the man and returned, panting. "He says it's eighty-five meters back."

"Could that be the net down there?"

Li peered at the shadow. "Not unless it's floating close to the surface." Then he shook his head. "No. The net would have had to break for it to be so long and thin. Hu would have noticed."

A ball of ice formed in Tang's stomach. The Argentine submarine fleet might be ancient and slow, but if he got one tangled in his nets, his ship was in deep trouble. For one thing, he would need to cut the net and run.

If the submarine sank because of his actions, that would cause an international incident. Beijing was perfectly content to let Chinese ships fish wherever they felt like fishing, but they would draw the line at damaging a sovereign naval vessel, especially if people died. That could only end in imprisonment and disgrace.

The worst of all scenarios, of course, would be that the submarine managed to untangle itself and come after them. He doubted they had torpedoes, but the Bofors 40 mm deck guns were more than enough to sink an unarmed factory ship... as the Argentine Coast Guard had already proved.

What could they do?

The decision was taken out of his hands. Something tugged on the lines of the netting.

"Cut and run!" he shouted, and ran towards Hu. It was a disaster, but anything else would be worse. With luck, no one would know it was their ship that had caused the accident.

The seas behind them began to froth so violently that he heard the sound over the wind, a noise like distant thunder or an approaching train.

Tang turned to look.

The sea was a mass of white foam, the surface moving and rippling. It took Tang a moment to understand what he was seeing.

The net had reached the surface somehow, and it had split open to reveal its wriggling cargo of squid and fish, glistening in the grey light.

Then the net seemed to explode.

Tang watched one fish—he couldn't tell what it was—fly a hundred meters in the air, impelled by the power of the event. It described a perfect parabola before smashing itself to slivers on the deck ten yards away.

It left a huge dent in the steel bulkhead.

"Run!" Tang repeated.

But his crew were all frozen, staring at the thing that emerged from among the writhing fish.

A snub-nosed cylinder fifteen meters wide, bluish-grey and pockmarked, shot from the water as if mounted on a rocket.

Thirty meters of it hung suspended in the air, trailing streamers of foamy water, and then it fell.

"A monster!" Li screamed.

"It can't be..." Tang said. But he knew it was. Not a whale, no whale ever grew that big. One of the monsters from the nightmares of every sailor since the beginning of time rose before him.

The colossus hit the water with a splash that sent waves that rocked the ship.

"I said run! So run! Engines at full power!"

This time his order went through, and he felt the humming of the diesel motors vibrating through the deck as they strained to accelerate.

The monster behind them must have heard. It turned towards them and opened its mouth.

The monster roared a challenge.

"Move!" Tang told his crew.

But the cavitating screws didn't manage to accelerate the ship quickly enough. The monster rammed them from behind and threw Tang to the floor.

The second roar seemed tinged with pain. Had the propellers hurt the creature?

Tang didn't know, and would never learn. The monster reared up into the air again and its motion brought it down right in the center of the fishing boat, breaking it in half.

But Tang didn't drown. He was under the monster when it hit his deck.

CHAPTER 2

The faces looked back at him grimly. No one, but no one was happy to be there.

Hermes didn't give a damn. He didn't want to be a monster hunter. It wasn't the reason he'd been in the military for almost his entire life. But, like the people around this table, he'd been made an offer he couldn't refuse. The only difference was that the four men and one woman sitting with him didn't know it yet.

"I suppose you're wondering why I brought you here," he said. It would be strange if they weren't: it wasn't every day that you got a flight to Malta and three nights in a five-star hotel without anything else in the way of explanation.

Max Alexeyev, a tall blond man who'd been a Spetsnaz soldier until a month before, shrugged. "You're putting together a team." He pointed at Irina Olenko. "I know who she is, so whatever we're expected to do, it's not legal or above board. Those two look like they know what they're doing." This was directed towards the two Africans. Then he pointed to Balzano: "And he was on the news. If I had to guess, I'd think we're going somewhere none of us want to be, and there will be extremely dangerous people there. And even more dangerous things."

Hermes nodded. "More things than people."

Alexeyev nodded. "I suspected as much. If you don't mind, I'll leave before I hear anything that will make me a threat to your operational security. I don't want to live the rest of my life looking over my shoulder because you want to tie up loose ends. So I'd rather not know what you're going to do with the monsters."

"No one is going to come gunning for you if you decide to sit this out," Hermes replied. That was the truth. The strike they were planning—at least the endgame-was going to make global headlines. Everyone on the planet would know the details once the journos got hold of it, which meant that anything Alexeyev might know would be in the public domain anyhow. He could tell Max wasn't convinced, though, so he tried another tack. "Where will you go? You know you'll never get another job in Russia."

Max had been a model soldier, but his Spetsnaz unit had run afoul of an SRV program so black that even after Max blew it to pieces, no one admitted it had ever happened. The official line was that the monsters had migrated to Yekaterinburg without any human help. A spokesperson had actually shrugged on worldwide news and explained that the Ural Mountains were a very big place, and that no one knew what happened in the forests.

"I'll find something," Alexeyev replied.

"But you won't find anything without dinosaurs. I'd like to show you a video. It's not sensitive to the mission itself, so you can rest assured that it won't put you at risk. It's from a military operation in Africa. It's a short clip. Would you stay for it?"

Alexeyev nodded. Reluctantly, but he nodded.

The clip showed a group of African soldiers getting massacred by what could only be described as monsters. Upright saurians that ran them down and tore them apart.

"This footage was filmed by the CIA," Hermes told them. "But it was abandoned at the site when things went sideways. They thought they were going after a regional Boko Haram HQ. They weren't expecting to run into those things." He looked around the table. "What you're looking at there is the battlefield of the future. Genetically modified creatures are being funneled to every terrorist group and insurrection on the planet. Even the mob has expressed interest. Human forces will need to learn to fight both alongside and against well-trained and well-armored saurian." He turned to Alexeyev. "You're not going to be able to run from this. And I'm offering good money."

Max thought about it for a long time. Finally, he sighed. "All right. I'll bite. What are you planning?"

"I want to take out the factory building the creatures," Hermes replied.

"Why would you do that? You don't look like the type to run a dangerous operation just for the good of humanity."

"There is nothing in the world that concerns me less than the good of humanity," Hermes replied with a half-smile. "But this is actually a legitimate commission from a major government."

"One of the dodgy ones, I bet," the South African said. Giniel Voornarcht was a South African mercenary with red skin from a lifetime spent in the sun and a long scar running from his left eye down to his neck. He was actually the person that concerned Hermes the least. The fee was more than the man usually commanded. If one person would join, it was Voornacht.

"You'd be surprised," Hermes replied.

"But I won't be enlightened."

"Naturally not."

"Good. I like the compartmentalization. I'm in," the South African said.

"Me too." Irina Olenko had no real choice. She'd defected from Russian intelligence and her options were to lie low and surround herself with armed compatriots or disappear from the face of the Earth, where her few remaining days would pass in the most sadistic torture and abuse that some very skilled SRV bastards could dream up.

"I'll help," Javier Balzano replied. He was dark-haired and brown-eyed, though his skin was actually lighter-toned than Voornacht's. "I've seen what happens when these creatures are loose." Then he looked around the table. "But I think I'm not like the other people here. I'm a soldier, but I've never seen combat. Well, not real combat against another army. And I'm not special forces."

To Hermes' surprise, it was Alexeyev who came to Balzano's aid. "What I saw on the news... Did that really happen the way the reporters said it did?"

"Yes." There was no duplicity in this guy. He was exactly what it said on the tin: an officer in the Argentine Army—a very minor institution even on a regional scale, but one that held to the traditions of an eventful past.

"Then you're a badass. I don't care if you never went through elite forces school." Then Max turned to Hermes. "I suppose I don't have anything better to do. What the hell. I'll do it."

Every eye turned to the remaining African. Unlike the rest of them, this guy was wearing his uniform, the dark green of the Gabonese Army. "That video from Africa, where did you film it?" he said.

"On the Nigerian side of the border with Niger."

"That's a thousand kilometers from Gabon," he replied.

"I'm aware of that," Hermes said. "But that mall where the people got attacked was thousands of kilometers further than that... and the monsters are there, too. They'll get to Gabon. And besides, you have experience with these creatures that none of the soldiers who've fought them can match."

Now the eyes on the big black man were curious. "Our friend Major Dini Louembe is the man who tracked the dragon in Ndogo Lagoon."

There were some half-hearted nods. With all the monsters popping up in Europe and North America, few people stopped to worry about Africa.

"He is probably the most experienced tracker of genetically modified reptilian life forms available today."

The heads nodded. All of these people had been out in the wilderness long enough to respect the skill involved in following an animal in an environment that was not built for humans. Besides, he looked the part. Even seated, you could tell that he was tall, well-muscled and fit.

He seemed unmoved, however. "I am here because my government asked me to be here. If they recall me, I will leave." Then he grinned at Alexeyev. "And if someone decides that I know too much, they'll have to come and get me if they want to kill me. The Gabonese wilderness is not a fun place to do that."

"If you make it back," Max said darkly.

Louembe shrugged. "No one lives forever."

"Good. Since you're all aboard, and you know why Major Louembe is on the team, I can tell you a little about the rest of your companions. Let's start with Colonel Balzano whom you've probably already seen on TV. He is with the Argentine Army, and his experience actually comes from fighting survivors. These were actual reptiles from the dinosaur age, not genetically modified versions of the monsters. In Antarctica. He was the highest-ranking survivor of a large expedition and, according to witnesses, the main reason there were any survivors at all. He has fought these creatures and lived to tell the story.

"Max Alexeyev was a Spetsnaz officer who tangled with creatures escaped from a lab in Yekaterinburg. They were under the protection of the SRV, so his fight was two-pronged. The fact that he came out victorious with only four men at his disposal is quite impressive.

"Mr. Voornacht is a long-time mercenary from South Africa. His area of influence spans from Namibia to Sierra Leone, and he has seen the blood diamond factions employing the creatures in tactical ways. That knowledge will likely be very valuable for us." Hermes carefully avoided sharing his speculations about which side of the blood diamond wars Voornacht had fought on, mainly because Louembe would have very strong opinions on the matter.

"And finally, Irina Olenko was in Antarctica after the Argentines abandoned their base, and she is an expert on what happens after creatures with certain genetic information die. It's not pretty." Irina had the palest skin of the lot and black hair.

"She's a rogue geneticist turned assassin," Alexeyev said. "She's on every wanted list in Russia."

"Yes," Hermes replied. "But if things had played out just a little differently, the same would have been said of you."

That got him a grunt.

"There's one person missing. We'd like to know who's coordinating," Balzano said.

Actually, the Argentine Colonel was more correct than he knew. The final piece of this team was a man who went by many aliases. Some called him Brown, others Sked, but everyone who knew him knew that he was the guy you called for when you needed both field-proven muscle and a world class hacker... but wanted only one man in-theater, to avoid premature detection. Unfortunately, Sked had just laughed and walked off when Hermes approached. They'd have to do without that particular guy... but at least the talent in the room was impressive.

"As for me," he said, "I'm pretty much your basic Belgian commando turned mercenary troop general. I can shoot and I won't complain if we spend a week camping in the rain, but I also have decades of knowledge in how to organize teams for anything from a large battle to a tiny insertion." He grinned and held up his phone. "More importantly, I have just transferred the money to each of your accounts."

Alexeyev nodded. "All right, then. Tell us about this mission."

"We're going after the lab that produces the monsters. It's run by a man named Park Sun-Lee."

"That bastard is still alive?" Max said.

Hermes nodded. An added bonus of having Alexeyev on the team was that he knew the North Korean scientist by sight. After defecting away from the communist régime in his home country, Sun-Lee had been employed by the Russian government—or at least some shadowy splinters of it—until he'd defected yet again and gone freelance. "Alive and well and living in Africa."

"Where in Africa?"

"We're zeroing in on that right now."

The faces looked back at him, grim again. "Which means you don't know," Voornacht said, speaking for the group. "So how are we supposed to break their lab if we're still looking for it?"

"Because we have a man on the inside at one of their clients. An insurgent group from Northern India is going to take delivery of some really nasty carnivores in four days' time, and we'll be there when they do. They're supposed to receive information about the pickup point within the next twenty-four hours... and they'll need to jump through some serious logistics hoops to get their Hercules down nearby. If they can make it, so can we."

"Is there anything we actually know? Africa is a large continent," Balzano said.

"We know they're not in Gabon," Louembe replied.

"That doesn't account for much, though," Max interjected. "Gabon is a tiny speck. My money would be on the Congo. It's utterly lawless but overflowing with Chinese money. A natural place to hide something like that." He thought about it for some minutes. "Or maybe the border between the Islamic north and the tribal and Christian south. Somewhere near where they filmed that video you showed us. In Nigeria."

"We don't need to speculate," Hermes said. "We'll know for sure within twenty-four hours."

"All right." But he still didn't look happy. None of them did. While they were perfectly fine with operational security, soldiers the world over preferred to know the terrain they'd be expected to perform upon.

Hermes passed out manila folders. "We're not flying completely blind. I do have some information for you. In those folders is everything we know about Park Sun-Lee and the monsters we know they can create. Everything from the creatures Balzano faced in Antarctica to the most impressive of the non-generic mashups is in there. We also know that Park isn't working alone. His partner is a man named Philippe LeFray, although he has gone by so many aliases since leaving France we hardly know what to call him."

"I don't need to know his name. Just show me a pic so I know between which pair of eyes to put the bullet," Alexeyev said.

"It's in the file. The main thing you need to know is that we'd like to take LeFray, or whatever he's calling himself, alive." He nodded towards Louembe. "Gabon is only the first of a list of countries who want to put him on trial."

"Why?"

"For dumping monsters into the mangrove swamps. It tends to disrupt the ecology," Louembe said. "And I suspect that after he gets out of jail, the French will want to drop him down a deep hole. Rogue geneticists are quite an embarrassment."

"All right," Alexeyev said. "I suppose the Frenchman will live, but nothing you can do or say will keep me from putting Sun-Lee down like the rabid dog he is."

Hermes met the soldier's gaze unflinchingly. "He's all yours."

***

Philippe finished putting the final touches on the shipment. The cavernous loading bay—a concrete cave shaped like a gigantic mail slot—was covered in fine grit and sand. Conditions were very much not the kind that you'd use for delicate biological specimens.

Except the things in the crates weren't delicate biological specimens. They were kept asleep for transport not because they might suffer in transit but because the guys with the guns who were taking delivery of the things would get themselves massacred if their packages arrived awake.

The animals had been hit with a sedative that would keep them under for at least twelve hours, and they would travel with a man who would shoot tranq darts through special openings after each interval.

It had taken the ground crew two hours to load them into their special delivery crates. That gave the transport team ten hours before they needed to re-tranquilize. It should be plenty of time for them to be out of the country... but he didn't want the men going for one of their eternal Eghajira breaks.

"If you don't hurry," Philippe told the Tuareg chieftain in charge of the men, "you'll have to deal with a whole herd of angry raptors."

They weren't raptors, but a special breed of large-format Compsognathus dinosaurs taller than a man, but what was the use of asking these men to know that? They were hired hands, utterly uninterested in the kind of creatures they were transporting... but they'd all seen *Jurassic Park*. Some things wormed their way into every corner of the world. That and, for some strange reason, *Lambada*, which was the ringtone for every one of the mens' phones.

The man he was speaking to nodded and went briskly about his business while Philippe cursed Spielberg for the millionth time. Those old movies had made working with dinosaurs dangerous. Not a day passed without the project losing at least one workman who thought weaponized carnivores would act like those in a blockbuster film.

These creatures were to regular dinosaurs what a guided missile was to a cannonball: both could be dangerous, but one was utterly deadly.

Philippe had designed them that way, working from the base DNA and tweaking until the things—despite the tiny brains—were as smart as a well-trained dog.

At first, he'd assumed it would be impossible to generate intelligent, trainable behavior in dinosaurs, but then he stumbled upon a video of a man training falcons to do pretty much exactly what he wanted these dinosaurs to do.

After that, things became easier. Instead of splicing mammalian genes into the very different dinosaur strands, he used the much more similar falcon DNA for the purpose. That insight shaved months off the process. Their dinosaurs might not be able to open doors like the ones in the films... but they could hunt and retrieve better than any dog on the planet.

And they had armored hides.

The attack saurians were a masterpiece. He was proud to have created them. A testament to his brilliance which even Sun-Lee accepted as superior. Sun-Lee was an excellent scientist, but his results were always linear, straight lines from point A to point B.

Philippe was an artist. He could make the disconnected leaps of intuition that defeated problems.

Together, they had created an empire. While others attempted to weaponize the newly discovered DNA sources, the combination of the Frenchman's inspiration and the Korean's perspiration had beaten the competition into the weeds.

Orders poured in from every corner of the globe. Some of them were even from legitimate government military agencies looking for an edge. They were becoming rich beyond their wildest dreams.

Philippe hated every minute of it.

There was nothing more he could do to help with the loading process, so he turned back towards the door. The air conditioning was bliss against his skin—even though the dock was roofed over and the sun couldn't burn them to blistered ruins, it was still unbearably hot out there.

He navigated the tunnels and took the elevator down into the cool depths of his office.

Closing the door behind him, he looked over the sketches on the walls. Dragons—winged, jewel-colored creatures straight out of myth and dream—looked back at him. Some had wings, some had webbed feet, some simply shone resplendently in rainbow hues.

They were all much more interesting than the coarse, utilitarian and utterly boring weapons their facility churned out like so many toasters or economy cars.

"Chiffon, where are you?" he said.

A creature climbed out from under his desk, hopped onto a chair, then onto his shoulder. About the size of a cat and covered in black fur, Chiffon combined an apelike agility with the spiderlike sense that something, somewhere was wrong with its movements. Something in the human hindbrain shuddered at the thought that something could move that way.

Of course, Philippe didn't find his pet disturbing. He loved the little ball of fur, and only regretted that he might have left a little too much of the arachnid genetic material in there. He would have loved to make a little brother for Chiffon, but sadly, he'd lost all his work leading up to the creature's creation the last time the French nearly caught up to him, in Panama.

Chiffon climbed onto his shoulder and chittered into his ear, and the desire to create something not because some terrorist group wanted larger fangs on their modified crocodile but because it would make the world a more beautiful place was suddenly too strong to resist.

"You know what, Chiffon?" he said, scratching the animal's fuzzy chin, "I think it's time to build you a playmate. Maybe something with dog and rabbit characteristics? Yes, that sounds nice."

He sat down to work and, as if on cue, the phone on his desk rang. It was Park, of course. He was the only one who ever called him.

"Yes?"

"We have a new client," Park said. "An Indonesian Jihadist group who want something to terrorize the beaches. Something aquatic."

Philippe sighed. "How big?"

"Big enough to bite off a leg. And aggressive. We need to be sure that, if someone dumps them in the water, they'll go straight after the swimmers and not waste time drifting along coral reefs or basking in the sun."

Philippe was already thinking of what he could build the monster from. Sharks were an obvious baseline, but perhaps dolphins would work better. It took a certain amount of intelligence to hunt humans, after all.

"When do they need them by?"

"Four weeks."

"Impossible. Aquatic creatures are going to require testing. Plus, putting up the production facilities is going to be annoying. We're going to need a lot of water. Tell them six weeks and start putting together the tanks. If you can get them done in four weeks, I'll have some fast-growing juveniles for you."

"All right. Thank you." The North Korean hung up.

Philippe knew Park was planning on killing him just as soon as he had all the basic designs in his possession. Since his partner was already in possession of walking and flying creatures, the water-borne weapon system was the only one he was missing... and once Philippe turned that one in, and they proved to work, he immediately became expendable.

But that was something he would worry about in a few weeks. In the meantime, he would keep accumulating money. It took money to disappear from the face of the Earth when a man like Park wanted you dead.

And he would build a rabbit-monkey-cat to keep Chiffon company. It wouldn't even cut into his schedule... unbeknownst to Park Sun-Lee, it wouldn't take too long to build what the Indonesians wanted. His mind already sang with possibilities.

It would be a beautiful thing once it was done, but nowhere near as beautiful as his new pet.

He bent over and retrieved a battered black document case from inside a drawer. It was the only thing Philippe had brought along from his old life. He'd purchased it at an office supply store in Libreville, and it had followed him out of Africa to Central America and back to Africa. Inside were the specs for what should have been his greatest triumph, but instead had been his worst disappointment. And his most painful betrayal.

The sheets of paper inside were yellowed and stained with moisture, but he recognized the creature they showed. They were almost exactly like the one they'd produced. A tear rolled down his cheek.

"Hello, Poupée," he said. "I think I know exactly what I need to do to make you work this time." He began to press keys on his keyboard, calling up the programs he needed.

Then he paused and looked back at the drawing of the large-headed spider-monkey-looking thing on the sheet.

"But this time, I'll be watching you much more closely. I've learned, you see."

Then he got to work.

CHAPTER 3

High above his head, a brightly-colored bird circled the two-lane road on which they were driving. Salah Ag Ilbak shuddered. Where he came from, a bird circling overhead could mean just one thing: that something was about to die, or had already done so.

In his homeland, it would most likely have been an animal, and you could tell the size of the creature by the number of carrion-fowl overhead. A desert mouse might merit one, but if a camel or a man found misfortune on the endless arid wastes, you could see the congregation for leagues.

Here in the wetlands, where the air seemed thick and dirty with all the captured water weighing it down, people seemed to be everywhere. You could hardly drive for a few kilometers without coming up on a settlement: a few cinder-block houses and sometimes a town with paved roads. No wonder birds flew everywhere: they were waiting for the mass of humanity to drop dead and give them a feast such as birds had never been given before.

The smells of habitation were everywhere. Not just the clean smell of diesel fumes and exhaust, but the smells of cooking, of garbage piles... of people packed closer together than the world had ever meant for them to be.

He selected an empty stretch of road, out of sight from villages, and pulled over. His convoy did the same, obeying without question. That was as it should be: he was their chief, and they were his family. No honorable Tuareg would ever defy his leaders, and Salah had made certain that only honorable men were selected to drive the six trucks slated to make the delivery.

As the men descended from their vehicles, Salah pointed up at the sun. None needed any further explanation: it was noon, time for prayer.

The men faced northeast and did their duty before God.

Only after that was finished did they come together to smoke and discuss their progress.

"We're making excellent time," Brahim, his sister's son and the man entrusted with their computers and GPS systems, said. "At this rate, we will reach the delivery point a full day before the clients arrive."

"And the roads?" Salah asked.

Brahim smiled. "Unless it rains extremely hard, these are the best roads of the trip. Ivory Coast is not the Sahara, Uncle. The roads here are in constant use, and in constant maintenance."

"The people here are infidels," he reminded his nephew.

The man bowed, understanding what his uncle meant: never take for granted that one who couldn't even be bothered to follow the word of God would do his duty when it came to infrastructure maintenance. And it would be even worse if the country didn't have a large Muslim population to watch over them.

Then Brahim smiled and shrugged. "You are right, of course, but even infidels need to be able to move around their country. I'm confident we will arrive in plenty of time."

Salah grunted. Brahim was the man he was grooming to take over as chief. He'd told no one, of course, but no man lived forever, and a wise ruler cared for the future of his people. Though his nephew might not be as serious as Salah's father, or even as Salah would have preferred him to be, the younger man was a product of a different world. No longer could the Tuareg tribes wander happily in their desert; the world around them was closing in, and its presence would soon be felt. A man who understood that was necessary in order to guide his people.

And Brahim understood. He could use the technology of the outside world and even spoke English and French. He was the bright hope of the tribe.

Salah smiled at his thoughts. Though he wasn't as young as he'd once been, he wasn't planning on dying just yet, and he wanted to be able to pass along some of the knowledge the young man would need before then.

Although Brahim would be shocked to hear it, Salah knew just how he felt. Salah had been the young man once, fighting his own father tooth and nail to move the tribe away from the traditional forms. Other Tuareg people were moving from horses and camels to diesel... but Salah's father wouldn't hear of it.

Salah had respected the old man, just as Brahim, who surely itched to make even more changes, respected him.

Unfortunately, Salah's father had died before teaching Salah how to lead, and that had caused the tribe to suffer while he gained the knowledge. The tribe ended up stronger in the end... but the learning curve had been brutal.

Tuareg lived in one of the most inhospitable places on Earth. And that was why their clients trusted them. If you needed to move material—especially valuable material—around near the Sahara, you called on Salah's clan.

Everyone knew they were trustworthy: if you gave them something, that would be delivered, on time and in one piece. Unlike many African trucking concerns, the value of the cargo made no difference to Salah. His word was sacred and unbreakable.

As was that of his men.

"Let's get moving, then," he said.

"Why the rush? It's our first time in Ivory Coast."

Salah smiled. It was a moment for teaching. "In the first place, we have been given a job, and we must complete it before you go out on a sightseeing tour. After the job is done, I have no problem with you spending some time visiting the villages." He'd been young once, too, and knew that a blind eye from the elders was sometimes imperative in a man's upbringing. Though he was devout, Salah wasn't stupid: he knew a man must see wickedness for himself and make his own decisions. A man without experience was nothing but a hollow shell—not even the word of Allah could hold them together. "There's another reason, however. I want to be certain that the place selected for the handover is adequately isolated. You've seen how many people are around us here... if this airfield is near a town, I want to understand the risk."

"There is no risk, Uncle. All people would see is trucks unloading crates and men loading them onto an airplane."

"These are not normal crates. They're not even made of wood. And they hum. Anyone who gets close might be made curious by the noise and want to look inside. And what then?"

"Then we fulfill the difficult part of the contract. No one looks into the boxes."

Salah smiled. "Your zeal is quite becoming. But I prefer to leave the country without hurting any of the locals. That kind of thing can get out of hand, and if they close the border..."

Brahim snorted. "They'd have to man the borders first, before they can close them."

"Still. I prefer to be careful. Onto the trucks."

They obeyed without further comment.

***

Melanie Viña lay on a thick branch in a tree on a hill, high enough that it afforded a commanding view of the neighboring countryside but still hidden from casual observation by the uppermost branches. She watched the trucks roll in through the scope of her Remington MSR sniper rifle, still trying to get used to the feel of the new weapon. She swore by the M40... but she didn't want anyone linking what she was about to do with the Marine Corps. If that happened, it might come back to bite her in the ass.

She was a little over a click from the airfield and, unless the people she was expecting to pick up the shipment at the airfield were a lot more sophisticated than she expected, they would be packing weaponry more suited to a gunfight at close range in which a lot of lead flying through the air would serve you better than precision shooting. They certainly wouldn't be expecting a sniper.

She smiled at the thought that anyone could be so naïve. Unless the odds were horrendous, precision shooting would always carry the day. It was one of the main reasons engagement reports always seemed to show a huge difference in the number of American dead when compared to the enemy. It was because American troops were expected to know how to hit what they were shooting at while most of the people the Rangers and SEALs were shooting at had only the minimum training in firearms.

And the next few hours would give the terrorists coming in to pick up their cargo another good example.

Of course, she would need to take at least one of them alive... but that was a problem to be considered later. The first order of business was to make sure they couldn't get away.

The shipment consisted of six trucks. Big single-body Mercedes-Benz chassis with enormous wheels of the kind you'd want if crossing the desert. The trucks were festooned with shovels and metal ramps that were likely used to dig them out of deep desert drifts. None of them had trailers; the cargo bays were integral to the tractor.

Definitely desert transportation, which was a clue she would be able to use no matter how things played out over the next twenty-four hours.

The drivers didn't seem to be armed, at least not ostentatiously. She imagined that a convoy crossing borders in this region would have some sort of protection... but these guys didn't seem to be anything but what they appeared to be: truckers hired to take stuff from one place to the other.

But they had to know what they were carrying, didn't they? And if they did, then they weren't innocent by any stretch of the imagination.

Still, if possible, she would try to keep their casualties to a minimum, especially because the truckers were the people most likely to know just where the monsters were coming from.

The airfield itself was a typical grass strip located out in the country. The fact that it was located in Ivory Coast was irrelevant; it could have been in Costa Rica or the Philippines or Australia. The philosophy would have been the same: trees cleared away and the grass strip maintained by hand or perhaps using a single wheeled vehicle, an ancient tractor of some sort.

The only thing that made this one notable was that it was really long. Someone wanted to be certain you could get a good-sized cargo plane in here. It didn't take a genius to guess that this was a smugglers' strip. In Africa, most of the cargo was probably diamonds and things like stolen shipments of copper, but you'd get some drugs on their way somewhere else as well.

And now monsters. Big ones.

Melanie gritted her teeth. She was determined that this batch of creatures wouldn't reach their destination, and was further determined to put a bullet between the eyes of the guys building the things. While the animals might be frightening, the true monsters were the men who built them and sold them to the kind of people who'd let them loose in a shopping mall.

She carried a wallet-sized photograph of a girl, a thirteen-year-old with dark, curly hair and braces: Melanie's niece. Her name was Stephanie Viña, and she was fourteen. At the moment, she was in a hospital, fighting for her life after the mall attacks.

But that wasn't the only reason Melanie had come out to Africa and spent most of her hard-earned life savings—twenty years of pay, including combat pay, from her time in the Marine Corps. She was mostly here because of one person: Sergeant Cora Gimenez.

Her best friend for years, a woman she admired and respected, had died in a monster attack in the Indian Ocean. It had been all over the news, but no one she asked was clear on exactly who had built the massive sea creature that had ended her life. She'd called in every favor she could, had gotten hold of friends of friends with contacts in the CIA and the NSA, and still no one could tell her if the monster had come from Africa or from a rogue US company or a Russian lab. All they could say for certain was that the African concern was the biggest player.

No one on the US side had any idea where they were based. The only data that arrived came out of Europe and said that there would be a handover less than a click away from her position.

So she'd entered Ivory Coast by boat and made her way slowly towards the interior. Her dark skin, inherited from her Cuban grandmother, as well as her knowledge of Arabic gleaned during a tour in Iraq, created a cover for her among the locals. She pretended to be Egyptian, and no one batted an eyelash.

Her contacts in-country consisted of exactly no one, so getting to the airfield overland was her own responsibility.

It proved much easier than she feared. Not one person during the entire hundred-and-fifty-mile bus ride had so much as looked at her wrong. Most people were all smiles and helpfulness. Everything she'd heard about traveling alone in Africa, and the resentful glares of the locals had proven to be completely false.

Of course, it might have been different if they hadn't thought she was African herself.

Still, it was a pleasant enough ride and she made a few friends on the way… friends who looked at each other knowingly when she got out and headed towards the airstrip. They probably thought she was involved in illegal activity and was going to catch a plane.

And in that, they were exactly wrong. She was involved in illegal activity and was there to keep a plane from ever taking off.

***

"These are CSK-181s," Alexeyev said, placing a hand on the fender of the bright green all-terrain assault vehicle. "They haven't been sold to anyone outside of China. How did you get them?"

"That doesn't matter," Hermes replied. "What matters is that no one will try to link us to any specific government based on these."

"Except China."

"If we get caught on video, a quick look will confirm that we're not Chinese."

"Great, just what we need," Voornacht interjected. "For the Chinese to be mad at us for stealing their equipment."

"These aren't stolen. They've been redirected. And in the extremely unlikely event that anyone sees us, they'll have been abandoned by the time anyone can put together a team to come looking. Remember: we just need to find out where the factory is. According to my informant, the shipment is coming by truck. I doubt they'll have come too far."

Voornacht didn't look convinced. "Trucks can go pretty far," he said.

"Carrying crates of attack dinosaurs? That doesn't sound like a good idea to me." Hermes gestured towards the vehicles. "Climb in."

The two drivers were former Belgian soldiers who Hermes trusted implicitly, both because he'd known them for more than ten years and because they didn't know details of the mission and would be paid only after Hermes himself arrived safely home. He was riding with Louembe and Irina Olenko, while Voornacht, Alexeyev and Balzano were in the second vehicle.

Ivory Coast was going through a peaceful period, with a temporary cease-fire in the on-again, off-again civil war. Hermes' sources had been unanimous in reporting that it was perfectly possible to move around the country without being molested.

In that case, the heavily-armored and well-armed assault vehicles might be overkill, since they could have crossed the country, gear and all, in a couple of minivans. But Hermes knew Africa well enough to know that a small show of force went a long way, and that no one would attack an overtly military vehicle without first checking closely which faction they belonged to. The continent wasn't a well-drawn battlefield with clearly-defined friends and foes. It was an often chaotic, ever-shifting landscape of threats that needed to be analyzed and defined. Hermes had often told his European colleagues that if another sublime tactical genius, a Rommel or Napoleon were to grace the face of the Earth, he would likely come from Africa, raised to greatness from a bush war.

Of course, he'd probably need some help on the strategic side. It was quite difficult to get trained in big-picture military ops when your operational scope consisted of twelve pickup trucks, a few hundred troops with AK-47s and a Fiat G.91 fighter plane from the 1950s left behind in a different war by the Portuguese. But some of these wars had been won with that, and some with less.

So their enormous Dongfeng Mengshi CSK-181s motored unmolested inland from the coast. They had a four-hour drive to the airfield, timed to allow them to arrive just as dusk was falling. Hermes wanted to be able to scout around in the dark and figure out who was where.

Since the clients were obviously going to be arriving by plane—his source said they had an ancient Hercules that had once belonged to Pakistan—he was mainly concerned with two groups: the men driving the trucks and the airfield's security people, who doubled as the local army unit.

It consisted of four men.

He turned to Irina, sitting next to him. She was peering intently into a tablet. "How are the drones?"

"Number six isn't charging its battery as well as I'd prefer. I think it was damaged in transit. The rest look okay."

"How many do we need?"

"Three. I'll keep the rest as backup."

He squeezed her leg and she smiled slightly in response. They'd shared a lot together, and had been lovers on and off for more than a year after returning from Antarctica. They had been off until the night before, when a knock at his door preceded Irina, wearing a shy smile and a negligee that was anything but shy. "I'm always nervous the night before a deployment," she'd said.

Now, however, she was all business. "I have two of them set for night vision. UV and IR, while the third will act as my UV illuminator and fire drone. If we need to hit something from above, that one will coordinate with the other two to get a precise fix on the target."

"What about comms activity?"

"The IR drone has the black box, but I won't know if it's working until we get there and see what they're using. I can deal with cell phones and sat phones, but I can't jam a radio."

"No one uses radio anymore."

"Then they're idiots. Sometimes, the old ways really are best."

It was incredible to him just how many talents Irina had. Though Alexeyev was perfectly correct in saying that she'd been a biologist specializing in toxic creatures and manmade viruses, for some reason, her handlers at the SRV had seen fit to train her in electronic warfare as well.

He'd asked her why, and she said it was for a specific mission that had either been canceled or that they never got a chance to send her on before her career got derailed when they went after the remains of the monsters at the Argentine Antarctic base. That particular mission had ended with Hermes and Irina as the only survivors… without any way of calling for help. Only the fact that Irina was from some godforsaken town in Siberia whose winters made Antarctic summer look like the Caribbean had saved them: she knew how to survive in extreme cold, and they'd made it to Halley Base, much to the surprise and consternation of the British soldiers there.

Being handed over to the Belgian authorities with a note of protest was much better than the alternative: the Russians really, really wanted Irina back.

"Want to stop for some dinner?" he asked.

"Do you really think that's a good idea?"

"We're running early. I don't want to arrive before dusk."

He leaned up into the front seat and ordered the driver to pull over in front of a roadside restaurant, a place of cinder blocks with plastic chairs and tables in front of it.

"As a biologist, I'd like to point out that this is how you get dysentery," she said. "And stopping to go to the bathroom every three minutes is a good way to lose a gunfight."

"And as an African by adoption," Hermes replied, "I'd like to point out that if we stopped at a place like this in Europe, you wouldn't say anything."

"Yes, I would. Dysentery isn't racist and it doesn't care what continent it's on. It's just a bug."

"Oh, come on."

She sighed and followed the men out of the cars.

***

"And what have we here?" Melanie said. "This is getting interestinger and interestinger."

She congratulated herself once again for choosing the right perch. Had she not insisted on getting a tree on a rise, she might have been able to see the airfield, but she wouldn't have been able to watch the rest of the area.

In this case, that would have meant missing a good chunk of the action.

Seven men and a woman had just entered her field of operations when they descended from a couple of Humvee-like assault vehicles of Chinese design. They'd alighted five hundred meters from her position and were moving purposefully, setting up equipment. She saw three drones and several guns, although they were right at the far range of her thermal scope. The only reason she'd even seen them was because she wanted to be certain that none of the guys from the trucks were getting too close, so she made periodic checks around her position.

It looked like these guys were setting up to fight their own private little war, and the only candidates to be on the receiving end were her friends with the trucks and the guys who'd be picking up the dinosaurs.

Unfortunately, that meant that she might end up on the other side of a pitched battle from these new players. She needed information, and if these guys decided to whack everyone, that would prove difficult to obtain.

"Damn. Why do even the easy missions have to get complicated?"

But then she buckled down to start rethinking her strategy. No one liked a whiner, especially not Cora Gonzalez, the woman Melanie was out to avenge.

She'd figure it out.

***

Irina cursed. "The trucks are already there," she reported.

Hermes nodded gravely, but she saw his features tighten, a certain sign of stress which she'd learned to identify even when he had his poker face on. "Do you think they've already made the delivery? Maybe our info was bad and we missed the party."

"I can't be certain," she replied, "but if I had to guess, I'd say we're on time. These guys don't look like they're in a hurry to go anywhere. They actually opened the trucks and did something inside. I couldn't see what, but again, if I had to guess, I'd say the cargo is still in there, and the animals are being fed."

"But why arrive so early?" Hermes said. Then he answered his own question. "It's either because they didn't want anyone to see where they came from, which means the production facility is very nearby... or it means they had a long drive and didn't want to be late, which means the factory could be anywhere."

Irina nodded. "And since this is a military operation..."

"Murphy's law will be in full effect. The factory is probably in South Africa or something. We're going to have to go look at the license plates on those trucks. Can your drones get that?"

"No."

"Of course not. We'll need to send one of the men. Louembe could probably sneak in and steal their tires without anyone hearing him. Alexeyev can probably do it, too, but he'd likely decide to kill them all and blow up the trucks in the process. Spetsnaz people aren't big on subtlety "

"I'd say you didn't send either for now, and I'd also say we should get on the other side of the cars and hunker down," Irina replied, heading for cover.

"Why?

"Because we have more of that Murphy's Law going around."

Hermes followed her behind the assault vehicle and ordered the rest of the men to do the same. "Can you be a little clearer?"

"Yeah. There's a sniper on a tree half a kilometer away."

CHAPTER 4

Javier Balzano checked the weapon they'd assigned him. He hoped he wasn't going to have to shoot anyone, and had expressed his desire to be part of the rearguard in order to avoid getting blood on his hands. He would cover them if they retreated or needed help, of course, but he preferred not to be part of any offensive action. Though he'd come into contact with some very unusual monsters in Antarctica, this wasn't really his war.

He thought at least one or two of the others would react the same way, but there was no reticence. They all seemed to have a personal axe to grind with the people building and distributing monsters.

Louembe appeared most indignant of all. From what he'd said the night before, he viewed it as a personal insult that some random men from Europe and Asia would assume that Africa was too weak to deal with a violation of this magnitude.

It was an interesting attitude, Javier thought. If the same thing had happened in Latin America, no one would have looked at it as a colonial invasion, but as a logical solution to a specific problem: an enterprise like this one needed wilderness and reasonably weak defense forces, not to mention bribable police. Africa, like Latin America, had those things in abundance, without the risks inherent in trying to do this work in Central Asia.

But perhaps it was easier for him to say that since he was descended from the very colonial powers the Africans were angry about.

The more he thought, the more the mission seemed surreal, which was why he was familiarizing himself with the gun. Concentrating on an unfamiliar weapon required him to stop thinking of other things.

But the novelty was very thin. It was pretty much a standard FAL rifle which someone had modernized. He half-expected to find the name of Fabricaciones Militares stamped onto the weapon, as the Argentine weapons' manufacturer had a long history of updating the FAL... but these said DSArms, a company he'd never heard of.

Judging by the reactions of his comrades, it appeared to be a good choice of weapon. Voornacht and Louembe gave the rifles a quick look, grunted and moved on to something else. Alexeyev barely lingered longer. It made sense: other than the AK-47, the FAL was the most ubiquitous assault rifle in the world if you discounted the proprietary weapons the major governments used. It was a good gun.

They'd spent the night sleeping on the ground, with the two vehicles between their own position and the sniper, never giving the man a target.

"All right," Hermes said, once they'd finished their coffee. "The plane is supposed to get here at around nine-fifteen local time. We'll move into position as soon as we hear it coming."

"What about the sniper?" Alexeyev asked.

Hermes smiled. "We don't think he's with the drivers or the clients."

"Ah. Guesswork. That's comforting," the Russian sneered. "Even if you're right, he can still blow our brains out."

"I'm aware of that. We're going to stage the raid from the trees out of the sniper's line of fire." He scratched a quick diagram in the dirt with a stick. "Have a look. This is the runway. We think the plane will stop here, and these are the trucks. Here's the sniper, and the tree line adjacent to the airfield. There's a dirt access road here, ending at a gate that we can drive through without suffering any damage. If we come in this way and then park beside the plane here, the sniper can never see us from his position."

"That kind of limits us if things go wrong," Alexeyev observed. "Or if he has something that can get through our armor. Why don't we hit him with the drones?"

"Because we just don't know who he is. He might be a CIA observer or a representative of the local army. He might be a random poacher."

"I don't know. I think if someone's up a tree with a rifle in a place where a terrorist group is going to take a delivery, we should consider him a combatant."

Hermes held up a finger. "I was thinking of the following. Instead of putting three drones up and holding the others in reserve, we can use all six, and have the backup team on the sniper. If anything goes wrong on the ground and we need to expose ourselves, we'll take him out."

Alexeyev grunted. It was obvious he didn't like it. "Who's on the point team?"

"You, me, Voornacht and Louembe, plus the driver," Hermes replied.

"All right. It's crazy, but I'll do it." He turned to Irina. "You must promise me that you'll take that sniper out if we need it. Immediately, no questions asked."

"I will."

"And if we manage to capture the people we want to grab, what then? Can we also take out the sniper?"

"No," Hermes replied. "We're only hitting the sniper if things go bad. We just don't have enough information at this point."

Alexeyev said something in Russian which sounded dirty.

Louembe looked at the sky. "I think it's time. Listen," he said.

They all shut up and the sound of propellers filled the air. Even in a jungle staging point thousands of miles from his home base, Balzano recognized the drone of a Hercules. He smiled.

"All right, people, saddle up."

They each knew which vehicle to climb into and which seat to occupy. Javier jumped into the second assault vehicle and immediately made his way to the rear seat on the driver's side, allowing Irina to come in beside him. She took a few seconds, as she needed to be certain all the drones got into the air and clear of the tree cover before joining him.

As soon as she closed the armored door, the driver gunned the engine and raced after the first CSK-18. This vehicle would park under the trees where the sniper couldn't see them. Balzano and the driver would take cover behind suitable trunks and cover the men going into the center of the fray, while Irina Olenko piloted the drones.

He hoped things went well. If not, it would be the first time in his life that Balzano would fire at other human beings. He hated the idea, but he'd signed up for this mission and taken the money.

He just hoped he could do it.

***

Max Alexeyev grasped the handle on the inside of the front passenger door. It was little more than a steel tube, but that was the beauty of military vehicles: there was nothing in this truck except what really needed to be there. Basic seats, handholds, lots of space to store guns and a shitload of armor.

The rush of entering battle never changed. Normally, he had to jump in, or fly low on some helicopter in the middle of the night. Someone who'd never seen combat might think that kind of insertion would get the blood pumping much more than driving in to face some unsuspecting terrorists very far from home and a bunch of truck drivers. They'd be wrong. Even something as prosaic as driving into the battle over a bumpy road in the full sunshine and heat of the African morning was a rush.

He'd missed it and, for the first time since they'd decided to go their separate ways, he found that he wasn't thinking about Marianne.

Good.

They stopped under the trees, out of sight with the engine running while they waited for the plane to land and come to a stop. They didn't want to spook the terrorists, so they waited for Irina to give them the signal to attack.

…And waited. Max understood it was necessary to give the bad guys time to open the loading ramp and begin to load the plane, but in that case, Hermes should have had them wait until the plane was on the ground before the assault vehicles rolled.

Unless he wanted to take advantage of the roar of the aircraft's engines to cover the sounds of their trucks approaching. Or unless he wanted to get everyone in the vehicles so that they could have a nice thick layer of armor between themselves and the sniper.

Then he started thinking about the guy with the gun somewhere in the treetops, looking down at what was happening here. Hermes should have sent a couple of men to take him down, or at least to capture him and figure out what the hell he was doing in-theater. A sniper could only shoot what he saw, and while the vehicles had to run on relatively cleared paths, two guys on foot could stay in the trees. Maybe all the stress they were feeling could have been avoided and the guy would turn out to be nothing more than a wildlife photographer who'd chosen a really good vantage point. But that would have been a truly unfortunate coincidence. That perch was an ideal spot to cover the airfield and its entrances.

He shook his head and laughed silently at himself. Colonel Garkov had told him, in no uncertain terms, that he would never work out as a foot soldier because he thought like an officer, always looking at things from every angle and trying to figure out ways to do it better.

Max recalled the conversation.

"A soldier like that," Garkov had told him in his office in the Spetsnaz base in Vladivostok, where Alexeyev's unit was doing joint exercises with the Frogmen stationed there, "is worse than useless. Once he starts thinking that way, he'll begin questioning orders. And that will lead to problems, because a unit that thinks its leaders are imbeciles is not a confident unit."

"But isn't that better than having them obey stupid orders?" Max said. Looking at it now, he squirmed at the memory: it was a sign of just how inexperienced he'd been in those days.

"No. I'd rather have them follow bad orders, even take unnecessary losses, than to question the chain of command in a situation where it's necessary for them to obey. For an army to function, its officers—even the morons who made it there because they have uncles who are generals—need to know that their troops will do eastly what is asked of them."

Max had shifted uncomfortably in his chair. Even then, he must have been a fast learner, because he'd only said, "Yes, sir."

"Which brings me to you." Garkov indicated Max's file. "You're clearly one of the good ones. You got selected for Spetsnaz training even before you saw much real combat. Hell, it says here that the only time you were anywhere near a firefight before you got into the special forces program was once when a Chechen terrorist crashed a car a couple of blocks from a warehouse you were guarding, and you helped in the arrest."

"That's correct."

Garkov blew a raspberry. "Whoever recommended you for further training should have seen that as a red flag. You abandoned your post to do something more interesting."

"The police would have been killed if I hadn't realized the man had an AK-47 under the seat and shot him, sir."

The colonel sighed. "The problem isn't that day. It's today. You had the men around you change position without authorization."

"They were in the line of fire."

"Except it was an exercise, and the only live fire we were using were a few mortar shells to give you guys some sense of real action. And they were slated to fall right next to the place where you convinced your colleagues to redeploy. If the sergeant hadn't seen what was happening and called everything off, the Russian Army would have one less headache—you—but we'd also be mourning the loss of five good soldiers whose only failing was to listen to a smartass."

Max swallowed. He knew he was in trouble when he got pulled off the exercise, but hadn't understood just how badly he was fucked until now. "Yes, sir," he said.

"We have a special punishment for exceptional soldiers who are convinced that they're smarter than anyone else." He grinned evilly and allowed a long pause so Max could sweat. "We make them prove it."

"What?"

"I'm going to send you up for advanced leadership training, with a recommendation that any unit you ever lead be used well away from any other unit. If I have my way, you'll end up doing black ops behind enemy lines until someone finally gets lucky and plugs you. But they won't listen to me, of course. They never do."

"You're... you're making me an officer?"

Garkov laughed. "Oh, no. Not yet. You'll be taught to lead small units of men in combat situations. There are commissions available, but you have to be good at it to get them."

"Oh." Max hadn't known whether to be relieved or disappointed. "And when will I start?"

"I'm expecting an email from the man who runs the course, but I expect to be able to ship you off in two weeks. I'll be glad to get you out of my hair, and even happier to think that, in a year or two, you're going to be staring at a target in the middle of the night in a village that's no more than a pimple on the devil's ass, probably in the Pakistani mountains, and some wet-behind-the-ears recruit is going to be questioning your orders. Only then will I believe that life is fair."

"Yes, sir."

"In the meantime, I can't have you contaminating my men with the thought that they can all do this and will be given the chance to lead teams, so you will now go and tell the team that is digging the trench for the sewage pipe in the southeast corner of the base that they're relieved of that duty and should report here. You'll be relieving them." All joviality had left Garkov's features. "I want the trench done before you leave. Maybe all the digging will give you a chance to think about what nearly happened to you because you disobeyed a direct order."

Max grinned as he recalled the conversation. Garkov had been right: from the very first day he'd led a group of men, his troops had made his life miserable by not obeying his orders the way he wanted them to… but neither the blisters from digging or the experience as a leader had managed to cure him of his tendency to reevaluate every single command decision.

He shrugged. At least Hermes didn't seem like an idiot… but no matter where he'd been in combat, a Belgian mercenary would never approach the competence of even the lowliest Spetsnaz soldier. That was just a natural law.

"Go, go, go!" Irina's voice came in over the headset in his helmet and the CSK-18 accelerated with a diesel roar.

Though he'd done a lot of missions in his life, they'd mostly taken place at night in Central Asia, surrounded by his own comrades and the operatives of Russia's covert agencies. If someone had suggested that one day he'd be driving into combat in the middle of the African day in a Chinese assault vehicle to capture some men who were trafficking dinosaurs while following the orders of a man from Belgium… he would have had that person's vodka ration revoked and probably sent up for psych evaluation.

And yet, here he was, and it felt just the way it was supposed to feel.

The CSK-18 burst through the insignificant gate and onto the rutted grass encircling the airstrip. Though the single runway was well-maintained—albeit also grass—the area around it was a muddy mess.

It made no difference to the big assault vehicle. It had wheels that reached Max's waist, and could have probably driven over the entire continent without encountering anything it couldn't go over.

Up ahead he saw an ancient Hercules plane painted grey. Men were chocking the wheels—probably unnecessary and maybe even dangerous on grass—and the propeller blades were coming to a halt. Its markings reminded him of those used by the Pakistani Air Force for its transport planes, but someone had painted over any identification with a slightly darker shade of grey that could be made out in the bright light.

The driver's orders were to position the vehicle in such a way that the plane would block the sniper's line of fire. He did it with verve, driving straight across the grass in the shortest possible line. Four men who were standing in the CSK's path nearly didn't dive out of the way in time, and a huge forklift carrying a long row of crates on a platform took too long to back away.

The CSK-18's bumper bar slammed into the huge load and pushed it aside as it powered through.

Max was impressed; the assault vehicle barely slowed. He looked behind to see the giant forklift tipping over onto its side and dropping grey crates everywhere before the small windows on the assault vehicle precluded any further sightseeing.

Once the vehicle was in position, the driver slammed on the brakes and Hermes ordered them out. The mission was simple: shoot anyone armed and capture at least one of the truck drivers. They were the ones who could lead them to the factory floor, wherever that might be hidden. The truckers had been there and they'd driven from there to here.

Max had a second to get his bearings as the people on the ground reeled. It was pretty obvious that no one expected an attack—this was just a cargo run well out of any combat zone. Ivory Coast was neutral territory, not involved in any of Asia's territorial squabbles. Safe.

He scanned the field. The truckers had unloaded their vehicles, and a large number of high-tech looking grey crates stood beside the runway. Behind them, a bunch of the same crates had crumpled and splintered where the forklift had crashed.

And that was all the time Max had for sightseeing. A man wearing grey camouflage ran down the loading ramp to see what was going on. Unfortunately for that man, he'd sensed something was happening and was holding his sidearm in one hand.

That was a mistake; Max hit him with a short burst from the rifle. Respecting the unfamiliar gun, Max aimed for the chest as opposed to the head, but apparently a FAL—even a high-tech one like this—was just a FAL, and this one acted just like the ones he'd trained with when studying enemy weapons. Plenty of recoil, but it packed a punch.

The guy on the ramp dropped like a stone and rolled the rest of the way.

Even before he'd reached the grass, Alexeyev was on the move. His job was to secure the interior of the aircraft and make certain that no one could hole up in there and make their lives miserable. He would be exposed for some meters, but Hermes had promised covering fire.

Just as he was reaching the plane another guy in grey camo started down. Max shot him without even bothering to check if he was armed. Now that the shooting had started, you had to assume that terrorists buying dinosaurs were going to shoot back.

He dropped two more as he ran up the ramp and then paused.

Just as a FAL was just a FAL, there weren't too many things you could do to make a cargo plane different. This one was set up with an empty area behind a bulkhead. Some webbed seats could be folded down from the walls... and that was it, other than acres of grey paint and a few safety and security markings in red and white.

There was no place for anyone to hide, and the door would likely lead into a small crew cabin and then the cockpit.

He hesitated a moment and then decided fast was better than stealthy. He hoped no one was watching him on security cameras as he sprinted the length of the plane and slammed into the aluminum door which folded aside to reveal a small passenger area with ten seats. It was empty, so he didn't even slow and crashed into the last door.

As he entered the cockpit, he saw a hole in the windscreen and instinctively dropped to the floor. Something wasn't right.

He looked up at the copilot. The man, a dark guy with a mustache, was slumped over to one side. Blood flowed from a bullet hole in his forehead.

Max crawled over to the pilot's seat and found the same thing.

Then he crawled out, keeping his own head down.

One thought went through his head as he moved: sniper.

They should have taken the guy out when they had the chance, even if he'd taken out two of the bad guys.

***

Melanie grunted. She'd nailed the pilot and copilot, but the third guy in the cockpit had been too quick for her. He'd gotten on the ground and disappeared from her sight before she could get a bead on him.

No worries. Even if they had a backup flight crew—which would make sense, given that they would likely only be on the ground long enough to load the crates and get the hell out of Africa—they'd need a plane to fly out on.

Her next objective was to deny them that.

She began pouring bullets into the two engines on the starboard side, the ones not blocked by the fuselage, concentrating on the area behind the props. Hopefully, the armor wouldn't be thick enough to stop all her rounds. Then she shot all the tires she could see.

She was about to fold the rifle and get herself down the tree and out of the area when another thought struck her and she took aim once more, this time hitting one propeller blade on each of the engines on her side of the plane.

There. That Herc wasn't going anywhere.

But the trucks were. Movement through her scope showed that the half-dozen Mercedes-Benz single-bed trucks that had brought the crates to the airfield had started up and were driving in her direction, leaving the unloaded boxes behind. Apparently, the men who'd irrupted into the transfer had let them go... or at least they weren't actively firing on them.

That was actually a good thing for Melanie. The only road out of the airfield big enough for a convoy that size ran right past her position... and it meant that she could take one of the men at her own leisure as opposed to trying to sneak one out from under the noses of the soldiers who'd just busted the delivery. Those guys didn't look like they had a sense of humor: she'd just watched them cut down everyone who came out of the plane.

She finished packing her rifle and climbed down the tree and hurried over to the road. There wasn't much time, so she stood in the middle and observed the overhanging branches.

There. That one would do. She climbed up onto it and waited for the convoy to approach, glad that her pack was light enough to allow her to climb like a monkey and also that she'd had the foresight to pack a sidearm, even though it meant getting her stuff into the country was a little more difficult than it would have been had she only brought the rifle.

Fortunately, the officer who'd pulled her aside to check her bags hadn't questioned her permits. Melanie still didn't know if they were real or forged—she just knew that they'd worked like a charm and that when she got back, she owed a couple of supply sergeants big time. She knew better than to ask where the hell they'd gotten the contacts, however.

A rumble on the wind announced that the trucks were on their way, and she clenched her teeth. She hoped the dire state of the dirt track would keep the drivers from moving too quickly, but even if it didn't, she had to drop onto the last truck—that would be the only way to keep the driver of the vehicle behind from spotting her.

They came into sight, and didn't seem to be moving too fast. She could see the trucks bounce up and down along the road.

Melanie was satisfied to see she'd chosen her perch perfectly: the convoy would parr right under her feet.

She let them go by, one by one, trusting her camo, combined with the general green-ness of her surroundings, to keep her from sight.

As the cab of the final lorry passed under her, she lowered her legs and dropped.

Even at full extension, it was a good six feet to the roof of the truck's cargo area and she landed hard and lost her balance. She rolled towards the back of the lorry, desperately trying to grab some kind of handhold before she fell off the back.

Just as she was slowing, the truck hit a pothole that launched her into the air. She watched the back of the vehicle drive under her and she began to fall towards the road.

Instinctively, Melanie reached out and grabbed a handle on the side of the door, a solid, round one.

With a wrench of her shoulder, her progress was arrested and she found herself halfway up the side of the truck, her boots dragging in the dirt. Knowing she would pay a price, but ignoring the pain, Melanie pulled herself onto the rear bumper.

She was on her way. When these guys stopped, she'd be there.

***

Voornacht shouted, "I've got the trucker under control!" He was standing over a kneeling man, pointing his rifle at the guy's head.

"Good," Hermes replied. The rest of the men, dark-skinned, with beards that made them look darker still, had broken and run for the trucks. They didn't need those, though. One was enough, and it was also easier to keep an eye on one prisoner than a bunch of them. "Let the rest of them go. Shoot them if they turn this way. And get that guy into the Jeep."

A crack behind him made Hermes turn, and he saw a crate explode outward, splintering as something emerged.

Something grey and green. Something big.

Something angry and suddenly fast. The grey monster sprinted straight towards them. Hermes realized it would reach Voornacht before him and began to shout a warning... but he knew it was useless before the words emerged.

Voornacht, however, didn't need the warning. Spurred by some sixth sense—or maybe just by the fact that he'd heard the crack as well, the South African dove to one side.

The creature's fury now had a single target: the kneeling driver.

It slammed into the prisoner at enormous speed and, with a single wrench of the mouth, flipped the man into the air as if he were a rag doll. In a lightning move, the monster snapped its jaws around the driver's neck as he came down and shook the man a couple of times.

Then, apparently satisfied that its prey was dead, the monster turned towards Hermes.

He froze for a moment, and stared at it. This wasn't a grey lizard like the ones in his coloring books when he was a kid. This was a mottled green and grey monster whose skin looked like the camouflage patterns on jungle uniforms. Down or hair grew on its belly. From the top of the bulbous head to the end of the muscular tail, it must have been three meters long. And the thickness around the jaw gave the impression that it was built for strength of bite.

The creature charged.

Hermes snapped out of his trance. He'd never been one to tighten up in battle, and it wasn't time to start now. He rolled to his right, getting off a burst of three shots as he went. He aimed at the evil little yellow eyes.

The FAL's bullets were quite powerful, but the creature didn't fall. It skidded to a halt on the runway grass, shook its head a couple of times as if to clear it, and turned back.

Hermes knew he needed a little room to maneuver. "Irina," he called over the radio, "I need you to take out that sniper right now."

"Yes, sir," she replied coolly.

He ran towards the crates. Considering the fact that another monster could emerge at any moment, that might not have been the best idea, but it was the only cover he would be able to reach before the much faster creature could tear him apart.

He wouldn't have made it if it hadn't been for Martin, the driver of the assault vehicle, who hit the monster with another burst from the side.

That distracted it and, even more furious than before, it went for Martin. The poor man had no cover. He emptied most of a magazine into the reptile before it ripped him in two.

Hermes cursed and fired. The thing didn't even seem to feel the bullets.

At least Voornacht had managed to get out of the way. He and Louemba were hiding behind the CSK-18.

Hermes watched with disbelief as the big man from Gabon climbed onto the roof of the assault vehicle, completely exposed, and began to fire at the monster.

He was aiming low, at the body.

Hermes wanted to shout at the man to aim at the head, that even if he hit something vital, the creature would get to him before it bled out, but Louembe seemed determined to put as many bullets into its chest as humanly possible.

As the monster lunged at his feet, he skipped away, landing on the CSK-18's trunk without missing a beat. Finally, Louembe ran out of ammo and sprinted towards the Hercules. Alexeyev strode out to cover him.

But the Russian didn't fire a round. The genetically modified dinosaur was staggering to a halt, bleeding from dozens of wounds.

As they watched, it fell onto its side and lay panting on the ground.

Seconds later, the panting stopped.

Hermes walked over to Louembe and said: "That was the bravest thing I've ever seen. But foolish. Why didn't you shoot it in the head? You couldn't miss at that range."

Louembe raised an eyebrow. "You've never dealt with crocodiles, have you? They've got a tiny brain lost in a mass of skull. Unless you get really lucky, shooting them in the head only makes them mad. Well, this one looked like just a big crocodile standing on its legs to me, so I treated it like one."

At that moment, Irina's voice came on the line. "Hermes. You can move about freely, the sniper's gone."

"Did you take him out?"

"No. He left before you ordered me to."

"Hmm." It was something he'd have to think about later, another complication. In the meantime, he had a bigger problem: the man they'd grabbed to take them to the factory was dead and the truckers were motoring away. They'd need to follow them... and now they knew Hermes' team was coming.

But Voornacht and Alexeyev were looking at something else. "What do you want us to do with that?" the South African asked, pointing at the crates.

Hermes focused on them and realized that they were all moving about, and some were making ominous thumping noises. Each one held a monster just like the one that had so nearly killed him—and which *had* killed a good soldier and also the man they needed to show them where the monsters were being built.

"Burn them. Burn them all."

CHAPTER 5

Philippe watched the incubator like a hawk. It was completely unnecessary since there was a timer counting down that would tell him when the process was done and, furthermore, there was nothing he could do if things went wrong, but the habit was stronger than he was. Back when he designed the first accelerated incubator that could deal with mammalian genetic material as well as reptiles and amphibians, he'd had to stay awake for days at a time to ensure a viable result.

In those days, viable meant anything that could survive more than a few minutes.

His gaze fell on the label for the unit he was using now. It was written in Chinese, and he had no idea what it said.

But he knew what its presence here meant: it meant the lab he'd left behind in Paris had been reverse-engineered by people who knew what he'd been doing, and then the French government had either sold the technology or, more likely, been a victim of industrial espionage. From the look of the incubators in the facility Sun-Lee had built for them, the tech had long since been industrialized and now appeared to be completely reliable.

Speak of the devil, the man himself walked in. "We have a problem," the North Korean said.

"What?" Philippe replied without taking his eyes off the readout. Sun-Lee tended towards unnecessary alarmism.

"The delivery for the Paki... I mean the northern Indian freedom fighters was intercepted."

Philippe looked up. That actually *was* bad. Bad as hell. "What do you mean, intercepted?"

"I mean there were people waiting at the airfield, armed to the teeth. They killed the clients, and grabbed one of the drivers. Salah just called me. He's really pissed, and says we need to get his man back."

An icy ball formed in the pit of Philippe's stomach. He knew that Park Sun Lee had survived unscathed after being part of the innermost, most top secret programs in two of the most brutal clandestine services on the planet: Russia and North Korea. And he'd done it the old-fashioned way: by being a bloodier bastard than the people around him.

"I had nothing to do with the leak," Philippe said.

A long, cold silence followed. "I know," Sun Lee replied. Which probably meant he'd been listening to all of Philippe's conversations, electronic or otherwise. Which Philippe already suspected. "If you did, we wouldn't be having this conversation."

The ball of ice in Philippe's gut became even more solid. It felt nearly as frigid as the North Korean's dead, impassive stare.

"So what do we do now?" he said, forcing the words through his constricted throat.

"We move to the backup base."

"We have a backup base?"

"Of course. This one only exists as a test run, to see where the project failed. Now we know, and we can advance to the next step. We need to pack anything critical and move it right away. Here are the coordinates. I've left Mahmoud instructions to take you there when you've finished packing." He turned to go.

"Wait," Philippe said. "What about my equipment?" The incubators weren't going to fit in Mahmoud's modified dune buggy.

"All duplicated in the new HQ. So don't waste any time and get going. I don't know how long we have."

"And the new shipment we're building? It's in the big tanks."

Park shrugged. "Leave one of the junior scientists to oversee it. If no one crashes our party, we'll ship as scheduled. If not, we'll have to delay the delivery while we duplicate the work. Now copy anything sensitive and hit the purge command on your computer. That was programmed to nuke the whole thing beyond recovery. It's unfortunate, but we don't really have many choices right now." Park hurried away.

Philippe nodded as he realized this misfortune might play into his hands. Unlike the land-based creatures, the big sea monsters were delicate and difficult to gestate. Only Philippe could keep them alive, and Park knew it. Until their production was fully automated like everything else, it meant Sun-Lee had to keep Philippe alive.

That gave him time to plan his escape.

As he gathered up papers and files, the incubator, ignored in its final moments after the obsessive vigil, pinged.

He dropped everything and opened the door to the suitcase-sized piece of equipment.

"Hello, my dear," he said.

The tiny creature lying inside looked so much like the lost, betraying Poupée that he almost wept. It looked up at him with eyes that communicated an intelligence well beyond what something that size should have had.

Of course, he mused, *most creatures that small weren't completely riddled with human genes.*

He gingerly pulled out the plastic bassinet on which the animal lay and studied it.

"Perfect," he said.

The industrially-produced incubator had done what even Philippe's gentle ministrations hadn't managed a decade before: it had created a perfect version of his most ambitious experiment ever. In his hands lay a creature that could think for itself and learn to... well, Philippe didn't really know what its limits were. The last one had betrayed him before he could study the question properly.

This time, he'd keep a closer eye on it.

And he would never give it a reason to come to hate its creator.

***

Smoke and the smell of charred monster flesh floated in the heavy jungle air.

"Now what?" Max said, surveying the carnage. Their entire plan was contingent on keeping the hostage alive... something they'd failed miserably to do. "Looks to me like we're totally fucked."

Hermes held up a hand. "Give me a second," he said. Then he snapped his fingers. "Search this guy."

The surviving driver bent over and quickly turned out the dead trucker's pockets. A phone, a clipped-together wad of bills and some coins emerged. No identification or passport.

"Irina," Hermes called. "We've got a cell phone for you to play with."

Irina walked over. She was as calm and collected as if she always went toe-to-toe with monsters twice her size armed with teeth like daggers. She studied the phone for a minute then smiled. "Two generations out of date. I can crack this in an hour."

"I don't need you to crack it. I need you to figure out who the lead trucker is. Then I need you to track that man's phone back to their base."

She thought about it. "Not as easy."

"But can you do it?"

"Maybe. Definitely, if the target phone is as old as this one. I'll go back to the Jeep and get to work on this." She walked away. "But you might start thinking of plan B. It's possible we'll need to follow the truckers on the ground."

Max felt the seconds ticking away. He had a clock in his head that told him how much time they had to get out of a hot zone. It was nothing definite, but he trusted his sixth sense implicitly. "We need to get out of here," he told Hermes. "There has to be someone in charge of this airfield, and they probably saw what happened here, or at the very least heard the shooting. Every soldier in Ivory Coast is going to be here in a few minutes."

Hermes hesitated before answering. Then he nodded. "You're right. This isn't a failed state. The civil war might have weakened certain institutions, but it's still a working country. I'm so used to African operations being in territory that either my employers control or that the enemy does, that I forget that neutral sites also exist. Old habits and all that." He lifted his head, looked around and shouted. "Everyone in their Jeep. We're leaving."

"What about him?" Max said, indicating the dead Belgian who'd been driving the Jeep with his head.

"We bring him with us. We'll drop him in a river somewhere people won't find him. I hate to do that, but his presence would just create too many questions. Even if the body is found, there are no bullets in it. People will assume he was mauled by something."

"And the trucker?"

"Leave him."

They picked up the mangled corpse of their fallen comrade. Hermes grabbed him under the armpits leaving the boots to Max. That was fine by him: the bloody section was the upper body.

They took him to the nearest assault vehicle and tossed him unceremoniously in the trunk.

Hermes spotted Irina: "Are your drones stowed?"

She nodded and they set off, taking a road out of the northern side of the airfield, avoiding the main entry, which was where any soldiers would appear from, and also the secondary gate they'd come in by, which was where the authorities would expect them to leave through. They found a small gate and this time, took the time to cut through a padlock and then leave the gate closed behind them. They even replaced the lock with one they had in their equipment: finding it locked might fool the guards into thinking no one had used the gate... and if anyone had seen them, they'd need to remove the lock or break the gate. All of that would take time. The Argentine, Balzano, took the place of the fallen driver.

The road was bumpy and dusty, but Max barely noticed. He felt the post-engagement lull, the exhaustion of having the adrenalin wear off. It had been a good fight, even if one of the enemies was more than a little unconventional.

The motion of the vehicle took him back to the days when he spent endless hours riding Jeeps similar to this one over the steppes of Central Asia. Dust, dirt, and potholes the size of elephants were like the softest lullaby his mother ever sang to him.

Even through the encroaching haze of sleep, a single thought jarred continuously: they'd failed.

So what now?

***

Melanie dropped from the truck as soon as it came to a stop in front of a roadside restaurant, a clapboard shack from which wafted the smell of cooking fish. She concealed herself in the forest to avoid being seen.

The men from the other vehicles milled around for a few minutes and sat at a table. They were angry: she could hear them arguing in a language she couldn't understand. Not Arabic or French. She thought it might be Berber, but not because of how it sounded but because she guessed the men were nomadic tribesmen from the desert areas to the north.

She needed to decide what to do. Was there any way she could approach the men without immediately being captured and questioned, or worse?

Finally, she shrugged. Hiding in the woods wasn't going to get her anywhere, plus, she hadn't eaten since early that morning, and the trucks had been driving nonstop for three hours. They would likely have to stop for fuel soon, and when they did, someone was going to spot her on the back of the rearmost truck. So she strode out of the trees, adjusted her pack and walked up to the counter.

"What's for lunch?" she asked in broken French.

"Fish," the man replied, giving her a gap-toothed grin. "It's good. Fresh. I caught it in the river this morning."

His French was even worse than hers, which surprised her. The people on the bus and in the capital had spoken fluently, so quickly that she couldn't follow. Was he an immigrant? A member of some tribe that hadn't accepted the centralized education system? Or something else? She suddenly realized that she didn't really know the first thing about this country she'd decided to operate in. Online research and the CIA worldbook only went so far.

She studied the fish. They were a little bigger than her hand. "Can I have two of them?"

"Yes. Two thousand francs."

He said it much too hopefully and Melanie had to suppress a chuckle. If she laughed, he wouldn't budge from the price.

"I only want two, not five. Seven hundred francs."

He shook his head vehemently. They exchanged a couple more volleys and finally ended up at a thousand francs for the fish and another five hundred for a Coca Cola in a glass bottle.

The fish was excellent; it was the best meal she'd ever had for three dollars.

After silencing the rumbling of her stomach, she considered her plight. She needed these men to tell her where they'd picked up their load. If she went up and asked them, she'd become food for whatever scavengers roamed the forest. The only thing the animals wouldn't gnaw on was the bullet the men would put between her eyes.

Nothing brilliant occurred to her, so when the men showed signs of being about to leave the restaurant, she decided that a dumb plan was better than no plan at all, and she approached the grizzled, grey-haired man in his mid-fifties who was clearly the leader.

"Hello," she said in Arabic. She hoped they spoke the language. If she had to switch to English, the game was up. These men would never trust an American.

The driver looked up sharply, but his suspicion seemed to subside when he saw the person addressing him was a woman.

Good, she thought, *let them underestimate me.*

"You look like an honorable man, the leader of honorable men," she said. "I am in need of assistance." She looked around the restaurant. "And though this is a good place, I know I can't trust the locals to help."

Finally, the man responded. "And why do you think we would be any different?"

When she heard him speak Arabic and, better still, realized that his Arabic was halting and imperfect, Melanie nearly wept with relief.

This might actually work, she thought. But there were still many risks she had to take; any one of them could easily derail what she needed to do, and then she would be back to trying to follow the drivers. She had no other way to reach the men she wanted to punish.

"I've been robbed and lost everything but what I have in this pack. My money, my passport, everything," she said. Then she took the next risk: "I need to get back to Timbuktu in the next two days or my friends will leave me behind. I'll give you all I have left, a hundred American dollars, if you take me there." If she'd guessed wrong, if these men were from the south and not from the north, as she surmised... she would just have lost her anonymity for absolutely no gain.

"We are a trucking company, not a roving band of taxi drivers," the man replied.

"I'm begging you. I'm desperate."

The man looked her over; she hoped the demure pose and the Arabic approach would lead him to believe she was a liberated woman from the Islamic world. She already knew she could pass for Egyptian, but she would much rather pretend to be Lebanese if the situation called for it. Lebanon was famous for being a liberal, multi-ethnic place where the Arab world's intellectual and cultural leaders resided.

Well, at least it used to be before they intellectually and culturally decided to murder one another. But the regular people were still full of a *joie de vivre* that would help her to disguise the fact that she was a Westerner. Anyone would simply dismiss any strangeness as a Lebanese person acting Lebanese.

His gaze lingered a long time on her hair. She could almost hear his thoughts: this woman was either not an Islamic woman, or she was lapsed to the point she would allow everyone to see her without her head covered.

But she knew he wasn't an Arab. She'd heard him speak. Were the desert tribes as strict as other groups? Less so? More so?

The old man sighed. "Though I believe you're abusing Allah's call to aid one's fellow man, I will help you."

"Thank you," she thrust the crumpled bill in his direction.

He shook his head. "If your story is true, you need that more than we do. We've already been paid for this trip." He paused. "And if your story isn't true, then that is no concern of ours. We will do our duty before God."

He said the last part in a louder voice, probably for the benefit of his men. It was a clear warning that she should expect no camaraderie, not even that of occasional traveling companions, from his troops. She was on her own, and expected to keep herself to herself.

She sighed; it was going to be a long, hot, dusty and most of all lonely drive... but now that she knew they were taking the Timbuktu road, she was a lot more confident that she might actually make this work.

***

Adam Lai looked over the boardroom as he entered, counting supporters and people who'd want his head on a platter. It was still his company, but only by the slimmest of margins. Many of his directors were extremely unhappy, even among his supporters.

He smiled. At least they'd read the brief he'd sent. "So," he said without preamble. "What do you think?"

"This isn't what we do," Imar said. "We're in construction. Heavy industry. Consulting. Not... I don't even know what you'd call this. Peacekeeping? Non-proliferation? This is a job for the UN, or individual governments. Why get mired in this?"

His younger brother was incandescent, and he was probably right to feel that way. From the point of view of a shareholder, he was right: getting involved in the current fight to stop the spread of genetically modified monsters would water down their profits.

Of course, Imar would vote whatever Adam decided was best for the company, even if he had to make a little less money. He would always vote to keep control of the company in the family's hands. And that assured he would support Adam.

Others were not so certain. He let every one of his department heads express their concerns and put their arguments forward. Every one of them told him to reconsider. They thought he should think it over. They were in Malaysia, far from the world of monster attacks, after all.

"Gentlemen," he said sternly. "I'm afraid it's not me who has to think things over. It's you. Have you already forgotten that we were one of the first victims of weaponized biology? Have you already forgotten all the men you lost to these animals? The brightest young minds in each of your departments," he caught each of the men's gaze in turn, "were savagely cut down in their prime, brilliant futures shattered, all because some people had decided to test monsters where those men happened to be. Maybe the reason I haven't forgotten is that they nearly killed me, too.

"But this isn't a personal thing. It can't be. It's about the survival of society itself. What kind of a world will this be when a terrorist group can simply release a vanload of tiny carnivores bred for aggression and hunger, into a school? They won't have to convince suicide bombers to give their lives for an extremist cause, they won't have to expose themselves. Just drive up, drop off their charges and drive away. Everyone in this room has become wealthy by my side. We started out together, not knowing if we were going to have a company by the end of each month, and now we know we're all going to die extremely rich men. Well, I for one, would like the world to hold together a few more years so that my children can enjoy the life I've broken my back to achieve for them.

"I've never asked you to support something just because I said so. I've never felt any project, any direction for the company was important enough to create a rift among the board members. But this time, I am.

I'm asking each and every one of you to support the creation of the Suppression Division. I'm not asking you as businessmen, and I'm not asking you as company directors. Partly, I'm requesting it of you as fathers and uncles. But mostly, I'm requesting it as humans. You need to decide if money is more important than being able to look yourself in the mirror or less so.

"I'm opening the vote."

Ten minutes later, Lai sat in his office.

That could have gone better, he reflected. The board, men he'd trusted, men he thought he could count on, had not only voted against his proposal, but, in a lightning turnaround, they'd also voted Imar as the new Chairman and asked Adam to take a leave of absence.

"Only temporary, of course," they'd said.

"Until you can take some emotional distance from what happened to you," they'd also said.

It was bullshit, pure and simple. The board had kicked him out of the company his grandfather had founded, that his father and uncle had nearly run into the ground, and that he'd built into one of the biggest corporations in Malaysia, trailing only the Government-owned petroleum holdings and the major manufacturing concerns.

Like any CEO who doesn't own a controlling interest in the company, he knew the day would come when the board would force him out. He just expected it to be a very different board that would do it, far in the future after his supporters had retired. Not a board filled with old friends and family.

Furthermore, he'd always imagined that, when the day came, he'd feel crushed, a broken shell, lacking the energy to live another day after a titanic struggle to retain control. He thought he'd probably die soon after losing his job, possibly by his own hand, but more likely from ennui and a lack of desire to go on.

Maybe the fact that he'd been blindsided, never expecting the swift, final resolution heading his way, explained that he didn't feel broken or suicidal. He felt... free. Relieved. Energized, even.

He knew exactly what he wanted to do with the rest of his life, and even without his salary as CEO, he had plenty of income from the company. No one had taken his shares.

Lai decided he would forge ahead with his project without the company. He didn't really need it, after all.

The best part was that he'd already put the first step in motion. He hoped it would work out.

***

Youssef completed his prayers and stood, folding his prayer mat. He needed to get moving if he wanted to get everything done this morning. The souk would be open already, and it was a beautiful, warm day for doing his shopping. If the price was right, he might even be able to buy something for little Mahmoud. He started towards the main exit from the square.

Suddenly, a crack sounded, then another. He stopped dead in his tracks. Had that been gunfire? Before he could come to a decision, the crowd in front of him, which had been filing towards the exit in cramped but polite fashion, suddenly turned around and, to a man, began rushing back his way.

That settled it. He no longer thought, just turned with them, half of his attention on trying to avoid being trampled by the people around him, the other half on running away from the sounds as fast as his feet could carry him.

There was no conscious decision involved in the flight. His conscious mind had abdicated the decision-making process to that part of his brain responsible for instinctual processes, the primitive portion that told humans to run in the presence of saber-toothed tigers and poisonous snakes. The fact that the threat was thoroughly modern made no difference: the reaction was too basic to change.

He scurried around a corner, the dun-colored walls of the complex herding him towards another square but, more importantly, away from whoever the armed men were.

His city wasn't violent, but the war had only been over for seven years, and the walls still sported the pockmarks from the gunfire... and the citizens still remembered that when shots rang out, you ran the other way.

By virtue of his original position at the back of the crowd, Youssef found himself leading the charge to escape. He hoped no one was crushed by the running mass of bodies. He knew he couldn't stop: the press behind him would be tremendous.

He reached the square first, bursting around the final corner without slowing.

That was where the primal portion of his brain woke again and screamed at him.

Backwards! Go backwards! Danger! Flee!

But that was impossible. Even as he stumbled to a halt, the crowd behind him pushed him forward.

Straight into the waiting jaws of the dozens of slavering prehistoric creatures waiting in the square.

Youssef didn't even have time to ask God's help before the nearest of the monsters, twice as tall as a man, struck with a lightning-quick motion of its jaws and tore his head off his shoulders.

CHAPTER 6

"Gotcha!" Irina said, pumping her fist in the air.

Alex looked over at her and raised an eyebrow. She flashed him a triumphant smile and spoke in Russian: "I've located the trucks."

"The ones from the airfield?"

"Those are the ones we're chasing, yes? Of course those trucks. They're on the A5 road, fifty kilometers north of the border."

"In Mali?" He held up a hand. "And don't say 'is there any other northern border?' because if you do, I might be forced to use violence."

She smirked. "You might find me more difficult to intimidate than your little Siberian girls."

"I've heard of you. I won't underestimate your skills. Speaking of which, how the hell did you find them so fast?"

"I didn't. They found me."

"What?"

"The owner of the trucking company called this phone a dozen times. He obviously wants his driver back but, better still, he was the only one who called. I had a friend in Odessa run the number for me to see who it belonged to. Turns out I could have done it myself... it's listed in the Yellow Pages."

"Figuratively, of course. You're using a leaked directory," Alex said, trying to show he knew how intelligence people operated.

"Like hell figuratively. Literally." She turned her phone around, swiped away the map she'd been poring over and showed him the screen. A directory showed an entry for a trucking company in... he expanded the image... Bamako which listed a name, a number—he assumed this was the one Irina was referring to—and showed an image.

The image was very clearly one of the Mercedes-Benz trucks they'd encountered at the airfield. Standing beside it was a man who could have been one of the drivers, a guy who looked to be in his mid-fifties.

"That is Salah Ag Ilbak. He owns the company, and he also owns the phone we're tracking."

"What else do you know about him?" Alex asked. "How many men does he have?"

She laughed. "This isn't the Russian Army. We don't have access to the SVR's man in Bamako to put us up to speed about enemy strength. I can't tell us anything we didn't already know except his name and his position."

Alex grunted. She was right. And the transition from real soldier to mercenary was going to take a lot of getting used to. He was already disliking it, and he'd barely even gotten started.

Irina leaned forward and tapped Balzano on the shoulder. "We need to stop the vehicle," she said, switching to English.

"Why?"

"Because we're going the wrong way."

Their mini-convoy halted at the side of a dusty, potholed road. Hermes emerged from the other vehicle, a quizzical look on his face.

"They're on the A5," Irina informed him.

"That isn't the road to Bamako," Hermes replied.

"Then they aren't going to Bamako," Irina said. Alex smiled to see that he wasn't the only one she was abusing today. Apparently, she was only pleasant to be around when the boys were playing soldier... when it came to discussing her own field of expertise, she became a mixture of Stalin and Margaret Thatcher. Probably because most men would tend to dismiss her as just another pretty face. "They're a hundred and fifty klicks to our north and seventy-five east. This road goes to Segou, unless they're thinking of stopping along the way."

"They're not going to Segou," Hermes said. "They're going into the desert."

"That's a pretty long drive," Irina remarked.

"But it's the only destination that makes sense. The monsters have to be coming from somewhere without people. And the Sahara fits the bill perfectly."

"So, what now?"

"We need to follow them as fast as we can go. Because there aren't all that many cell towers in the open desert, and once they get off the cellular phone grid, Irina is not going to be able to find them again."

***

"We need to stop for a few hours," Salah told the woman. He had asked her to ride in his own truck for the duration of the journey. It was actually Samir's truck, but Samir was in the hands of the men with the guns, so he'd taken it upon himself to drive.

It was better this way. The woman would have been a distraction for the younger men. He'd met her like before, and the word to describe her was 'dangerous'. Even though she acted respectful of his age and position, sometimes she forgot herself and spoke of things no woman should know, and of places he only vaguely recognized from stories told to others. This was not a demure woman of faith, keeping her family on track. Glimpses shone through of a woman of the world. Or perhaps just a very worldly woman. Neither would be a good influence on the men.

He wondered who she really was, and what she was doing on the way to Timbuktu. Her story was believable enough—brave tourists from all over the world came to see the glories of that city, after all—but she didn't seem to fit the naïve tourist trope. There was something about her eyes, the way she gazed steadily at the world, missing nothing. If she'd been a man, he'd have either cultivated her friendship or given her wide berth.

"You have been good and honorable to me," she said. "I cannot complain about a delay."

He nodded, unsure of what to say, and turned right onto another road that ran parallel to the river.

She said nothing, merely staring at the blue water of the Niger River. After a couple of kilometers, the pavement ended and the true desert road began: a barely visible track somewhat cleared of the larger rocks. Fortunately, there was no sand here. That would come later, as they approached the place where the foreigners were building monsters.

Seeing her steely-eyed gaze, he sought to reassure her. "I have a cousin here. He has some items I need to pick up."

She seemed to be measuring him. "And since you've already been paid for this trip, that is a good thing."

"Yes. It is free. Very few things in this life are free."

They reached the village where Jamal was waiting. It was a cluster of adobe buildings huddled in a semicircle on the shore. There was no room to drive a truck inside, but his cousin had parked his own vehicle, a battered Toyota pickup, outside the houses.

Salah descended from the truck and walked over to where his cousin stood. The man was fifteen years younger than Salah, his hair still black as the day he was born, and his face held concern after they released their embrace.

"I would have preferred for you not to ask me for this."

"I would have preferred not to ask. Do you have them?"

"Twenty rifles. And a bonus. A rocket launcher."

"I am not a man of war. You will have to teach me to use that. The rifles... all of my men have used rifles before. Even automatic ones. It gets dull out in the desert, so when we can get ammunition we shoot at rocks with an AK-47."

"Then you will have no problem with these. They are also the Russian guns."

Salah nodded. That was good. Unfamiliar rifles would trip them up.

"And the launcher? Can I see it?"

Jamal lowered the back gate of the pickup truck and pulled on a green-painted crate. Then he looked back and scowled. "Your woman seems interested in this."

"She is not my woman, merely someone who asked for a ride. She appealed to our charity."

Jamal nodded. He understood, but he didn't like it any more than Salah did. He quickly covered the box with a blanket that lay on the pickup's bed.

The woman arrived. "If you're going to be here a while, do you think I can look around in the village? I'd like to see that tall building."

"The temple," Jamal nodded. "It is very beautiful. This is a safe place, so feel free to enjoy it."

She walked away, disappearing between two adobe buildings. Even before the woman reached the village, two children ran out to see who the stranger approaching them might be.

Salah turned back to Jamal. "Is she to be trusted?"

"She is of no consequence. I accept that she has her own agenda, and we know nothing about her, but she was in the middle of the jungle in Ivory Coast. No one knew we would stop there, not even us, until you called. We just happened to be the first people she saw who could solve her problem of getting closer to Timbuktu. She would have hopped in any car going her way."

"A loose woman."

"Perhaps," Salah replied. "But I get the sensation that she would only be loose when she decides it. She could climb into the car of the worst degenerate in Africa and she would be perfectly safe."

"Perhaps you should leave her here. I'll make sure she gets to Timbuktu safely."

Salah was sorely tempted, but after a few moments, he shook his head. "I gave my word. Let's load up the weapons."

It was the work of a moment. Then, Salah spent time speaking to Jamal and talking on the phone. The woman returned, he said his goodbyes and they rolled away.

***

"We need to make another stop," he told her some hours later.

She nodded her assent. It was almost as if she'd become a completely different passenger after leaving the village, much less talkative, lost in deep thoughts.

He much preferred this version.

This stop was much shorter. As agreed, the men were waiting on the side of the road outside Diré. There were twelve of them: three he knew by name, and the rest he knew by sight. They were all part of his clan, but cousins of cousins, men who'd left the desert for the towns.

These particular men had all been summoned to Diré from surrounding villages where they were hiding or in semi-retirement. All of them had seen conflict in the past few years. Many men had, with Mali so unsettled. All of them had fought honorably for the Tuareg against the oppressors in the south. They were just the men he needed to complement his own drivers.

Within minutes, they had been distributed among the trucks and they started down the road. Timbuktu was just forty kilometers ahead. He would be relieved to be rid of his burdensome passenger.

He said a prayer that she was telling the truth, and that Timbuktu was actually her final destination. If she tried to wander the desert without proper protection, it would not end well for her.

As if reading his thoughts, she suddenly spoke.

"Let me go with you," she said.

"It is only a few more minutes to Timbuktu," he replied, unsure what else he could say.

"I don't want to go to Timbuktu. I want to go with you."

He stared at her, eyes completely off the road, the one thing he always told young drivers they should never do. "You have no idea what you're saying."

"You're going to attack the men who asked you to transport the monsters. You think they betrayed you to the people who ambushed you. That's why you've got an RPG and a shipment of AK-47s in the back. That's also why you just picked up a small army."

He nearly ran off the road.

"I don't know what you're talking about," he stammered.

"You know exactly what I'm talking about. And I know exactly what is happening. We both want the same thing, and I can help you achieve it."

"You? You are a lost woman. Probably fallen beyond even Allah's capacity to redeem."

"Perhaps you are correct. But I'm still useful. From what I saw back there, I'm the most highly-trained soldier in this convoy."

He laughed. "Girl, your joke grows thin."

"I am not joking. I'm a US Marine sniper. And before you say something stupid, like that snipers aren't real soldiers, you'd need to know something: I'm a Marine first, a sniper second."

He paused for a long time. "For both of our sakes, I hope that isn't true."

"It's true. And you need me." She opened her bag to show him a rifle that made the AK-47s they'd loaded hours before look like something from the stone age. "Your men are going to attack a factory or a lab of some sort. They'll have defenders up on the roof or in other places where they can cut you to pieces before you even know where they are. I can cover them from a kilometer away if we need to. They'll die before your men are exposed. You can go inside and wreak whatever havoc you desire."

"And where will you be once we go inside?"

"Right behind you," the woman replied. "If you'll lend me a regular rifle, I'll use that. If not, I have a handgun in my bag, too. And when I run out of bullets, I also have a knife."

"And if I say no? Will you shoot me in my cab? I am not armed right now."

She stared at him for a moment, then sighed and shook her head. "No. If you throw me out at Timbuktu, I'll follow you through the desert the best I can until you lead me to the place you're going. Then, if you left anyone alive, I'll kill them."

"If there is anyone alive in there when we're done, then I will not be alive." He studied her set features. "Why are you so eager to attack a lab in Mali? Has your government decided to cut costs by forcing its assassins to travel in borrowed trucks?"

"No. This is personal. I lost a friend to the people who build monsters. Worse, though, there's a little girl in a hospital back home fighting for her life. She was mauled in an attack. I'm going to hunt down the animals who did this, with or without your help. She is my niece." She shrugged. "If you let me come with you, I can probably save some of your men. If you don't, I'll pick up where you left off. But I'm not backing away."

Salah sighed and nearly forgot himself so far as to take Allah's name in vain. He caught himself in time, but still his anger simmered at the woman.

Nevertheless, when they reached Timbuktu, he continued onwards without stopping, the woman still seated beside him.

***

"We lost them," Irina cursed.

Hermes had transferred to the lead vehicle. "Why?"

"They're off the cellular grid," she replied. "We're getting into some serious desert here. No towers."

"Well, we had a good run. What's their last position?"

"A couple of clicks north of Timbuktu."

Hermes leaned forward. "Javier, step on it. Let's get to the point where they disappeared as fast as we can."

"I'm already going as fast as we can," Balzano protested.

"Nonsense," Hermes replied. "These things can go much faster. We haven't even left the road yet. Step on it."

The Argentine obeyed and Max felt the acceleration press him back into his seat. At first, the man seemed tentative, but then seemed either to resign himself to the fact that they were going to crash or begin to enjoy the sensation of driving at insane speeds on public roads in a vehicle that was more like a tank than a car.

Max shrugged. It wasn't the safest thing he'd ever done, but it was certainly less risky than jumping off a helicopter into enemy-held mountains. He didn't expect to die in bed of old age, but he also didn't think Balzano would kill him. Somewhere out there was a bullet with his name on it, and it wouldn't be denied by a road accident. He dozed.

Thirty minutes later, they reached the spot where the trucks had gone off the grid.

The road they'd been following tracked alongside the Niger River, a fertile area which kept the real desert at arm's length. Once they got out of Timbuktu, however, all doubt vanished.

It wasn't the Sahara you saw in the movies. There were no enormous dunes of bright yellow sand. The dunes here were low, peppered with nearly round shrubs, and the sand was a pale color. Max expected the vegetation would disappear as they went deeper into the desert.

"Let's see if we can find tracks," Hermes called. "Twelve trucks went through here somewhere. They have to have left marks. And Irina, get a drone up. We need to find them... or traces at least."

Max got out with the rest of them as they trudged and drove around an area the size of Gorki Park searching for six sets of truck tracks.

He sighed and wiped the sweat from his brow. The sun beat down hard on his head, and the only sunscreen any of these yahoos had bothered to bring was weak: SPF 15. He'd look like a lobster by the end of it.

This had 'long day' written all over it.

***

"Get off of that," Philippe said. "You'll break it and I haven't even calibrated it yet."

Poupée looked down at him from atop the nutrient tank. She cocked her head quizzically, as if trying to make out what he'd said.

She was frighteningly smart. The original version of this same little animal, the one that had broken his heart, had been intelligent, but not quite to the same level: this one had been decanted two days before and already recognized her name. She would soon be testing her tiny vocal chords.

She seemed human, almost. But unlike a human baby, the monkey-like creature had an animal's instinctive learning curve, accelerated by a couple of genetic tweaks Philippe had thought might be fruitful to make the resulting creature even more intelligent. It didn't need years and years under mother's care to learn the basics. In fact, the little creature had learned to move on all fours in the Jeep coming to the new lab. By nightfall, it was walking upright.

"Come here," Philippe said.

Poupée stared. He pulled a piece of candy out of his pocket.

"Come here," he repeated.

The little creature sniffed the air, trying to gauge what he held.

"Come here."

Poupée jumped down and snatched the piece of candy from his hand before retreating back up to the top of the cylinder. She munched on it for a couple of seconds, staring at him all the time.

"That's right," he said. "Good." He held his hand out to her. "Poupée." Then he brought it back and touched his own chest. "Philippe." He repeated the gesture. "Philippe."

The little creature's eyes burned with intensity. They remained where they were, staring at each other for long minutes before he finally decided he needed to get on with his calibration of the equipment. He turned to go.

"Phleep," Poupée said.

He froze. It sounded exactly the way it had sounded a decade before when Poupée's homonymous predecessor had learned to speak. Up until the last time he saw her, the little creature had been unable to pronounce his entire name. The tiny anatomy was limited to making certain sounds.

But that wasn't the important thing. The important thing was that this new version from one of Sun-Lee's industrial vats had done in a day what had taken the original weeks. It meant that Philippe's original design was working better than it ever had before. The building and incubation procedures had been much more precise this time around.

Better still, it meant that, if he was careful to conceal her abilities and diligent in training her, Poupée could become an ally in a place where he had no friends.

The new lab wasn't an above-ground warehouse like the old one. This one looked like a cold war bunker complex, except on a massively larger scale. Philippe suspected it must have been built by one of the region's demagogues as a military complex, probably a nuclear weapons lab. The entrance was a camouflaged tunnel a hundred meters long, big enough for large trucks.

Had they gone far enough east in the desert that Kaddafi might have built it? Maybe the reason his nuclear weapons complexes were never found was that they weren't in Libya at all, but in Mali or Niger or Algeria. Sun-Lee had been extremely careful not to let Philippe know exactly where the original lab had been... and that meant that he couldn't calculate where they were now by the length of the car ride.

He shook his head to clear it and remembered that Poupée wasn't his only pet. It wouldn't do to neglect his other little creation, even if Poupée was destined to supplant her in every way.

"Come with me. Let's go say hi to Chiffon," Philippe said.

CHAPTER 7

The complex was a darker shadow in a rocky patch of ground where the dunes gave way to packed dirt and stone. Through the night vision goggles, it looked like a warehouse.

Melanie grunted. "I wonder how they keep the satellites from spotting them."

"No one with satellites cares what happens in Northern Mali," Salah replied.

It was the kind of attitude she expected to encounter as an American in Africa. The US was famously indifferent to the plight of the continent, of course, but this time, it didn't sound like the criticism was specifically aimed at Americans. She suspected the comment contained unspoken anger at Russia, China and, very likely, the major Arab countries, too.

"Well, if we fail to take these guys out, I'm pretty sure someone is going to take an interest. If I got information that could lead me all the way here, the major intelligence agencies can do it, too. Even more quickly than I did."

"You have the same problem everyone from dry places does," Salah said. "You don't listen. I didn't say they *couldn't* watch. I said they don't care. And these monsters? The people building them will sell them to anyone. I've driven to that airfield dozens of times. I've delivered to Arabs, to Europeans, to Chinese. No one will attack the complex as long as they guarantee equal access."

"And why are you attacking it?"

"Because they betrayed us." Salah spat. "It was the North Korean who did it, I can assure you. The other one, the Frenchman, he's human, but the boss is colder than a witch's heart."

"But why?"

"Because he doesn't care, either. He sold out his clients. We were expected to be collateral damage."

She was glad she couldn't see his face.

"There's not much movement," she said.

"They're in there," Salah replied. "Dozens of them. Men in white coats and soldiers in green uniforms."

"Green uniforms? Not much good for desert warfare."

"I think the Korean wants them to look like the troops from his country. The uniforms are like the ones you see in the news."

"You seem rather well-informed on world events."

A long silence ensued, followed by a sigh. "We're not all savages in Africa," Salah said quietly.

"You're right. I'm sorry. In fact, the only real savages here aren't even African. They're in that building over there. How about we put them out of their misery?"

"You don't think they're going to send out patrols?"

"If they were going to do it, they'd have done it by now."

Every star in the universe seemed to be out, aided by the fact that there was no light pollution to speak of. It was almost light enough by starlight alone that she was tempted to do without the night scope.

But no. You didn't put your allies' lives in danger that way. You used the tools, even if you didn't think they were necessary. She locked the night scope into place, making certain everything was adjusted correctly and lined up.

"I'm ready," she told Salah. She took a deep breath and aimed the rifle at the roof of the building, and the dimly-visible hangar doors that fronted the warehouse.

It certainly didn't look like the people in there were expecting company. In fact, it seemed like the place was deserted. Except she believed Salah's words implicitly when he said that this was where he'd picked up a load of deadly animals just two days before.

She believed his words because she saw his eyes when he said them: they burned with the righteous anger of a man betrayed.

Did mine do the same? she wondered. *Probably, or he wouldn't have allowed me to come.*

She heard a rustling from behind as Salah's troops filed past her position, a tiny column of fighters. Some were obviously attuned to the desert, making almost no noise as they advanced. Those guys would have been dangerous to any foe without IR. Was night vision tech widespread in the Sahara? She had no clue; none of her training missions had ever been aimed at fighting in the region. She hadn't been part of any of the teams selected for African missions while the Libyans were still a dictatorship.

The men crept up to the front door and waited. The hangar doors where the trucks entered were closed but Salah had told her that there was a single-person entrance on the front of the building as well, and that they would try to get in that way.

She wondered what kind of tech they had for the entrance, but it turned out to be a lot less impressive than she expected. The rearmost of the men stood up. They were holding something heavy between them. As she watched, mouth agape, they simply ran at the door and rammed it.

It swung open and she pulled her scope away: she didn't want to lose night vision in the sudden flood of light.

Besides, the men were in. There was no further need for a sniper to cover them from a distance.

Had this been a Marine incursion, she would have held position, covering the building in case the enemy tried to go over the roof and come at the Tuareg warriors from the rear. But it wasn't, and Melanie wanted her part of the action. She deserved to put a bullet through the forehead of at least a few of the men responsible for putting Stephanie, her niece, on life support.

Melanie wanted to get in there *right now*, but she forced herself to take a deep breath and scan the roofs and surrounding area one last time. Only when she was absolutely certain none of the enemy was around did she lay her rifle in its pouch, close the zipper and stand. She spoke to her gun, a habit that she'd formed because she spent more time with it than with anyone or anything else in her life over the past five years. It wasn't something she could help: "I'll be back in a bit, girl. And if I don't make it, be shoot true for whoever finds you out here."

She sprinted for the door, trying to make as little noise as possible.

It wouldn't have made much difference; no one inside would hear the rustling of her clothes. The clatter of automatic weapons fire cut through the night. AK-47... but whose? If there was one constant in the developing world, it was that rifle, the magnum opus of a man whose name was legend among soldiers for more than seventy rears: Mikhail Kalashnikov. Everyone used it.

Melanie slowed as she approached the entrance. The shooting was still going on, and she didn't want to walk into a firefight without a careful look.

The hangar was empty of trucks and combatants. The only thing visible were a couple of bodies about halfway across its expanse. She jogged up and knelt beside them: a guard in a bright green uniform and a young Asian woman in a lab coat. They'd both been shot multiple times.

"So much for fire discipline," she sighed.

The loading bay was well-lit and very obviously empty. It was just a big arched roof covering a concrete slab where trucks could park and be loaded without being cooked by the Sahara sun. The loading docks themselves were concrete bays like one would encounter at the rear of a mall in suburbia.

She sprinted across the open space, remembering to zigzag in case anyone decided to take a pot shot at her. She jumped up onto the platform and took cover beside a cargo door.

No one appeared, so she looked inside quickly, then pulled her head back.

Nothing. Just a wide, empty corridor heading deeper into the complex beyond. She chose the centermost and ran until she came to a curve. A quick look confirmed the next segment was empty, too.

About halfway to the door at the end of that one, the shooting started again, punctuated by screams. She couldn't make out the words, but the guns were still AKs. She burst through a doorway to find Salah standing grimly, watching as his men riddled another three corpses with bullets.

He turned to her, eyes afire. "I think we will both be disappointed," he said. He said it calmly, as if he'd been standing on a beach as opposed to a complex where an enemy was producing terror weapons. "I fear the men we seek are not present today."

"Surely we haven't seen the whole complex," she replied. "Where are the labs? The offices? We've only seen a few dormitories."

"I don't know the answer to that question. In fact, I've never been deeper into the building than the corridor behind us."

"Then why do you think they're not here?"

"Because there are almost no people here. Every time we've been here before, the place was full of scientists. Also, there are always several trucks in the loading bay. Now it's empty."

"Let's hope they're asleep, then."

Shots echoed from an open doorway up ahead and one of Salah's men fell to the ground, screaming and clutching his stomach.

Melanie dove into the open apartment beside her. The rest of the Tuaregs did the same. She crouched beside the door and poked her head out for an instant to check the situation.

The shooter was still in the doorway, standing in the open as if daring anyone to leave cover to engage him. It was a good position for a guy with an automatic rifle: he could spray the entire room or concentrate his fire using localized bursts if anyone moved. Salah's four uninjured people were pinned behind what looked a large metal trash container. Salah himself was behind a column.

She had no idea where the rest of the crew might be, but none of her allies was in position to lift their weapons and shoot back.

Which left it up to her. She obviously wasn't as good with a handgun as with her Remington, but the range was maybe ten yards. If she wasn't able to put one between the guy's eyes at this range, she would give back her EGA.

The trick was to do it without getting turned into Swiss cheese.

She looked around the room she'd sheltered in. It held a bunk bed in which only the bottom bunk had been slept in, one chair and a tiny desk. Her eyes landed on a square alarm clock with red digital numbers. Old school stuff.

Melanie picked it off the table, tore the plug out of the wall and hefted it.

Perfect.

She returned to the door and lobbed the clock across the room to where the other small apartment area opened up.

It crashed against the wall and clattered to the floor.

The bad guy with the gun opened fire and bullets tore into the drywall across from her.

She only waited long enough to see the first shot strike and exposed herself for a single second, took a bead, fired off a shot and moved back.

The rifle fire stopped. Melanie took a second to think. She didn't want to poke her head out to see what was up because if she'd missed, the guy would be waiting for her to reappear from where she'd taken her shot.

So instead of getting her head blown off, she dove across the corridor, rolled and ended up behind the same trash container as her allies.

On the way, she looked to see where the shooter was. All she saw was the bottom of his boots. He was on his back in the doorway.

She stood, dusted herself off and spoke. "It's clear, let's go." Then she ran towards the doorway, gun in hand, just in case.

There was zero need. The green-clad guard was dead as a doornail, a single bullet hole in his forehead. She looked at it critically for a moment and made a mental note to get back to the range: she'd aimed for the bridge of his nose, and the shot had missed high and to the left. It hadn't come back to bite her, but an inch further off and she would have missed and probably gotten chewed up by the AK-47.

Speaking of which, she relieved the guard of it and put the strap on her shoulder. This fight looked like it was going to turn into a question of who could fling the most lead into the air, and she didn't want to be the one to bring a handgun to an automatic rifle fight.

Melanie refused to look at the guard's face too closely. The black boy she'd drilled looked young… and she really didn't want to know just how young. There were child combatants in African conflicts, and she didn't want to be the one who stole some poor mother's twelve-year old.

Especially considering that a good part of the reason she was here was that a young girl was in the hospital.

So she stepped away quickly, resisting the urge to look back. There would be time to think about what she might have done later, once they were out of this building and her mission was complete.

The corridor behind the guard was carpeted, which seemed wrong, somehow. You weren't supposed to be running towards an unseen enemy with an AK-47 in your hand over grey corporate carpet. You needed a jungle around you, or maybe a mountain village in Central Asia.

The next door opened into another large room, and the sense of having invaded a corporate headquarters deepened. It looked like a cube farm: people should have been sitting at the desks, bent industriously over their laptops, suffering from paralysis by analysis.

Instead, the room, though brightly-lit, was completely empty. Salah's men spread out and began to check the cubes, but Melanie was more concerned about the doors that opened up along the walls.

She went into the nearest one and her heart sank.

It was the lab, the place she'd been searching for. There could be no doubt about that. A number of vertical steel cylinders the size of water tanks lined the walls, while an enormous square table in the center glistened with glassware and tubes.

But the place had been smashed. The glass was in pieces, the tanks against the walls pierced in several places.

The molten remains of a computer terminal still stank of burned plastic.

Someone had abandoned this place with no intention of ever coming back.

Salah stood beside her. "It is as I feared," he said.

"So now what?"

"If they had gone into the cities, I would have heard. There's only one place they can go from here: deeper into the desert. It will take some time to locate them." He held her gaze grimly. "But we will find them in the end. No mouse moves or vulture flies in the desert without the Tuareg knowing about it."

"I will help," she said.

"I fear you won't be of much help. Your element is not the deep desert. You should go home."

"I– What's that?"

A rumbling sound reached her from somewhere deeper in the complex. She strode over to have a look, rifle at the ready. It didn't sound like an engine, the sound was deeper, something you felt in your bones.

"It's coming from the back door," she told Salah.

They approached carefully: the door was a large double-paned one, one panel opening in each direction, but it had no windows they could study the other side through.

The door burst open without warning, and a grey, waist-high mass emerged. Melanie caught only a single scent of rotting fish before the wall of water knocked her off her feet.

The flood washed over her head. For a terrifying instant, she was six again, stranded in the middle of a pool at a friend's house. As the other children looked on, she realized she wasn't going to make it to the side, and she went down. The last thing she saw before her head went down was her mother, fully clothed, diving in after her.

This time, however, there were no strong arms to lift her out and, for a split second, Melanie nearly panicked.

Then her training kicked in and she relaxed, remembered her years of struggle to overcome her fear of water, which culminated in her becoming city freestyle champ. She tried to swim.

Her hand encountered the floor, soggy carpet leaving no doubt about which way was down. She pushed up against it to see if she could reach the surface. She got her legs down and stood.

Her head broke the surface.

And realized the water level was just below her chest.

"Nice," she said to herself, shaking her head. "You'll be drowning in a bathtub next."

Though the water was no longer a threat, she realized it was pulling hard. The wave that had hit her was receding, and it was pushing her through the doorway. She tried to grab onto something, anything, but nothing came to hand and she floated through the entrance, her feet only occasionally touching the floor.

Only then did she realize the lights had gone, and that the cube farm's emergency lighting didn't reach into this particular corridor.

The darkness wasn't a problem, though. Allowing the current to push her along, she unclipped her flashlight from her pants and prepared to check where she was going.

Then she thought better of it. The beam would just give away her position. Would it be better to see and be seen or simply to drift in the dark?

The water was rushing through a thick grate in the floor, and she thought she would be sucked through.

But the grating was too fine for that, and she just stood there, struggling to stay on her feet as chairs and other office detritus slammed into her. Eventually, the rushing flood slowed to a trickle and she turned on her flashlight—potential enemies be damned—to see that the drains were clogged with everything from desks and monitors to…

Salah.

The man lay facedown in a shallow pool, unmoving. She knelt beside him and turned him around, trying to feel a pulse, anything.

Nothing.

"Not on my watch," she swore and began to breathe into his mouth and pump on his chest. Despite all the training she'd had in the military, now that the chips were down, the reanimation course that came to mind was one she'd stumbled upon by the Tarrytown Fire Department in New York state one day when she'd happened to stop because a sign said there was a town's fair happening.

She moved her hands to the rhythm of the old BeeGees staple "Staying Alive". One, two, three, four pumps. Breathe into his mouth.

One, two, three, four pumps. Breathe into his mouth.

"Come on, Salah," she said in English.

The grizzled, ashen features remained unresponsive.

One, two, three, four pumps. Breathe into his mouth.

A stream of water gushed out and he coughed. Wide open eyes suddenly stared back up at her. Hands like claws grabbed the front of her shirt.

"Relax. You're going to be all right."

For a second, the bewildered stare remained, and then the hands slowly relaxed. He said something in Tuareg. And then he held her gaze.

"Shukram," he whispered. *Thank you.* "You saved my life."

"We are in arms together," she replied.

He struggled to his knees, and she helped him to his feet, still coughing out water.

And then she heard the rumble again.

"I think there's more water coming," she said. "We need to get out of here."

Salah shook his head. "Not water." He pointed, his finger trembling, over her right shoulder.

Melanie turned around and, Marine or no Marine, she screamed.

An enormous mound of flesh sat within what looked like it had once been a colossal water tank before someone had blasted it open.

The mound had a neck ending in a head the size of a refrigerator.

When Melanie screamed, the head turned towards her and the thing opened its mouth to reveal teeth like swords. The neck snapped in their direction.

Melanie couldn't move. She froze in place, waiting for death to engulf her.

Something crashed into her and dropped her onto the sodden ground as the teeth missed by less than a foot overhead.

Salah got off her and began dragging her towards the exit.

Melanie pushed him off and got to her feet. They ran for the exit as fast as Salah could go.

Even so, the monster's mouth nearly got them as they reached the door.

"Damn," Melanie said, "this corridor is wide enough for two of those things."

"They must have been planning to take it out this way."

But the monster, large as it was, wasn't built for land, or at least not to be graceful on land. They turned to see it waddling towards them.

It didn't take a genius to realize it wasn't going to capture them. It was just too slow.

Melanie regretted having lost her rifle in the flood, but she took a bead on the thing's eye with her handgun. At this range she wouldn't miss—and if she couldn't kill the monster, at least she would blind it.

Voices from behind, two men shouting in Tuareg, broke her concentration and made her turn.

They were two of Salah's fighters, pointing at the monster and jabbering.

Her annoyance turned to delight when she saw what one of the men had on his shoulder.

"Give me that," she said, grabbing the strap that held the RPG.

The man pulled away until Salah said something to him, then he handed over the rocket launcher, reluctantly.

They retreated to the end of the corridor—she saw this one was another of the ones that led to the loading bay.

"Get back," she said.

Then she knelt on the ground, aimed the rocket—at this range, and with a target that size, she wasn't even particularly concerned that she'd only had a few days of training with RPGs—and pressed the big red button.

At first, she thought the impossible had happened and she'd missed.

But a couple of beats after the missile disappeared, the monster seemed to explode from within.

Melanie wiped away the blood that had sprayed on her face, handed the spent tube back to the soldier and smiled.

"That felt even better than I thought it would," she said.

Then she walked away.

They would need to wait for daybreak before deciding what to do next.

CHAPTER 8

"We're too late," Hermes said.

Max said nothing. What could he say? The only thing he could think of was to point out that it was extremely obvious that it was too late. That didn't seem productive.

Two bodies, stiff and wide-eyed, lay on the floor of the loading bay. They'd been dead for a while.

"Not a professional job," Max said. After all, if Hermes could state the obvious, why shouldn't he? The two corpses were riddled with bullets. The fact that they held no weapons meant little, but Max supposed that, even before they were killed, they posed no threat. They looked more like office workers than guards.

"No. In fact, if I had to guess, I'd say it was done by our friends, the truckers."

"Why?"

Hermes shrugged. "When criminal organizations have problems, they fall out. Who knows? Maybe the truckers didn't get paid. Maybe they were the intermediaries in this deal and the dinosaurs we burned belonged to them, and they lost a bunch of money. It could be one of a million things."

Max looked around. This didn't look like a little misunderstanding between small-time crooks. This looked like the fury of a Jihad.

But Hermes was right about one thing: they didn't have enough information to speculate.

So they walked further into the facility. The lights were off, which made sense, at least: if you were going to come into a facility and kill everyone inside, it would be easier if they couldn't see you.

It made little difference. The loading bay doors were open, resulting in an illuminated—and oven-like—interior. The bright tropical sun lit the entire bay.

Flies buzzed around the corpses, not even dispersing when they approached.

"Should we tell someone about this?" Balzano asked. The Argentine, Max noted, didn't get too close to the bodies.

Hermes shrugged. "Not really our job."

Max suspected that meant no one would ever know what happened to the people who worked here. Without a working air conditioner, they would probably mummify in the baking heat, and be covered as the facility inevitably filled with sand.

He suspected that most of them wouldn't be missed.

But he also suspected that Balzano would bear watching. The expression on his face was that of a man having a crisis of conscience. In their line of work, that was a serious liability. If he decided that the next of kin needed to be notified and he called the wrong people... not only could that ruin the operation, but it could also get the rest of them on a bunch of shitlists if he started reporting what he'd seen.

Max made a mental note to talk to the guy.

It would have to wait, though. They needed to clear the rest of the building.

Voornacht and Louembe swept past, rifles leveled, only glancing at the bodies long enough to ascertain that they were, in fact, dead.

Max let them take point. He shared Hermes' conviction that they would find absolutely nothing of value in the huge warehouse complex.

So when, just a few meters further ahead, Louembe's deep voice came back to them from a corridor, it came as a surprise.

"Mr. Cevert, I think you might want to see this."

Hermes nodded to Max and they pushed forward into a small area with residential apartments built into it. The entire area was pockmarked with bullets and Max could see three bodies: two on the floor in the middle of the room and a third in the doorway.

Louembe knelt beside one of the nearer corpses, and it took Max a second to figure out what he was doing, and another moment to believe it once he understood: the man was tearing the lab smock off a dead young woman.

"Look," Louembe said. "Here."

He stood and took a step back, pointing at the bare, pale skin, puckered with several bullet holes.

Max gasped. The largest wound hadn't been made by a bullet. The flesh was torn in a semi-circular pattern.

Something had taken a bite out of the woman... and then walked away, leaving bloody footprints on the concrete.

"The creature fed after the other men were gone, and after she was dead. No bleeding, see?" Louembe said. "I'd say it's a lot smaller than the ones at the airport. Maybe a meter and a half tall. Maybe a little less."

"How many?"

Louembe shrugged. "Only one came here. It might be the only one, there might be a thousand of them. I can't tell."

"Don't they move in packs?"

Louembe cocked his head. "I know what you're thinking, Mr. Cevert. You're thinking the famous African tracker will be able to tell just by the fact that one claw print is slightly larger than the other that the animal is part of a well-adjusted family that hunts together on alternating Mondays and Thursdays. That's not how tracking works, no matter what you might have seen in the movies." He turned to look down the hall. "And that goes double for creatures who were probably released from an incubator just a few hours ago. Who knows what instincts have survived the genetic modification, and how those were affected by being surrounded by a building instead of a jungle?"

Hermes nodded. "Call Irina and tell her to stay in the Jeep. And tell Jerome to keep his rifle close and the engine running. I don't want to lose another driver."

Max made the call and they headed deeper into the complex, flashlights ablaze. They'd long since left behind the bright light of the hangar doors, and the only natural illumination they encountered came from bullet holes in the wall and roof, where the corrugated skin happened to intersect with the corridor they were following.

"Whoever hit this place was not short on ammo," Voornacht whispered.

Max chuckled quietly. "And they weren't exactly crack shots by the look of it. If it weren't for the evidence to the contrary, I'd say they couldn't even hit the walls."

"I'm not so sure," Voornacht replied. "Did you see that guard we passed? Someone dropped him with one shot, right in the head."

"Even the incompetent get lucky sometimes," Max replied, darkly.

He was thinking of a mission in Beirut, near the Green Line. They'd been sent in to teach one of the Muslim factions the lesson that you could kidnap all the American assets you wanted, but you never, ever, for any reason, took a Russian. The mission had entailed murdering three entire families and harvesting fingers to show the misguided leaders the error of their ways, before the leaders were killed in turn.

They had approached the target building from behind—from Muslim-held territory so that no one would suspect them of being enemies—the grisly harvested digits in a sack. They kept close to the buildings, hugging the dark patches along the street.

They should have been invisible to all eyes, and the idea was to overpower the sentry at the back entrance, a man who would probably be much less alert than his peers looking across the Green Line at the Christian sector of the capital.

They had gotten to within twenty meters when a shot rang out and Sergeant Mihailovich, who'd been just a few steps in front of Max, went down in a spray of blood. He'd been shot perfectly between the eyes.

"Shit!" Max said. "Sniper! Hit them with everything we've got!"

They opened fire on the back door, a spray of lead shattering concrete already bearing the scars of a hundred firefights.

Individual shots were the only return fire.

"He's there," Max said, bringing his rifle to bear on the spot where the muzzle flash had betrayed the shooter's position.

A barrage suppressed return fire and, when they reached the position, they ignored the dead sentry and entered the building like the wrath of a vengeful God.

Only much later, when they were aboard the transport heading back to Yekaterinburg did Vitaly approach.

"Did you see the sentry?" he said.

"No, what about him?"

"He was a kid, maybe fifteen. And this is his gun."

He handed Max an American revolver, something that would have been accurate to maybe ten meters in the hands of a skilled marksman.

"This killed Mihailovich?"

Vitaly nodded. "It was the only weapon he had. He was probably aiming at someone else. You. Me. Our guys on the other side of the street. We'll never know."

Max shuddered. It was on such things that the fortunes of war balanced. The difference between life and death might be just how badly a scared kid missed what he was aiming at.

He snapped back to the present, reminding himself that woolgathering in a place where they already knew they would find animals that wanted to eat them was another good way to get dead.

Louembe held up a hand and they stopped.

"What?" Hermes asked.

"The floor up ahead… it's wet."

"Dragon pee?" Voornacht rumbled.

"Not urine," Louembe said. "Smells like swamp water."

"Ah, one of those famous Sahara Desert swamps," Hermes said. Despite being Belgian and not French, Max could hear the Gallic shrug in his words, delivered deadpan in the darkness. "What do you recommend?"

"I see no reason not to move forward, but perhaps you should let me scout ahead."

"Agreed."

Louembe disappeared into the hallway. A tense minute later, his head popped back out. "It's clear... but it's strange. Like a water pipe burst, except it's not clean... there's a strong smell of fish."

"Fish smells won't kill us, let's go."

The next room was an office area that had been trashed and subsequently flooded.

Max entered an office and called. "There's computer equipment in here... looks like it was destroyed, but maybe Irina can do something with it."

Hermes walked over and studied the computers. "This makes no sense."

"What doesn't? The trashed computers?"

"No, that makes sense. The guys who came into this place shot everything and everyone they found. What doesn't seem right is how they got trashed. Not one shot was fired here." Hermes looked out into the office. "And the rest of it is weird, too. There are a lot of workstations, a ton of sleeping areas that have seen recent use. Several labs." He gestured to offices around the central area. "So where are the bodies? The truckers, or whoever, were in no mood to take prisoners. We should be waist deep in dead people who came here to build monsters. But we're not. It looks like a skeleton crew got killed."

"You think they ran when the deal at the airport went sour." It wasn't a question.

"Yeah. That's exactly what I think."

"They could be anywhere in the world."

"I doubt that. I doubt it a lot. You can't move an operation this size just anywhere. It's got to be in Africa. Or in Russia."

Max nodded. "Only if the government allows it."

"Or the Mafia."

"Like I said, the government."

"Look out!" Louembe's voice preceded the big man through the door to the main office area. He dove aside just as a creature followed him through.

Max didn't hesitate. A quick burst of three shots to the creature's chest brought it down. Thankfully, it was much easier to kill than its big brother at the airfield; it went down and stayed down. "I like these guns," Max told Hermes.

They rushed over to where Louembe was trying to secure the door. "There are more of them?"

"Yes. But that's not what I'm worried most about. I'm worried about what they were eating."

"If they were eating it…"

"The one I saw was already dead… but if there's another one somewhere, we want to leave."

"No one is leaving," Hermes said. "We need to secure the facility long enough for Irina to have a long, hard look at every piece of technology around. We're not leaving until she does."

Max grunted, but said nothing. Maybe being brought up in Russia had made him a cynic, but what had been a very clear objective—to kill the people building monsters—was suddenly beginning to look like industrial espionage was also part of the deal. He would be watching to see which pieces of equipment Irina spent her time on.

"If we're not leaving," Louembe said, "then we either need to hunt down the animals or contain them somewhere. I spotted five at the carcass."

"Carcass?"

"I couldn't really see it in the dark. All I can say is that it was something big."

"Big like a person or big like an elephant?"

"Big like a whale," Louembe replied. "And it smelled like one, too. A bunch of these little guys were feeding on it. It was hard to take an exact count, but I think there are still four more."

Max knelt by the dead one. "Compsognathus," he said.

Hermes raised an eyebrow. "You have hidden depths," he remarked.

"I was caught in the middle of one of the very first outbreaks of monsters. I've kept up with what people have been reporting about them. These were all over the news last summer. Some holiday-makers in the Indian Ocean ran into a serious pack of these little monsters. The only difference is that those were smaller than this example. But they look the same. If they're not Compsognathus, they're related." He stood. "What we need to bear in mind is that, apart from the teeth, these guys have got a seriously wicked claw on the rear feet. You'll probably want to keep away from that."

"Carnivores, I assume," Louembe said.

"Yeah. And I know the news reports aren't exactly trustworthy, but they made them out to be vicious maneaters, attacking without provocation."

Louembe raised an eyebrow and kicked the dead dinosaur. "I'd guess they hunt in packs. They don't seem like they could do much against some of the big stuff from dinosaur times."

Ever since he'd found himself surrounded by the SVR's dinosaurs in the Ural Mountains—and barely living to tell the tale—Max had made a point of learning everything he could about prehistoric monsters… he knew the Gabonese soldier's assumption was an oversimplification. Over the hundreds of millions of years that dinosaurs had ruled the Earth, there had been all sizes and shapes. Sometimes the dominant forms on land weren't all that much bigger than this one.

And Compsognathus had apparently been a successful variety.

Hermes interrupted the chain of thought. "Whatever they were, they're trying to get in here."

He was right. Scratching sounds came from the door, echoing through the darkened room like it was some kind of bad horror film.

The twin panes of the door rattled against each other.

"That clasp won't hold them long," Balzano observed.

"That's why you have rifles," Hermes replied drily.

Balzano laughed and shook his head.

The five men took cover behind the nearest cubicles. The walls were the ideal height for that, about five feet tall. They stood there like men in a trench, training their FALs on the doorway and waited.

Not long after they had taken their positions, the clasp burst away and four creatures bowled into the room. They stopped, and appeared to be sniffing the air. As always when dealing with smaller dinosaurs, Max was surprised by just how birdlike their movements were, especially the way they bobbed their heads when they walked. Spooky.

But there was little time to admire them as biological specimens. In Max's previous contacts with dinosaurs, he'd spent most of the time running from them. It was nice to be on the side with the overwhelming force for once.

The room thundered as all of them opened fire at once. The dinosaurs died almost instantly.

"All right," Hermes said. "We need to check the rest of the building carefully. Once we're sure there's no more of those things around, we can bring Irina in." He turned to Louembe. "Take me to this carcass of yours."

***

Irina cursed. She looked around at the pile of broken and slagged computers the team had dredged up for her. She cursed again.

The computers had been intentionally destroyed. Many had been set on fire. Others had been hit with an assortment of blunt objects.

"This is going to take a while," she told Hermes.

"We don't have any other leads."

"Of course we do. We can find that driver and beat the information we need out of him. Or your mysterious Malaysian principal can bribe someone else into getting us more info. He has to have something, and we're already in-theater."

"We don't know that the enemy is even in Africa anymore." His eyes softened for a second, and she knew he was about to ask her to do something specifically for him. Not for the mission. Not for the good of mankind, but for him. "If you can't do this, my only other idea is to follow the truck tracks. They head into the desert, and we'll have to re-equip with water and supplies if we want to follow them. I'm not confident how long those tracks will last. We need this."

"I'll do my best, but…"

"That's all I can ask. Thank you."

She did her best. More than most people would ever have believed possible. For a single moment, after hours of searching for a functional unit in the mess of broken computers, hope flared: she'd finally found a hard drive which seemed to be neither melted nor dented. She whooped in triumph when her reader managed to open it.

Almost immediately, however, the triumph turned to frustration. The drive held a bunch of pictures of someone's dog and, presumably, a wife or girlfriend. It was a big drive which had probably held much more than that at some point, but the rest of the data had not just been erased, but completely destroyed. Scrambled fragments were still on the disk, testament to the fact that someone's wipe program had ripped the files into incoherence before removing them from existence.

She wasn't going to recover that.

But before reporting to Hermes that it was hopeless, she gave it one more shot, grinding through every single piece of equipment in the complex. The only thing working was the computer in the guard house. It seemed to be about twenty years old, wasn't connected to the internet and had nothing on it except a few gigs of porn, and nothing particularly imaginative at that.

A despondent group made camp a few kilometers outside the complex that evening.

***

The world seemed composed of smoke illuminated by blue neon.

Lai sat in a bar in Bangkok, watching the floor show in fascination. He'd known places like this existed, but he'd never imagined he'd be sitting there, watching a woman do improbable things with her nether anatomy…

He looked away. The man who'd agreed to meet him, a Thai national with red contact lenses named Saelim, sat across from him. He was the one who'd suggested the basement dive known only as Grunt's Place. A big woman in a blond wig sat beside the man. Both were covered in clouds of smoke: hers from a vanilla-flavored vape, his from a traditional cigarette.

It had been years since he'd been in a place where you could smoke indoors. Everyone seemed to be doing it, and the acrid smell and thick air transported him back to his youth.

"Can I have a cigarette?" he asked.

"Of course," Saelim responded. "And I apologize. I would have offered, but you didn't strike me as the type."

"Too rule-abiding?"

Saelim smiled. "I would have said too refined."

Lai accepted the proffered light and puffed like he was in college. He coughed after that, but took another drag. It made him feel young again. Young and angry with the people who'd made smoking one of the modern world's sins. He looked back at Saelim, who was watching him with an openly curious expression. "It has been a long time since I smoked," he explained.

"And you chose to start again today?" He looked around the bar where men and women drank, smoked, watched the floor show and concluded illegal deals that ranged from simple prostitution to murder for hire. "Unusual place for it."

Lai smiled. "Wrong. It's the perfect place for it. I won't run into anyone I know in here. The friends of CEOs don't come to this kind of bar. Worse, they don't let the CEOs come either. They're all afraid of how it would look and want our peccadilloes to be discreet." He turned to the woman. "I don't think we've been introduced."

"They call me the Elephant Woman, Mr. Lai. But you can call me Ellie," she replied in a deep, hoarse voice that immediately had Lai checking for an Adam's apple. If one was there, he wasn't able to spot it under the folds of skin. "I can get the people you need."

"I need professionals. The very best."

"You already hired the very best," Saelim informed him. "From what I heard, you sent them out on a mission in Africa."

"Yes. But I need more of them, this time. And a base here in Thailand for them to operate out of. Oh, and an office and apartment for me, all of it secure from both physical and electronic interference."

"Can we make another run at Sked and Akane?" she asked.

Lai shrugged. "They already told me no personally, but if you think they're really good—"

"They are the perfect people for this kind of thing," she interjected.

"—then by all means try. But we need a backup in place. The Irina woman is good, but I think we need more people on the electronic side. Real hackers."

"We can get them."

"Good. And I'd like the strike force to be about twenty strong. If Hermes is willing to stay on, we'll keep him in command, but just in case, I'd like to see a few profiles there, too."

"I can get them in front of you for the fee you discussed with Saelim," Ellie said. "And the goon squad, the regular mercenaries, will be priced in the range he quoted. But the skill players... they'll want to negotiate with you personally. It might get expensive."

Lai laughed. "I can cover it. But even better, if we do it right, I'll be able to rent this team out anywhere in the world. We'll be the go-to option for everything from consulting to muscle when it comes to monster problems. And we won't come cheap."

Now it was Ellie who laughed, a deep, rumbling chuckle. "And here I was led to believe that this was just some kind of weird macho vendetta," she said. "I prefer it this way. Much cleaner." She shook her head. "But then again, I should have known. You were always reputed to be a cold-blooded businessman." She turned to Saelim. "I'll set up the interviews and get back to you with a time and a place."

Saelim nodded, and she walked off into the blue smoke. Lai followed her with his eyes, noting that she stopped at every second or third table to speak to someone.

"She seems well-connected," he remarked.

"Oh, Ellie has her finger in every pie in Bangkok and most of the others in the region. Even the Triads, the Yakuza and the Mafiya let her operate without interference... she's valuable enough that they actually turn a blind eye if she happens to stumble onto their turf accidentally. And she's too smart to do it on purpose."

Lai nodded. That was a good thing to know. He watched the woman performing on the stage. She was a different one, and she was dancing as opposed to doing unusual tricks. "Do you think she's for hire?" Lai asked Saelim.

Saelim laughed incredulously. "For hire, for sale, for rent. In this place, everything and everyone is for sale. Whatever anyone wants."

"I just want one night," Lai responded evenly.

Suddenly Saelim understood. "With her? She's a common whore... she probably hasn't bathed since the last man. I can get you something much better." He smiled. "More refined."

Lai sighed. "I'm tired of refined, Saelim. Just once, I'd like to live like a normal human being. So see if I can take her back to the hotel without overpaying."

"Of course."

CHAPTER 9

Salah sat by the fire while his men brought the food. "Are you cold?" he asked Melanie.

"Not really, but I'm not baking, either. It's a bit of a relief."

He chuckled. "I know what you are referring to. We could never love the desert if it wasn't for the nights that make it bearable. That's the reason people are creating monsters."

"What? I didn't follow that."

Salah smiled in the dim light. "The monsters come because the people in other places don't have the right balance in their lives. They're too packed together, and they don't have the cold nights to remind them that the warm days are a gift from Allah."

"There are other cold places in the world as well," she replied.

The Tuareg's smile grew wider and Melanie realized that she'd said exactly what he wanted her to say. She felt herself smiling as she waited for the man's reply.

"But those places don't have the hot days to remind them that the cool nights are a gift from Allah," he said.

He watched her closely, to see how she would react. She laughed and he seemed to relax at that. "There is wisdom in there," she said. "But I'll have to think about it some before I can understand its meaning."

"There is wisdom in that, too," Salah replied. "I have news."

That came as a surprise. The truckers had been sitting on their asses for a couple of days since they tore apart the monster complex and, despite Salah's assurances that they would find the place where they relocated to, Melanie was starting to think they were simply going to partake in the tropical pastime of getting things done whenever they got around to it.

It wasn't all bad: the taboo over her had been lifted, which meant the men were allowed to speak to her—and mostly they asked her about life in the US. When they realized she'd been deployed to a bunch of other places, it turned into a nonstop questionnaire about life in the US, Europe and the Middle East. Their interest in the world beyond their own borders, their desire to know if the news that reached them was real, bordered on a childlike innocence she could grow to love. The cynicism that every person over the age of ten showed in her own neighborhood when she'd been growing up—and everywhere else ever since—just wasn't present.

Better still, in two entire nights, not one of these men, hardened warriors from the way they spoke about themselves—to her trained eye, a couple might actually have been telling the truth—tried to hit on her. They spoke with the respect due a comrade-at-arms, and only obliquely, by the endearing shock in the way their eyes widened whenever she touched a topic which should have been improper for a woman, let on there might be anything different about her.

Obviously, Salah had laid down the law.

The effect was that she was comfortable there, with them. It almost felt like she was back in Mosul shooting the breeze with her squadmates. She could have stayed there for a few months without getting restive. Unfortunately, she didn't have that kind of time. Her accumulated leave was significant, but not endless.

"What have you heard?" God, she hated the eagerness in her voice.

But Salah seemed to understand. "Their Jeeps went to an old facility deep in the desert. We've found them."

Melanie wanted to spring to her feet and urge the man to hurry, but she controlled herself. "When can we go?"

Salah shook his head sadly. "In order to move in that direction, we must first go the other way. We are not prepared for the hamadas and the sand."

"What's a hamada?"

"A dry place of rocks. We need to return to El-Khalil and leave most of the trucks. These aren't the best vehicles for the open desert. It's better to take two old Dakar Kamaz trucks."

She rifled her memories for any recollection of military hardware with that name. She remembered that there was a Russian truck company named Kamaz, but the Dakar model didn't ring any bells. "What are those?"

"They are race trucks. Old ones, from 2005, I think. They used to run the old rallies that crossed the desert. They are perfect for what we need, and they can carry all our men and equipment. They were sold to an African company when one race ended. Apparently, they were supposed to be doing their last race and everyone was surprised when they both finished. They sat in Senegal for years until a friend of mine bought them and repaired them. He will allow us to use them."

"Even knowing we might not give them back? They sound like they might be expensive collector's items."

"He would never question it. He knows how things are." Then he looked at her critically. "Do people really give value to trucks as collector's items where you come from? That seems to go against everything a truck is used for."

"I don't know about these," she said. "But you should see some of the trucks one guy I used to go out with had built up." She struggled trying to remember the Arabic for neon tubes and low-profile tires and how to explain that the truck could no longer function on anything less than billiard-table-smooth pavement, but she shrugged and gave up. "You would be shocked at just how useless that vehicle was by the time he was done with it." She also didn't say anything about how useless that particular guy had turned out to be, particularly in bed. Why shock her host more than she already had?

"These trucks are not useless, though. They are exactly what we need."

"Good."

"We leave at dawn."

***

"You're not going to believe this," Irina said. "But I got something."

Hermes shook his head to clear it. He was sitting on the terrace of the Hotel Sahara Passion in Timbuktu, ignoring the billion stars of the Milky Way overhead. He knew he was falling into a tropical torpor, that combination of waiting for the hours to pass while one had nothing to do.

He knew the feeling well after spending months on end in shack-like bars along some lonely stretch of jungle river drinking the local rotgut while he waited for whatever warlord he was currently employed by to make up his mind to attack his neighbor.

Usually, though, he had booze, and the days melted into a soft continuum.

You couldn't really drink yourself into that state in Timbuktu, much less keep the alcohol flowing freely enough to keep it up. Mali was a Muslim country and, though Hermes had little respect for local laws—and indeed, had no clue whether there was an anti-alcohol law on the books in the country—he knew that some customs were stronger than law. And when you were forcibly stuck in a tiny city in an on-and-off-war zone, and your transportation stuck out like a sore thumb because not many people in Mali drove modern Chinese assault vehicles, you kept your head down. Which meant he was not only bored out of his mind, but bored out of his *sober* mind. A much more depressing proposition.

His state of mind wasn't exactly conducive to hopefulness. "What is it?"

"The truck driver. He's back on the grid."

He sat up, suddenly fully alert. "What? Where?"

"Six hundred kilometers from here. Some shithole called El-Khalil. Right on the border with Algeria."

"You're sure it's him?"

"It's his phone. I mean, I could call him if you want… but I don't think that would be a great idea."

"Get everyone. Tell them we're moving now." He pulled three one-hundred-Euro bills out of the pocket in which he put the denominations that were too large to be of daily use in Africa and sprinted down to the lobby. In a moment, he'd paid for their stay—the woman behind the desk looked more Swiss than Taureg—and, stopping only long enough to grab his bag, met the team at the car. Irina, as always, was last to arrive, but no one said anything; she had to pack up all the computer equipment she'd been using to try to get a lead on the quarry.

Besides, making a sexist joke at her expense was a good way to get your photos and location sent to every law enforcement agency on the planet.

They drove into the night, Jerome driving the lead CSK-181 at high speed, with Louembe dozing on the seat beside him. In back, Irina kept tracking their quarry's phone, and trying to do God knew what else, while Hermes himself simply stared out the window into the black night beyond the road.

His African wars had always been fought in the jungles of the Sub-Saharan world, never in the Arabic-speaking north. Things in the north were more structured, and mercenaries, though not unheard of, were in much less demand… and many of those came from places like Iraq or Syria: men who had fought in the more politically-motivated conflicts in the Middle East.

Hermes had avoided those. Getting swept along in a cause was a good way to get killed. Your men might decide they wanted to fight to the death, and that any price was worth victory. If that was the case, he supposed he could let his men die, but the problem was that his superiors might feel the same way about him. And Hermes was not yet ready to die for someone else's ideology or religion.

That, after all, was the reason he'd left Europe in the first place. Sadly lacking in wars of their own, the Belgian Army kept sending him on peacekeeping missions to places where the conflict went much deeper than the people sending the troops would ever understand.

Tribal rivalries that went back centuries over which countless atrocities had been perpetrated. Systemic poverty which meant that, for many, dying in the street was preferable to the kind of life that awaited.

And religion… always religion.

It seemed like everyone in the places he ended up in always felt that any price was worth paying if it harmed the other side. Worse still, the peacekeepers in the blue helmets were, as soon as they arrived, everyone's enemy.

Give him a nice, clean resource war. Gold, blood diamonds, oilfields. Warlords who fought over money were easy to understand, easy to predict. They knew that a functioning unit was worth more than some objectives, less than others… and they acted in accordance with those facts of life.

Actual engagement with the enemy was to be avoided unless you could be certain it could be done at a profit. Ambush. Strike at production centers. Steal resources.

And now?

Not only was he heading into the heart of the largest desert in the inhabited world, but he was doing it for what seemed to be the wrong reasons.

Of course, he was being paid handsomely for it. That wasn't the wrong reason. There was no better reason for a mercenary to be where he was.

The problem was that his principal, the Thai businessman named Lai, seemed to be a true believer. He hated the monster builders with a passion, for personal reasons.

Of course, that hadn't been enough for Hermes to turn down a check like the one Lai had offered… but it was enough to make him wonder if he'd done the right thing. Riding at full speed down an African road in a dark night did wonders for your focus.

He sighed and wished the shooting would start.

It wasn't good to spend too much time with his thoughts.

***

Melanie woke and, for a moment, she thought she was in a hospital. The hard mattress, the starched sheets, the sounds around her, voices and machinery running in the middle of the night.

And she was in a bed.

As full consciousness returned, she remembered they'd come to El-Khalil four days before. The first three nights, they'd all slept in tents near the trucks on the outskirts of town but then one of the local chief's wives had realized they were making a woman sleep under the stars, and Melanie had been moved into a room in a mud-brick house. It wasn't luxurious by any standard—packed dirt floor, a pitcher of water as opposed to a bathroom with faucets—but the bed was sheer delight.

So what had woken her? She was sure there had been sounds outside her door.

She remembered she didn't have a door: the mud brick hut had a curtain which was currently open to the night.

Melanie lowered her bare feet to the dirt floor, thankful that the accommodations forced her to sleep with her pants and shirt on. She crept out of her room, around the small house and looked out into the night.

Across the street, headlights illuminated the trucks and the tents where Salah's men had pitched their camp. Five or six people with weapons had finished rousing the sleeping truckers and had them huddled in a circle. Rifles were trained on her allies. She couldn't tell in the night, but she suspected the vehicles creating the light were the same ones she'd seen at the airfield.

She grimaced. If that were so, these guys were pros, and taking her eyes off them might be a mistake.

There was no other choice, however. Moving quickly, Melanie dashed back into her room, opened her bag, and pulled out her Remington, snapping the stock into position and then carefully inserting a night-vision scope with a laser sight. She needed to get everything right because there wouldn't be time to fix it later.

Then she crept back out of her room and, using a pair of indentations in the wall as footholds, she pulled herself up onto the flat roof. Only after she put all her weight on the packed mud did she stop to think that it might not have been designed as a load-bearing structure.

Whatever. She just needed it to hold for the next five minutes. After that, it wouldn't matter.

She lay on the roof and studied the scene. One of the men, apparently the leader, was asking questions in Arabic. The words carried beautifully in the cool, still night air. He was receiving silence in reply.

She flirted with the idea of taking him down.

There was no question of missing a shot at this range—her target was thirty yards away—but if she started shooting, she'd only be able to take out one of them before they took cover and fired back. Or maybe before they just shot Salah and his men.

Melanie thought she had a better way. She took a bead on the leader and then broke every rune in the sniper's book.

She turned on the laser sight.

A bright red dot, the typical Hollywood cliché, appeared in the middle of the man's chest, and stayed there.

His companions reacted in alarm, turning in her direction. If they were any good, they'd immediately know the cluster of houses had to be the source of the beam. They also needed to know that if they moved, she would shoot.

"Hello," she called out in Arabic. "I think we should talk."

"Show yourself," the leader replied, ignoring the dot on his chest.

"I'm not stupid. No one is going to show themselves until you put down your guns," she said.

"We're not stupid, either," the man replied. "I don't believe there's more than one of you out there, and as soon as you shoot, we'll make you dead."

"Your soldiers will make me dead, you mean. I won't miss… and you won't survive. Let my friends go and I'll let you take cover behind your vehicles. And then we can talk."

"We'd be badly outnumbered if we do that," the man called back.

"You look like big boys to me," Melanie replied. "I'm betting you can take care of yourselves. You have ten seconds."

To his credit, the man only hesitated for a beat before he ordered his people into position. They were smart enough to know the only place where a sniper could cover them was from her direction, so they put the cars between her and him. Interestingly, the orders he gave appeared to be in English.

It was interesting because the assault vehicles they were driving didn't come from any of the English-speaking militaries she was aware of.

Her red dot followed the man all the way to the vehicles. After they had placed themselves where she asked, she left the dot on the ground between them and Salah, a reminder that they weren't alone in the night.

"Salah, get your rifles and come over here!" she said.

The men complied, scrambling into tents and then rushing across the open space.

"It seems I must thank you for my liberty, once again. Although I must admit I don't think they were going to kill us this time."

"Why not?"

"They wanted to know if we'd been to the monster factory… and they wanted to know where the men had moved the factory after we were done with it." He paused. "I don't think these men are friends of the Korean."

"These are the men who attacked you in the airfield," Melanie said. "They most certainly aren't friends with the monster makers."

"That is only true if you believe that Sun-Lee didn't betray his own clients... which is not something I believe. I think the whole problem comes from the Korean. I never trusted him, and I trust him even less now."

Melanie reached a decision. "I think we need to talk to these people. Help me down."

She handed down her rifle and then hung from her arms waiting for the men below to grab her and pull her down.

"Come on, guys," she chided when it became clear they didn't want to lay a finger on her. "I won't bite."

Finally, one set of hands reached up and supported her thighs just above the knees. She allowed herself to drop, hoping he'd reposition if she needed additional support, and not drop her headfirst to preserve her modesty.

In the end it wasn't necessary. The fall was shorter than she expected in the darkness, and she was on the ground a second later.

A rock tore into the sole of her foot. "I need my boots. Cover them." Then she hesitated, sighed and called out in a louder voice. "I'm coming over to talk. Alone, in about two minutes. Please don't shoot me or my friends will bury you out here."

She quickly put her boots on and rushed out before things could deteriorate.

"I will come with you."

"You won't understand a word we say. I'm going to speak to them in English. Besides, I might need you to come rescue me."

"Do you think they're Americans?"

"No... probably not. But I definitely heard them speaking English among themselves, so I'm going to try it anyway. I'm going to stand right in front of that car there. If I move off that spot for any reason, I need help. Come get me." She wondered whether Salah's people could make their greater numbers mean something against much better troops. She hoped so, or she might find herself a POW in a war she didn't understand. And that kind of POW generally ended up in a long debriefing in an undisclosed location followed by a single round to the back of the head and a deep, unmarked grave.

She wouldn't accept something like that without a fight.

The Jeeps were kind of weird. They looked a bit like Hummer knockoffs, and were painted in the bright green of some Asian militaries.

There were no manufacturer badges discernible by the light of their headlights.

Melanie stood right beside the trunk of the nearest one, in full view of her backup, and held out her hands. "Talk to me," she said in English.

The man from before was crouching beside the Jeep. He stood and looked her over. "You don't sound Tuareg," he said. "Or Arabic, for that matter."

"I'm American," she replied. "And you don't look like you're operating here under the auspices of a legitimate government."

"I never claimed to be. Do you?"

"No." She looked at the troops with him. They seemed poised, at the ready, but not nervous. They also looked to be extremely tough. "Are you going to tell me why you've decided to come in here guns blazing?"

"We didn't shoot anyone," the man said.

"Well, you sure pointed at them. Everyone from my hundred-year-old grandmother to my drill sergeant reminded me that you only point guns at things you intend to destroy. Especially pretty guns like those."

"We wanted to be certain there were no misunderstandings," he replied. "We needed to talk."

"All right. We're talking. What do you want to know?"

Her interlocutor shrugged. She thought—though it was hard to tell in the dim light—that he was smiling ironically. "We want to know why you shot up the monster lab, and if you know where everyone went."

"I can tell you that. But first I need to know why you're asking."

"Because we want to finish the job. Except we don't know where the job is." He said it without hedging, without hesitation. It surprised Melanie enough that she almost believed the man. At the very least, the facts supported that explanation.

It was her turn to shrug. She didn't think telling them their motivations would change much, one way or another. "Fair enough. We attacked the complex because a guy called Park Sun-Lee double crossed us." For now, Melanie decided that she wasn't going to mention anything about friends or family members hurt by the monsters. This guy seemed to be taking her as part of the trucking team, and until that changed, that's how she would play it.

"We know about Sun-Lee. He's on our target list. Just point us in the right direction, and you can forget about these guys. They're as good as dead, guaranteed."

Melanie shook her head. "That's not going to work. Salah wants to kill these guys himself. Preferably with his own hands. He won't give you anything but the corpses."

The soldier shrugged. "That's all I really need. If he can deliver, I'm happy to back him up."

She was about to agree, but then paused. From what she'd seen of this crew, they were good at what they did. They had good equipment. They had good guns. And they looked like they had been well trained.

"Salah won't like it but, speaking for myself, I'd much rather have you guys standing next to me when we hit the place. Last time we found a skeleton crew, just a bunch of technicians and a couple of really incompetent guards. I doubt that's what we'll find this time around. They'll be expecting us."

"Then we'll come in and help out. That's what we're getting paid for, anyway."

"All right, let me talk to my people and I'll come back."

Melanie turned to go, her confidence shaken by the man's laissez-faire attitude about his role in a situation that could get his people killed. Maybe they weren't professionals after all. Maybe they were just well-equipped amateurs out on some kind of vendetta. It might be better not to have them anywhere nearby in that case.

As she took her second step, the man spoke again. "By the way, were you the sniper at the airfield? If so, I'd love to know how you became the spokeswoman for the people you were aiming at. You might say I love a good story."

She smiled, confidence restored.

CHAPTER 10

Philippe walked up the ramp that connected his new lab in the lowest subbasement of the complex to the vat areas on the floor above. His footfalls echoed in the enormous concrete halls, reverberating eerily in the dimly illuminated spaces.

There was no carpeting, no corporate feel. Sun-Lee's new factory building was a relic of the Cold War. While he suspected it had been built after the fall of the Soviet Union, there was no way to be certain: the brutalist concrete and straight lines revealed nothing, not even through wear. The building hadn't been much used: someone had built the structure and abandoned it in place.

The only way to guess where this complex might be was to judge by the lack of water damage on the walls: he was thirty meters underground, and there was no sense of humidity, no stains on the concrete.

"Philippe."

The voice stopped him cold. If Sun-Lee had been a normal human, he should have been asleep at this time of night, like the rest of the researchers.

But the North Korean slept very little. Philippe had never caught him resting.

He turned, half-expecting to find the man holding a pistol which would signify that this was to be the final conversation that he'd been expecting for weeks.

"Yes," he said, working to keep his voice level. "I was just going down to check on the latest batch."

The Korean shrugged. "I've told you dozens of times you don't need to worry about checking every ten minutes... the incubators work. They can take care of themselves."

"Even so, I feel more comfortable checking. Besides, the next ones to hatch are the batch that is supposed to replace the one that got intercepted at the airfield. I want it to be perfect."

Sun-Lee nodded. "About that, I think you should know that our old complex got hit. A commando raid. There were no survivors."

"What?"

"I sent Tinaan over there with a Jeep to see what was happening, since I hadn't heard from them in a couple of days. He told me someone had been in there and shot everyone. They even shot up the two water tanks and flooded everything. He checked all the bodies: everyone's accounted for, which is a relief. We don't need to worry about security leaks."

"Oh, good." Philippe tried not to think about the two young researchers he'd left behind on the caretaker crew. He hadn't known them all that well, and they had been the least valuable members of his team… but he'd been the one to select them for the assignment that had eventually killed them.

He expected to feel guilt, but the sensation didn't really arrive. He was numb, living his life as in a dream, waiting for the day Sun-Lee would end the suffering with a bullet between the eyes. It was hard to believe, at this point, that he'd willingly joined this project.

The North Korean shrugged. "Well, that's why we left only the unimportant people behind. The reason I wanted to talk to you is that we lost both the aquatic monsters, I'm afraid. One of them died when the water drained out and crushed it against a door. The other appears to have been hit by some kind of rocket. So we need to quicken a couple more."

Philippe nodded. "All right. I'll start them up as soon as I finish my check. The tanks here are a lot better than the ones we had. We should have been using them all along."

"Thank you," Park Sun-Lee replied. "And as for this facility, I imagine you can understand why we had to hold it in reserve. If we'd lost this one…. Fortunately now that we know someone is after us, I can prepare. Anyway, don't let me keep you. I'm sure you have important work to do… even if the new incubators don't require anything of the sort."

Philippe swallowed as he watched Sun-Lee leave. The veneer of humanity he wore was so thin you could almost see the evil core beneath. He shuddered and walked into the incubator room.

The factory floor, as everyone called it, was a truly colossal space. Row upon row of incubator cylinders disappeared into the shadowed distance. Somehow, this room felt bigger than the identical one two levels up which was empty; the humming cylinders made it feel vast. He checked the thermometer on the wall—forty degrees Celsius—a good temperature for incubators, not a lot of fun for the people who had to check on them.

That made little difference to Philippe. He'd been living in exile in hot, muggy tropical places, long enough that a little heat hardly bothered him. He gave the bank of incubators growing the Pakistani's latest batch of monsters a quick glance—he wondered idly how one negotiated for a replacement after a huge snafu like the airfield incident—and then ignored them. Sun-Lee was right that these machines never failed, and there were a couple of hundred of them in the room. He wasn't going to check each one, although he did kneel beside a few random tubes to see how the readouts looked. Everything was fine, and the product would soon be ready to release into the holding maze to see whether they'd come through the incubation process intact. The labyrinth was yet another reason this facility was much better than the one they'd abandoned—watching a newly-hatched batch of product run through the corridors was enormously informative.

The Indian revolutionaries and their Pakistani clients would receive a product of uncompromised quality.

Instead of checking each monster's vital statistics, he knelt beside the fourth tube in the second row and let out a low whistle.

Poupée appeared instantly, her big round eyes bright in the dim glow. "Phlip," she said. "I find thing."

Even though his models predicted it, the speed at which the little creature's vocabulary grew astonished him. Obviously, the fact that she carried a very small brain around in her head would soon put a limit on how much Poupée could learn... but where that limit would be was anyone's guess. So far, the rate of her development outstripped even the smartest human. She'd been born just a few days ago, after all.

But was she able to understand his instructions? What he'd asked her to do was not a simple thing like eat an apple. It was a complicated concept.

"Show," he replied.

She darted back into the hollow between the cylinders, and he sighed. The space was about ten centimeters to a side, and no human was ever going to fit. "Come back," he said.

The face emerged again, cocked to one side, questioning.

How did you explain the concept of not being able to fit through a hole to a creature who had almost no experience with... with anything, really?

"Come this way," he said.

"No show?"

"Yes, show, but this way." Philippe pantomimed going around the tank. "This way."

She paused, and he was convinced she wouldn't be able to understand but, just when he was about to give up, she scurried out into the walkway between the tanks and led him through the dim room. Every few steps, she turned back as if to check if he was still with her and gauge whether she was doing the right thing. He made what he hoped she would interpret as encouraging noises.

They reached the far wall and she immediately climbed into the hole which allowed bundles of cables to flow from this large room into the water tank chamber.

"I had a feeling this was where we'd end up," Philippe said. "Stay there."

Under the tiny creature's watchful gaze, he went to the door that divided the chambers, entered his code, and stepped into the much bigger space beyond.

Immediately, the temperature dropped several degrees and the feeling of the air changed. While the incubation room was dry and warm, the clammy air in the tank room stuck to his skin. This room smelled like the seashore in a port town, slightly piscine, slightly rank.

He let the echo of the closing door die down in the enormous chamber before walking along the metal-grate catwalk to the spot where the cables emerged and called softly to Poupée. "I'm here now."

When her head appeared between the wires, the big eyes were visible in the gloom. "Phlip there?"

He realized she didn't know there were any other ways between the rooms. Doors were a foreign concept to her. The only way she would have been able to understand one was to watch someone going through... and this was a doorway that saw only infrequent use.

"Yes."

She thought it over, and seemed to be satisfied. Then, without warning, she tensed and jumped out of the hollow, right in front of Philippe and landed on the handrail opposite the wall.

It was so unexpected that he actually tried to catch her, to keep her from falling ten meters to the floor, and probably to her death. But by the time he got his hand out, she was perched on the railing.

He stared in wonder. A monkey would have been able to do the same thing... but probably not at her age. A chill ran down his back as he thought of what he could do if, instead of building tiny humanoid pets, he got serious and started improving humanity. Imagine eliminating all the awkward, helpless stages and creating children that could jump, walk, learn, and feed themselves at this accelerated rate.

And that was just the development. Imagine tweaking the genome itself. Humanity could be improved so much. In fact, there were probably people doing that very research right now, as he—the true father of the science—designed killing machines while he waited for his boss to shoot him.

Poupée broke his reverie. She pointed out across the enormous space to one of the two tanks filled with salt water.

"What?"

"That's just a water tank. It holds water. A tank," he said, peering through the gloom at the container. You could have driven a small fishing boat around in that one. Unfortunately, these didn't have transparent glass walls like the ones in their original factory, but were built of reinforced concrete. Though he knew the plexiglass was almost unbreakable, he still felt better having the creatures they were growing safely behind a thick layer of cement.

"No. No tank." She pointed. "In."

And Philippe's heart froze. His original little monster, the creature Poupée was named after, had also gravitated towards the other monsters he'd created. By observing the different creatures and the animals in the jungle around her, she'd learned that she was deformed, learned that she could never be among the fairy princesses and beautiful socialites of the books he read to her... and resented it. Finally, her rage had grown so deep that she'd gotten together with the only other creature with human intelligence Philippe had ever attempted, an enormous dragon-like lizard named Harold, and tried to kill off her creator.

She'd almost succeeded, too. If Harold hadn't been too dumb to check on him after mauling him, Philippe would have died. As it was, he still needed a cane to walk, a decade later.

And now, an even better version—smarter, more agile, quicker to learn—of the same little monster was asking him about his creations.

Fortunately, there was no way she would be conspiring with what was in that tank. The thing in there was essentially a stomach connected to a brain that only felt one emotion—anger that anything near it wasn't in its stomach—and held only one thought—how to remedy the situation. The mouth and teeth, big enough to swallow a small car—after chomping it to pieces—were well aligned with that brain.

"That is a Mosasaurus," Philippe said. "Be careful not to get too close." He doubted the behemoth would even notice something Poupée's size, but it was better to be safe than sorry. "If you go close, it will eat you."

"Eat?" Poupée knew what eating was, but she'd always linked it to something she did, not something that could be done to her. She thought about that for some moments, and Philippe wondered if she could actually understand abstract concepts. He would need to let her develop more language skills before he could talk about it, though. "No talk?"

Philippe laughed. The thought of something with a brain that small—just a bundle of nerves focused on the hunt, really—attempting speech was hilarious. "No. It can't talk. Only eat."

"Eat P'pee?"

"Yes. It will eat Poupée, and eat Philippe. Whatever gets too close." The water level was kept three meters below the edge, but that wouldn't stop a stretching Mosasaurus from grabbing anything walking along the concrete ledge.

Poupée shuddered. "I show," she said, and darted along the railing.

Philippe followed, cursing the metal bridge for the noise it made. He knew any sounds would be lost in the huge room, but this was supposed to be a secret mission. He followed her down three equally noisy flights of metal steps.

The little creature approached the control system located against the wall between the two tanks and Philippe's heart sank. The blinking lights and monitors would be exactly the kind of thing that would attract a young animal's attention. He should have been clearer when he gave her this task. Well, he would give her positive reinforcement for the fact that she'd attempted it, and then give her clearer instructions, just as if he were training a dog.

He understood that intellectually. Unfortunately, his intellect was also screaming at him that his remaining time was ticking away. And his intellect was dragging his emotions into the discussion. He barely managed to refrain from screaming at Poupée.

It would be a struggle, but he'd let her lead him to the computers, tell her she was a good girl and have her try again.

As he waited for Poupée to proudly show him what she'd discovered, the little creature surprised him again. She scurried between the blinking rack and the wall and, once past the humming electronics looked back to see if he was following.

Philippe raised an eyebrow. He hadn't even noticed that there was a space back there, and even if he had, he wouldn't have been tempted to squeeze inside: it was dusty and dark.

He pushed through, being careful not to disconnect any wires—there were few people up and about, but any sudden loss of information through these cables would bring swarms of technicians out to check on them.

Beyond the rack, the passageway didn't end at the wall, but continued deep into the concrete to end at what looked like the door in a submarine bulkhead. It was a little over a meter tall, maybe fifty centimeters wide, and it had a large metal wheel in the center.

Poupée was staring at the door intensely.

"What?" Philippe whispered.

"No can go," she replied.

He understood. At some point the little creature had seen the door open. Now it was closed and she couldn't understand what might be going on.

He knelt beside her and held out a hand with a peanut in it. "Good work," he said as she snatched the nut from his outstretched fingers. "This is exactly what I needed to see."

He pulled his phone out of his pocket. He carried it around even though Sun-Lee's paranoia precluded its use as a communication device within the complex. There was no signal this far out in the desert, and there was no wi-fi connection in the building: every piece of networked equipment was hardwired to the LAN which, in turn, used an encrypted satellite uplink to connect to the outer world... only on certain workstations. And everything anyone did on one of those was seen by Park Sun-Lee's security people, a small combine of eight men and two women who dressed alike—in tan-colored shorts and shirts—kept to themselves and appeared to be fiercely loyal to the leader of the project. Everyone knew it was better to forego contact with the outside world entirely than to run afoul of them.

But a phone had other uses. He often whiled away the hours playing a crystal shattering game when he was too tired to work and too wired to sleep. And, in this underground warren of a factory complex, he often found the flashlight useful.

Before turning it on, he stopped and held his breath for a moment, listening for anyone out and about in the tank chamber. He heard nothing, so he turned on the light to study the door in more detail than he could in the prevailing gloom.

In addition to what he'd already seen, he spotted a small metal plaque on the bottom right-hand corner of the door, from which three wires ran into holes drilled in the wall. The reason they were there wasn't difficult to guess: anyone who opened it would set off an alarm somewhere on the other side.

He suspected that if one needed to open this door, the alarm would be the least of his worries.

"You did an excellent job," he told Poupée.

She looked at the door again. "No can go," she repeated.

He nodded. "If we have to go, we'll go."

Poupée paused and thought, her features wrinkling with the effort. "When?" she said finally.

She's projecting the future now, he thought with a shudder. *Human children don't really understand how time works until they're what? Three? Four? She's doing it in her first week.*

"When we need to go through this, we'll know."

Before turning away, Philippe stared at the aperture for a few more seconds. He didn't say anything to Poupée, but he was thinking that, if that door didn't lead into a long escape tunnel built by an African dictator who made Sun-Lee look sane, then their escape attempt would be quite short. If that tunnel didn't lead out, there was only one possible way for their flight to end.

***

Another night, another bar, another seedy contact. Lai was beginning to enjoy himself enormously.

The man called himself Viktor, and Lai would never have trusted him… except he came with several recommendations. Well, not the man himself—that guy appeared to be a solid slab of muscle to whom someone had handed a script and some cash and told to do a job—but the people he worked for. The message through the grapevine was: 'These people are cold-blooded, inhuman killers, but their product is worth the extremely expensive price you'll pay for it.'

"Have you arranged the demonstration?" Lai asked the goon.

Viktor nodded immediately. That question was clearly in the script. "We have safe rooms in the city where we can do the transfer." His accent was as Russian as his fake name and his ice-blue eyes.

"It would have to be done on someone of my choosing," Lai replied.

"Of course. However, my employers don't recommend doing it yourself," Viktor said. "You should bring someone less valuable."

Lai took a sip from his caipirinha. The cachaça they used in the drink in this place—if it was even cachaça—tasted the way he imagined kerosene would taste if you drank it. And they'd stinted on both the lemons and the sugar. Probably because the people who came here wanted hard liquor with few frills. He should have ordered something else.

He was still trying to find his place in this new world he'd plunged into. His access to money would save him many of the growing pains, but he'd need to become accustomed to the new place in the world. This conversation was a case in point: if someone had suggested in a board meeting that they send a 'less-valuable' employee to take a risk, the HR department would have had a collective aneurism.

Then he chuckled... the real reason they should have been having the aneurism is that HR departments had become pretty much the least valuable sector of the entire company once they decided to police how employees felt instead of making sure the right people were working as hard as they could on getting shit done.

"I have someone I trust. Is the process really all that dangerous?"

The goon shrugged. "I heard it's been made perfectly safe and that there are people walking around whose minds are in bodies other than the ones they'd been born in. But I don't know. Making copies of human brains and overwriting them onto someone else just seems like it has to go wrong at some point, right?"

Lai laughed. "You never went to sales training, did you?"

"What?"

"Never mind. I suppose the people you talk to have a specific need, and you fill it."

"Yeah, I guess so. Most people have already bought the stuff by the time they talk to me. I'm just a messenger on these deliveries. Oh, and if someone decides they don't want it after all, I'm supposed to break a few bones while they reconsider the product's benefits."

Lai laughed. "And maybe you didn't need to go to sales training. Anyway, you won't have to break any of my bones. All I need is for you to tell me where I need to be and when."

"I'll do more than that. I'll take you there myself right now. Call your volunteer and have him meet us here in ten minutes."

Lai tried to find a way to decline the offer without getting his bones broken, but was unable to find one. Explaining that he didn't want to be alone and under the control of a criminal organization without anyone else in the world knowing where he was probably wasn't the best strategy. So he shrugged. "It's a bit sudden, but I really don't have anything better to do."

"Good."

He made the call and, when his well-paid volunteer, Gonzalo, indicated he was at the door, Viktor stood and allowed Lai to lead the way out of the dark and dingy bar. As he walked to what could conceivably be his death, or kidnapping, or whatever, he realized he was completely calm. The sense of impending doom, that sense that he'd forgotten to do something, or that something would go wrong at any moment if he didn't personally see that it didn't was gone. It was a relief, and only now that he was existing without it did he realize what a burden being a CEO had been. He'd exchanged his peace of mind for the chance to turn his family from comfortably well-to-do to individuals who walked with the world's elite. And not having tens of thousands of employees and their families depending on the quality of the decisions he made was liberating in the extreme.

So he let himself be led to an unremarkable house just outside of Bangkok proper where a man with a suitcase full of electronics connected electrodes to Gonzalo's head and to another man who was already strapped to a table.

A few minutes later, Lai watched, amazed, as the other man, a complete stranger, began to talk to him. The man had Gonzalo's movements, he spoke in Gonzalo's cadence. And he spoke of things he and Gonzalo had agreed would be the way to identify each other when the time came. Lai had no doubts: Gonzalo's mind had been imprinted on the other man's brain.

Impossible things became much easier to accept when you saw them with your own eyes.

He'd asked only one question: "Is it limited to humans?"

"No. Anything with a brain… as long as you put the electrodes in the right place. And we have a guy on call for that. It's included in the price."

Lai had nodded and agreed to the purchase. By the time he left, a mere hour after getting in, Gonzalo was himself again, chatting as if nothing had happened, probably planning how he would spend his well-earned bonus.

Lai didn't care what the man did with his money. His mind was completely occupied with what he would do with the incredible technology at his disposal.

CHAPTER 11

For the second time in a week, Melanie found herself looking through her scope at the site where the infamous Dr. Sun-Lee had built the monsters that had nearly killed Stephanie. With any luck, they'd catch him at it this time.

Weirdly, it seemed that a completely different set of bastards had been responsible for Cora's death, which she found strange. From what the soldiers working had said, her friend had been killed by a creature very similar to the one she'd fragged with the rocket launcher. The Belgian guy, Hermes, had put the blame on a completely separate group of douchebags, and she was inclined to believe him: he appeared to know what he was talking about.

Her scope didn't show a big building in the middle of nowhere. The entrance to the complex was a big door built into the side of a rocky outcropping at the end of a desert road that no one would have taken unless they already knew where it was. How Salah's men had tracked anyone here was a mystery.

Rocks crunched behind her and she turned on her night-vision goggles. A big man approached; she recognized the Russian Spetsnaz goon, Max. He'd spoken very little since the two groups had joined forces, so she was a bit surprised to see him.

He reached her position and crouched beside her. "Anything?" he asked.

"No. Nothing at all," she replied.

"They know we're here, then."

"How do you figure that?"

"If Hermes' numbers are correct, and the size of the lab you guys trashed seems to indicate that they are, there should be about fifty people in that building, mainly scientists, but I'm guessing we'll run into some guys with guns who know how to use them, as well. And Sun-Lee will be armed as well. He's a snake."

"You know Sun-Lee?"

"Yeah. I saved his life a couple of times. Now I wish I hadn't," the Russian replied. "I destroyed his original lab, though."

Even though he was right next to her, Melanie could barely see him in the illumination from the stars, and she'd taken off her goggles. She definitely couldn't see his expression, but there was something about the small talk that didn't ring true. "You're not here to tell me your life story," she said.

"No. I'm here to check if our sniper is up to her job. This is a stressful situation for someone who has never been to special forces school."

Anger surged. "US Marines don't need special forces training. Why blunt our abilities with the teachings of lesser services?"

Alexeyev chuckled. "No one is disrespecting the Marines. No soldier in the world would ever do that. But can you back up the tradition? We'll probably need a lot of help to get inside."

"You won't find a better sniper outside Camp Pendleton. If it moves and it isn't ours, it dies, no matter how far away it is or how fast it's moving."

He stayed silent for a moment. Then he stood and put a hand on her shoulder. "Then I'll leave you to it. The strike is in ten minutes."

***

Demolitions fell to Max and Voornacht. Apparently, the South African had spent his career blowing up structures on battlefields everywhere from Africa to Bolivia. Apparently, if it was hot outside and someone without their own Army Corps of Engineers needed something to be delicately removed using lots of explosives, this was the man they called.

Max, of course, had been trained by the Spetsnaz to infiltrate enemy installations. He wasn't his team's explosive specialist, but everyone needed to know the basics.

The door was set five meters into the rock, and it was more than big enough to drive two trucks through side by side. This wasn't a job done on a shoestring by some nameless African insurgents; someone with real resources and equipment had built this opening. He assumed the complex inside would reflect the same situation.

They crept towards the opening. There was still no sign of life, but Max was convinced the people inside were waiting for them. His sixth sense told him they were being watched.

At least the South African knew his stuff. Voornacht moved like a shadow, and if it hadn't been for the night-vision goggles, Max would never have known the man was there, not even five meters away.

They reached the edge of the rock face and peered inside.

Nothing. No visible security cameras or guard windows, just a whopping huge door that needed to be removed before they could get on with their mission.

It was a beautiful place for an ambush, but short of actually opening the door, Max couldn't see how the defenders could hit them. The thing looked really, really solid.

Just as he was about to give Voornacht the signal to advance, he heard a grunt from above, followed by a sudden scrabbling, as if something was slipping down a slope. A body fell to the ground just three meters away from them just as he registered another sound, the unmistakable bark of a sniper rifle.

The rifle fired again, but this time he heard nothing more.

Before the sound of the third shot reached them, however, another body hit the ground.

Max wondered if Melanie had missed the second shot. A Spetsnaz shooter wouldn't have, not at five hundred meters.

His doubts disappeared when he checked the body nearby: the bullet hole, perfectly centered in the man's forehead, glowed brightly in his night-vision view. There was no way someone could make a shot that good and then miss their second attempt. Apparently, one of the douchebags they were up against had died silently.

Pausing only to glance at the corpse of the guy who'd been preparing to ambush them—he was carrying an AK-47 and dressed in some kind of ill-tailored guard uniform, something from the 1950s, by the look of it—Max signaled Voornacht to advance. They ran to the door and began applying the shaped charges to the door.

The explosives they had were mining charges that had been liberated from some copper operation in the Congo. Like their assault vehicles, the explosive strips were also Chinese. And like the rest of their plan, they'd been selected for effectiveness as opposed to subtlety.

Once they'd finished outlining a rectangle a little taller than a man with their charges, they connected the wires and, playing out cable behind them, ran to where they had the detonator set up. A Spetsnaz specialist would probably have rolled his eyes at everything they'd done wrong, but Max was reasonably sure they would be safe behind the rock outcropping.

"Ready?" Voornacht said.

"Go," Max replied.

Max watched as Voornacht clicked the control knob to the 'On' position, lifted the safety protection, a transparent box that avoided letting the button be pushed by mistake, and mashed the big red circle.

The earth shook and they heard an enormous bang. Max was suddenly grateful they'd chosen a large, solid rock to hide behind.

The South African chuckled. "I think we may have used a little too much explosive," he said.

Max was about to move towards the entrance when a voice in his ear spoke.

"Wait. Sniper says there's someone at the door," Hermes said. He must have moved to Melanie's position when he heard the first three shots. Smart, since the sniper wasn't looped into their radio channel; they simply didn't have gear for her. The crack of the long-range rifle broke the air and, a second later Hermes spoke. "She says it's clear. Go."

This time they didn't creep. Max and Voornacht sprinted out of their concealment and around the rock they were hiding behind.

As soon as the door came into view, Voornacht grunted and said: "See, I thought so. Too much explosive."

Instead of the neat, man-sized hole they'd been planning to create, the right half of the giant door was torn jaggedly open. They could have driven one of their assault vehicles through the resulting hole.

Light poured from within, illuminating a recently dead guard dressed in a bright green uniform lying half inside and half out of the building. The one Melanie had killed earlier had been blown a few meters further away.

Approaching obliquely to avoid getting shot at by anyone within, Max took a quick look through the doorway. "It's a long tunnel, curving to the right. There are lights on inside, and I could see about thirty meters. There doesn't seem to be people waiting for us," he reported.

"All right. Go in there and see what's up, but if you encounter any resistance get out and wait for us. We'll be there in less than a minute."

"Gotcha," Max replied.

He popped his head up again. There really was no immediate danger, so he stood and carefully stepped over the broken opening. It was easy to see what had happened with the explosive: the door, which had looked like solid armor from outside was, in reality, about half a centimeter thick. They'd completely miscalculated the charge.

It made little difference. The job had been done, and there was plenty more explosive strip in the trucks.

He led Voornacht far enough into the tunnel to be able to see around the bend. More featureless tunnel ahead, for about forty meters, and then it opened up into a larger space.

"No one here so far," Max reported. "But there's a loading bay ahead which would make a good shooting gallery if that's where they're waiting."

"Okay, stay there. We're coming to you."

Max glanced behind to see that several of the truckers were entering the jagged hole in the door. Armed with Ak-47s, they looked exactly like the people he'd been fighting in the mountains of Pakistan just a year earlier. Enemies became allies in the blink of an eye when you were a mercenary.

Hermes came in after them, accompanied by Louembe and Balzano. The Belgian approached, smirking. "You were supposed to cut a hole in the door, not knock the building down," he said.

Voornacht laughed. "It's not our fault if the bloody contractors cut corners. Apparently not even dictators can get quality service out of those guys."

Max was about to turn back and point out the salient features of the loading bay when movement at the door caught his eye. Melanie walked over the broken door and strode to where they stood. She'd exchanged her sniper rifle for an AK, and she definitely walked like a soldier.

He held out his hand. "I believe we owe you our lives," he said.

She took it, but shrugged. "Just doing my job."

He hesitated, but asked the question anyway. He had to know. "You took down four of them?"

Melanie held his gaze. "Did you hear four shots?"

"Yes."

"Then there are four bodies."

He nodded. "We need to go down there, but these lights make it quite risky."

"Salah's men don't have night vision equipment," she said. He noted that she, herself, had an American set of goggles hanging around her neck. "Without them, there's only the five of you to take on whoever is waiting for us."

"We just need to knock out the lights in the tunnel. They should be able to see using the loading area lights, but I don't want to give the defenders silhouettes to shoot at."

"I thought he was in charge," Melanie said, nodding to Hermes.

Hermes looked up and shook his head. "When it comes to hitting hardened installations, Max is the man. I'm more of a mobile battlefield in the jungle type of guy." He shrugged. "Not too many jungles around here, though."

Max turned back to Melanie. "Can you hit the lights?"

She rolled her eyes. "When?"

The troops appeared to be ready, so he replied: "Now would be good."

Melanie took a second to study the light fixture above them and Max tensed. Would she show her contempt for his request by doing a cowboy imitation and shooting long bursts from the hip? That would be bad; a ricochet would make you just as dead as a well-trained enemy.

Unfortunately, there was no choice but to shoot them out: the lights were six meters above their heads.

She didn't do anything stupid. Instead, she took careful aim at a light far enough ahead of them that the bullet wouldn't put anyone at risk even if she missed. She breathed out, held the AK steady for a second and squeezed the trigger.

The light went out.

"These things are crap to shoot straight with," she said. But she was already taking a bead on the next light out.

Melanie worked systematically, taking out all the lights in the tunnel, and then asked the group to move to one side and shot out the lights above and behind them.

She didn't miss a single shot and, as far as Max could tell, every bullet ended up embedded in the fixture. There were no telltale ricochet sounds. She was every inch the professional soldier. His team back in Russia wouldn't have seemed quite as professional: no one could pull off complete earnestness the way the Americans could. A Russian would make the shots with the same care, but he would make comments, either humorous or fatalistic while doing so.

Darkness fell over the tunnel, but Max could still see the loading bay up ahead. "Thanks," he said. "They still know we're here, but at least they won't be able to see us coming."

"Unless they have IR," Melanie replied.

"Unless they have IR," Max agreed.

Hermes came over to them. "Want to take point again?" he said. "I'll join you."

Max nodded. Hermes was the best of the rest of them in these situations.

They moved down the tunnel, glued to the walls—Max on the left, Hermes across from him.

As expected, the tunnel widened into a concrete maneuvering area, a place where whatever trucks had been expected to enter the complex could maneuver, load and unload. It had an unfinished feel, bare concrete with no fixtures. Even the stairs appeared to be missing, at least to judge by the fact that there was a door a meter up, under which someone had piled a couple of crates creating makeshift steps.

Clearly, construction had stopped after the initial concrete was poured.

The unfinished nature of the area seemed not to have made much difference as to how much it was used. Evidence of copious traffic—tire marks, accumulated sand, packing detritus piled in the corners—spoke of recent activity.

"I count seven entrances," Max said. "Three of the doors are open. I don't see anyone standing in there."

"Doesn't mean they aren't further back. They definitely know we're here," Hermes replied.

"I would go through the second open door, right there," Max suggested.

"Why that one?"

"It's the biggest. Probably goes somewhere important." He paused to look the rest of the doors over. "I'd also leave three of the truckers here to cover the rest of the doors, so if anyone tries to come out behind us, they can shoot them to pieces."

"Agreed."

"And before anyone goes anywhere, we need to put a couple of flash-bangs through the openings. As soon as they go off, we go in."

They called the rest of the group over and reviewed the plan. Max, Voornacht and Louembe would be the first through and, once they secured the passageway beyond the door, the rest of the troops would come inside, in groups of five.

Melanie pulled up wordlessly and shot out the lights in the loading bay, leaving the open doorways as the only source of illumination.

"Cover us," Max told Melanie. Then he led his men towards the door they'd selected, hugging the walls to keep to the darker area.

Once beside the objective, Max pulled the black cylinder out of his pouch. Flash-bang grenades wouldn't kill anyone... but no one had thought to bring regular grenades on the trip. That was a planning deficiency Max could understand: an attack on a lab shouldn't have required serious ordnance.

He tossed the grenade through, squeezed himself against the wall, closed his eyes and covered his ears.

As soon as the explosion stopped, he jumped into motion, diving into the opening—this one didn't have stairs to reach it and surveyed the situation.

There was no one present, just a hallway that ended at yet another door.

Max turned back to his companions: "We'd better check that."

They carefully tried the handle, reaching out from behind the wall. Nothing happened, and the door opened onto a concrete cross-corridor in a tall room where the walls only reached about halfway to the roof, ending four meters above the ground.

"It's safe," Max said. "Bring the rest."

They repeated the procedure, clearing one end of the corridor and then the other before allowing the rest of the troops to follow.

"What is this place?" Melanie asked.

"I'm not entirely certain," Max replied. "The corridor seems to open into a couple of short cross-corridors."

Melanie crept forward and peered around the corner. She came back with a perplexed look on her face. "You're right. And it turns again after that, all right angles, too. It reminds me of…" she looked around. "Of some kind of maze."

Max realized she was right. He turned to relay the conclusion to Hermes when a mechanical noise echoed through the open room.

Behind them, the door they'd entered through was suddenly covered by a steel curtain descending quickly. The noise they'd heard was the motors and chains that drove the mechanism.

It crashed against the ground with a rattle and, at the same moment, the lights went out.

Max put his night vision goggles on, and toggled from IR to night vision… neither was telling him much, but at least the IR was showing him the body heat from his companions.

The truckers didn't have night vision.

"All right," Hermes said. "How many flashlights have we got?"

***

Philippe watched the screen with the thermal imaging camera feed as the labyrinth sealed, red and orange blotches on one end of the large room showed the position of the invaders while slightly less vivid, but much larger colored blobs entered at the other end. Sun-Lee, standing beside him, had a rapt expression on his face.

"What have you sent in there with them?" he asked.

"The shipment we were sending to the Pakistanis."

"That's a pity. I assume that some of them will get damaged. We'd better start incubating a few more."

Philippe nodded. "I'll do that as soon as we get done here."

"Excellent," Sun-Lee replied. "How do you think they'll do against the men in there?"

"I think they'll tear them to pieces. There are just too many monsters for twenty soldiers."

Sun-Lee laughed. "Whatever happens, it should be a great show."

The two groups of colored heat signatures closed the distance between them.

***

"Stick together," Hermes said. "Max, you take point. Louembe, bring up the rear. Marine," he said to Melanie, "can you keep the drivers in order?"

Melanie shrugged. "We just need to explain what we're doing. A lot of them have experience in the civil war. They can follow orders and march in a line."

"Yeah, but half of them don't have flashlights. Just keep them in line, will you?"

She went off to speak to Salah, and Max headed in the direction they'd decided to go. As soon as he turned away from the flashlights, he turned on his night vision.

The passageway ahead of him dead-ended at a wall, giving them the option of going left or right. He headed left.

"Why this direction?" Melanie whispered.

"It takes us toward the center of the maze."

"Aren't you supposed to turn left at every intersection if you want to solve a maze? I think I read that somewhere."

Max shrugged. "I don't know. I just hope there's an exit along the far wall, so I'm going that way. I can actually navigate by looking up. If you look carefully through the goggles you can actually see the features on the roof. See? The support columns are visible."

"And if it's closed?"

"Then we shoot our way through."

She continued on in silence and Max wondered if they weren't being overconfident. Maybe they should have shot their way out the curtain behind them. It would have made a lot of noise and it would have meant giving the enemy more time to prepare... but perhaps regrouping to think things through would have been a better option.

Fortunately, he wasn't the one who had to make the decisions on this jaunt. That task fell to Hermes, and he was welcome to it.

Max reached the end of another short chute and, with a glance at the ceiling, turned right, keeping to the center. He was delighted to see that this corridor was longer, twelve meters at least, and crossed a couple of intersections.

He glanced into each cross-corridor, but all were extremely short, dead-ending—and blocking his view—after only a couple of meters. He forged ahead.

Moments after he passed the first set of cross-passages, Max heard a soft clicking sound behind him, like long fingernails tapping a blackboard. He turned back to see what was causing the noise, ready to tear whoever was giving away their position a new asshole.

Movement, a light-colored streak in his IR view flashed across his vision, emerging from the corridor on the left and disappearing into the one on the right. Max couldn't quite discern its shape before a flashlight beam hit him in the goggles and turned everything white.

"Dammit," he whispered as he waited for vision to return. "Point those lights somewhere else."

A moment later, the screams started: shouts in Tuareg, which Max couldn't parse, thinning out and tapering off into a loud yell. Then silence from the man... but not silence: the sounds of snapping and slurping filled the room gruesomely.

Max tore off his goggles and tried to take a headcount. There were too many people packed into the corridor, and everyone seemed to be waving their flashlights to and fro. He identified Melanie, Hermes and Balzano just behind him, but no one else in the tumult further back.

"Calm down," he shouted.

No one listened.

Another form, shadowy and taller than a human appeared to materialize from the left. This one stopped in front of them and reared back with a menacing hiss. One of the men began to yell in pain.

But the rest of them didn't, and Max saw several of the drivers raise their AK-47s.

"No!" he shouted, but it was too late. The staccato bursts of several rifles firing on full automatic filled the corridor and deafened him.

Even in the din, however, he heard the pinging of bullets against the concrete walls.

"Shit," Max said and dove around the next corner. He knew only chance had saved him from being mowed down by his own allies.

Someone landed on top of him, and a third person stumbled around the corner, too.

The fourth walked in more calmly, actually firing controlled bursts behind him as he went. Max recognized Hermes in the muzzle flashes.

The firing in the corridor behind them subsided and Max got to his feet. The person who'd landed on him was Melanie. The other man was Salah, nursing a bleeding arm.

Since it appeared to be safe to look back into the corridor, Max took the Tuareg chief's flashlight and shone it around the corner.

Carnage. In less than fifteen seconds, the formerly pristine concrete of the hallway had been turned into a charnel house. A huge lump of monster lay in the center of the passage, bleeding into a huge pool, black in the dim light. It appeared to have been shot a hundred times.

Four human bodies lay around it and Max checked them quickly. Three had been torn to pieces by automatic weapons fire. Max cursed when he recognized Voornacht among them, killed by friendly fire.

The fourth had a huge gash in his stomach, and smelled of an open digestive system. He was still alive, but Max gave him a few minutes at most.

The rest of the truckers and Louembe were nowhere to be seen. Max could hear them shouting somewhere else in the maze.

"All right," he said to Hermes. "Now we know what we're up against. Let's find Louembe and get the hell out of here. We should come back with RPGs or something."

"And how are we going to find Louembe?"

"We'll follow the blood," Max replied, pointing at the wall.

Five red streaks ran along the concrete at shoulder height where someone's hand had dragged along the wall and disappeared around the corner, and drops and streaks covered the floor in the same direction.

Before they'd taken three steps, however, two dinosaurs like the one they'd fought at the airfield appeared around the corner.

Max backed away, rifle raised, expecting them to charge at any moment, but the creatures lunged at Voornacht instead. They hissed and spat, pulling at the corpse.

Max and Hermes rejoined Melanie, who was tending to Salah's arm.

"Change of plans. We're going that way," Max informed her, pointing away from the primeval monsters behind them.

CHAPTER 12

Mehmoud crashed into a concrete wall and fell back into a sitting position. The pain in his forehead acted as a counterweight, bringing his panic into check. He could still feel the frantic beating of his heart, and his hands still twitched, but at least he was master of himself once again.

He listened, but all he heard was his own breathing, ragged and loud. There were no sounds of pursuit. The monster must have run after someone else.

The space around him was dark. He'd dropped his light when he ran.

"Brahim?" he whispered. "Can anyone hear me?"

Nothing. But now that he was under control, and that his breathing was nearly back to normal, he realized that the soft sounds coming in through the open top of the maze could guide him back to where his friends were.

Also to where the monsters were.

He gripped his rifle tighter. He knew the things could be killed. He'd been one of the people shooting at the one that fell earlier. It was just a question of seeing it before it could hurt him.

He pulled his phone out of his pocket and turned on the light. It might not be as good as a real flashlight, but at least he wouldn't slam into any more walls.

The sounds were coming from his right, so he headed that way, then turned right again at the next dead end and left when he was forced to do so again. He expected that should keep him moving in his original direction.

The light danced around in front, casting the maze in an eerie light. He'd been in plenty of caves out in the desert, but the sharp, square walls of the obviously manmade structure around him were somehow more threatening than the echoing organic forms of nature. Mehmoud knew that nature was indifferent. It could kill you just because it didn't care if there was a man in its midst. But this place? This place was here to harm you on purpose. The creatures within as well: they'd been built to hurt people.

He stopped to listen again. Now, the sounds of people calling to each other seemed to be behind him, back the way he'd come.

Frustration welled up as he retraced his steps. One moment, the sound of conversation seemed to come from one side. The next, from the other. He must have gotten turned around.

He looked back the way he'd come, and the sound seemed to come from behind him.

So he turned again. Now it came from the side.

Something clicked.

Mehmoud shone his light down a cross-corridor, but it only went a few paces before dead-ending. He chose a different one, one that was longer. He could still hear the clicking, but the way sound bounced around in the maze made it impossible to tell where the sound came from. If he had to guess, he would have said it came from the wall to his right.

Of course, that was a solid concrete structure. He tapped on it, and it didn't even sound hollow.

The next intersection allowed him to U-turn around the wall, so he did so.

Two bright eyes gleamed at him from the darkness. They were level with his own.

He raised the AK-47, already pulling on the trigger as the gun came up.

The eyes darted in his direction. He tried to bring the gun to bear on them.

Thus distracted, he didn't see the monster's hind leg shoot forward. He only felt the agony of the knifelike claw tearing through the skin of his stomach. Warm liquid gushed onto his legs, onto the floor, pouring out of the gaping wound.

Mehmoud wanted to lift the gun, to shoot the monster in the face, but his hand didn't obey his command. At least his finger was still on the trigger. He could hear the gun firing, feel it jerking in his grip.

And then it went silent, and the eyes came closer. Teeth were the last thing Mehmoud saw, and the stench of rot from between those teeth his last sensation on earth.

***

Philippe watched the carnage, disgusted by the events unfolding in the maze, one floor above the offices.

"I'll go set up the incubators for the replacement products," he told Sun-Lee.

The North Korean grunted his assent, too engrossed in watching their monsters stalk the intruders to pay attention to anything outside his monitors.

Philippe walked to the incubator room and searched for the past programs. He quickly found the one he wanted, codenamed Compo-Maxi-4, and punched in all the authorization codes.

The machinery started working at once. Pumps spun and liquid flowed. The gushing of nutrients into each cylinder's holding tanks began. Liquid slurries with the components he'd need to grow fully-formed attack creatures within days—proteins, amino acids, nutrients and the all-important calcium supply that would give their product strong bones.

He also heard the conveyor belts beneath the floor start up. Based on the tech used by pharmaceutical distributing warehouses, the miniature belts could transport fertilized eggs from the cold storage area to the correct cylinder, where it would be quickened, nurtured and force fed.

The sound was just what he needed to conceal his true purpose.

Philippe whistled.

Moments later, Poupée appeared, peering down on him from atop the nearest cylinder. "Phlip want me?" she said.

"Yes, I need your help." He paused, thinking how to explain such difficult concepts to the creature. In the end, he shrugged and simply told her what he wanted. "Do you understand?" he asked.

She gazed at him for some moments, then said: "Yes."

"Go, then," Philippe commanded.

He watched her scamper towards the stairs at the far end of the room. The other technicians ignored her; they were accustomed to Philippe's collection of pets and experimental animals.

Once she was out of sight, he checked the status on the incubators—all nominal, of course—and returned to the control office where Sun-Lee hadn't moved from his seat.

"We should have a dozen new creatures in four days. Five days if we want to make sure they're defect-free."

His boss grunted. "I don't think we'll need a dozen of them. They've only killed one so far, and shot at a couple more. Our clients are going to love these things, they just walk through bullets. I'm so glad we managed to tweak those plans we stole from ZooDef. Their original Compsognathus were much too weak to face soldiers, don't you think?"

Philippe said nothing.

***

"Aim for the heart," Max said.

"I can hit them between the eyes," Melanie replied. This definitely wasn't the time or the place for some special forces Bruno to put her shooting in doubt. Why was it those guys always thought they could outshoot everyone. They were good, but not Marine sniper good.

"I know that," the Russian said. "I've seen you shoot. But it's better to shoot for the body mass. Apparently, the skulls are so thick you have a much better chance of injuring something important if you shoot for the body."

"Ah." She hated when the big guys got all logical on her. She never knew what to say. "Thanks."

The clicking of the creatures' claws on the concrete floor was getting closer and closer. The fact that you couldn't see where they would come at you from was maddening. She and Max pointed their guns forward while Hermes covered their rear. Salah staggered along in between, obviously in some pain, but enduring stoically.

Each intersection represented an adrenalin spike. Every time they peered cautiously around a wall, she expected to encounter a hurricane of teeth and claws and scales.

They took turns clearing each cross-corridor. Max had wanted to do them all himself, of course, but she had put her foot down: this wasn't a place for misguided chivalry. To his credit, Max didn't argue when she explained the facts of life, just nodded and let her take the next one.

They were using the IR function of their goggles, which had proven better than standard night vision for spotting the dinosaurs, even with the light from the flashlights giving a certain amount of ambient illumination for the regular function to amplify.

The next turn was hers, and she poked her head around and pulled it back.

"Clear," she reported.

Max stepped through, covering the next few meters of corridor.

Despite getting split from the rest of the group, the plan hadn't changed. They wanted to make it to the far side. Louembe knew where they were going, and he was probably the best man to lead a group through a dark maze. And besides, smaller groups were likely better— she certainly didn't want a repeat of what had happened when they first encountered the dinosaurs... their own men had nearly taken her head off with their indiscriminate fire.

As if to confirm that they were still alive, every once in a while the maze would erupt in gunfire and shouting. Apparently, the larger group had chosen the path with all the dinosaurs—Max, Hermes and Melanie hadn't encountered any more.

Max motioned them forward, and Melanie rose from her crouch when Hermes' voice announced: "Behind us!"

She turned to see two of the monsters approaching side by side. The creatures moved cautiously, unhurriedly, but also unafraid of the four humans in front of them.

Melanie didn't hesitate. She lifted her rifle and, overcoming her instinct to shoot for the head, she pumped a short burst, perfectly centered on the torso of the creature to the left, just about where she calculated the heart must be.

The things didn't even appear to notice. They kept coming as if the bullets were irrelevant.

"Keep shooting," Max shouted. "They'll go down eventually."

Then he opened up on the creature on the right. The FAL he was using seemed to be a bit more effective than the AK, or maybe he just got lucky. The one he was shooting at stopped and hissed at them.

Hermes joined the fun and now all three were shooting the dinosaurs. The one Max had hit staggered under the barrage and turned tail, limping around a corner.

The other one was either dumber or angrier. Upon finding itself alone, the monster lowered its head and charged.

Hermes, who was closest to it, was bowled over, and Salah was trampled, too.

Melanie and Max concentrated their fire as it approached, bullets disappearing into its flesh. Blood sprayed.

Two yards before it reached them, it stumbled and dropped to the ground, headfirst. One baleful eye studied Melanie and then, without warning, the hind leg, off to the side, shot out at her foot.

Melanie saw it coming and tried to jump out of the way, but the strike caught her sole and sent her tumbling. She heard Max's gun bark four more times, and then he was kneeling beside her.

"Are you all right?" he asked.

"Yeah." She checked her shoe and saw that the claw had cut through the black leather. A quick probe with her finger showed her that the skin below was still intact. "I'm fine. Check the others."

Max pulled Hermes to his feet and proceeded to Salah. Melanie saw him kneel beside the old man. "I think you need to come," the Russian said. "I don't speak Arabic that well."

She rushed over and knelt beside the old Tuareg. In the light of the flashlight, she could see he was bleeding from several puncture wounds on the right side of his chest.

He gripped her forearm hard. "Tell Brahim..." he said. Then he stopped as if to gather strength for a final push. "Tell Brahim he is the chief now. Tell him. My sister will make sure he does his best."

Then he lay back, still breathing, but incredibly weak.

"We'll get you out of here," she said.

The man wasn't listening. He was clearly in shock, or maybe he'd just said what he intended to say, and was simply waiting for his God to take him. Melanie resisted the urge to shake his shoulder, to scream at him to stay strong. It would make no difference at all, except possibly to kill the poor man.

"We need to move," Max said.

"We can't leave him."

"We must. We need to get out of this maze. The monsters can pick us off here, one by one."

"Dammit," Melanie said. She bent down, trying to get her head under Salah's arm to support his shoulder and help him walk if possible, drag him if necessary. But she realized the man was no longer responsive. She checked his pulse. "Dammit," she whispered.

Melanie stood. "Let's go," she said.

Max paused. "Are you going to be all right?"

"Until later," she replied.

Max nodded, and she realized that this Russian understood. All real soldiers knew about doing your work now and mourning your friends later. It was part of the job description. Even for those who lost comrades in combat or in training.

But for some reason, she felt Max's understanding went a step deeper. He knew exactly what she was feeling, and he knew exactly what she would feel. He gave her the impression of having been there, walked the path of loss and returned. She decided to ask him about it once they got out of this mess.

The Russian took the lead, with Hermes—bruised but functional— bringing up the rear. She wanted to tell them that she could do her part, but the truth was that she needed a few minutes. The old dead man back there had shown her that respect was something that could cut across cultures. They lived in worlds so different they couldn't really even understand one another, but Salah had bridged the distance between them out of the wisdom and kindness of his heart. She hoped his nephew made it out of the maze alive so she could make good on her promise.

A skittering noise reached them and Max froze. He peered around the next intersection and shook his head. It wasn't coming from ahead of them.

"Nothing behind us," Hermes said.

The noise came again and Melanie realized it was coming from above. Something tiny was scurrying along the top of the wall, glowing bright red in her IR. "Just a rat," she reported, "on the wall."

They advanced to the next intersection.

"Clear," Max said.

On to the next.

Before Max could inspect it, Melanie looked up again. The creature on the wall was keeping pace with them exactly, and she realized it must have jumped at least one big gap to do so. Could rats jump?

"*Suivre*," a high-pitched voice said.

They froze. No one in their group had a voice like that. Melanie might have been able to pitch her voice that high, but she hadn't done so.

"*Suivre*," the voice said again. Is seemed to come from above.

Melanie looked up. No. Even if it wasn't a rat, that thing was too small to be a child.

"*Suivre*."

"I think it's coming from that thing up there," Melanie said.

"The rat?" Max asked.

She shrugged. "Or something else up there."

"Whatever is talking, it wants us to follow it," Hermes said. "That's what *Suivre* means. To follow." He said something in French, loud enough to be heard over the next corridor.

"*Moi, Ppée*," the squeaking voice returned. "*Suivre*."

Hermes shook his head. "I have no explanation for it, but I think your rat is talking to us. I asked who was out there and what they wanted and, as far as I could tell, that little creature—I think it looks like a monkey, not a rat—said 'me, Pepe,' or maybe 'Poupée.'"

"Ask it why?" Max said.

"*Porte*," came the reply.

"It says there's a door," Hermes translated.

"And we're supposed to believe it? How do we know it wasn't sent here with a speaker strapped to it to lead us into a trap?" Max said.

"We don't. But I don't have any better ideas. Maybe we should just follow it, carefully, and see what happens," Hermes said.

"I never like what happens when I do that," Max replied.

"I agree with Hermes," Melanie said. In fact, she was in the kind of mood where she hoped they would end up neck deep in shit. The way she felt after watching Salah die, she would have welcomed the chance to empty a few magazines into something.

Max shrugged. "All right."

Hermes spoke to the creature and it set off along the wall, stopping every few paces to chitter at them unintelligibly if they didn't follow quickly enough. After a half-dozen turns—and without running into any creatures—they came to another wall.

This one had a single armored door in it. A number pad with a red light blinking on it was embedded in the wall beside the aperture.

Hermes spat in disgust. "We'll never get through that."

The light on the door turned green and the pane popped open with a hiss.

"Someone likes us," Max said. "Or there's something worse on the other side of this."

"I'll take my chances," Melanie said. She pulled the door fully open and turned to Hermes. "Tell it to bring our friends."

But the little creature was nowhere to be seen. Whatever it wanted to do, it had apparently managed.

On the other side of the door was a staircase.

"Up or down?" Melanie asked.

"Down. The upper areas would be harder to defend," Hermes replied. "Dictators like their bunkers deep. The good stuff should be down there."

They descended. The metal stairs creaked, but no one came to investigate.

At the bottom was another door. This one also had a number pad, but someone had jammed it open with a rubber wedge of the kind janitors used. The thing was so prosaic, sitting there in the middle of a terrorist facility, that Melanie chuckled.

"You all right?" Max said. He was just ahead of her, in the classic position beside the entrance where he could rush in immediately while not being seen beforehand.

"Yeah. And don't be so concerned about me. I'll be fine until we make it out of here. Then, I'm going to want a lot of alcohol."

"I'm not worried about you holding up," he replied. "But I don't want this to ruin you forever."

"You're pretty nice for a gorilla," she said.

"And you're quite all right for a woman doing a man's job," he replied.

"Careful. I've broken noses for less," Melanie said. For some reason, though, she let it pass. The guy had proven he would work with her and respect her abilities. She was used to taking crap like that from her squad mates and if that was what was happening here, then she would allow it.

"I can imagine," he replied. "Want to hurt whatever's on the other side of this door?"

"After you," she said.

And the banter stopped immediately. He simply whispered: "Three, two, one…" and charged through the open door.

"Clear," he said a moment later.

Melanie followed him, with Hermes immediately behind.

A long corridor with several exits leading off to the sides greeted them.

"Labs," Hermes whispered as they reached the first door.

Melanie glanced inside and realized he was right: glassware of the mad-scientist type dotted the tables while unidentifiable electronics filled most of the rest of the room. She was delighted to spot a piece of equipment she recognized: a centrifuge that could spin four test tubes at once. Two big cylinders like the ones they'd demolished in the first complex loomed over the small space.

"Wait a second," she said.

She stepped into the room and put her hand against a mug of coffee beside a workstation. "This is still pretty hot," she told Hermes, who was standing beside the door. "Someone pulled out of here just now."

"Which means they know we're coming," Hermes said.

"I'd say trapping us in the maze was a pretty good clue of that," she replied. "Should I shoot out the lights?"

The illumination came from fluorescent tubes, plenty of them.

"I'd rather not tell anyone waiting for us exactly where we are," Hermes said.

"You think they aren't watching the security feed?" She pointed to an obvious camera in the hall.

Hermes pulled out his phone and peered at it. "Maybe in some central office, but they aren't doing it remotely. There's no wi-fi in here."

"Ah."

Max led them down the corridor, and she admired his grace. For such a big guy, he could move extremely quietly while maintaining a rapid pace. She tried to catch a noise from him, but there was nothing, not even from three meters away.

Suddenly, he stopped and held up his hand. Melanie and Hermes halted. Max pointed forward to where the corridor ended at a concrete wall. A cross-corridor ran between that wall and the furthest office. Clearly, that was the exit from the lab area deeper into the complex.

With an unexpected burst of speed, Max sprinted forward. Just before reaching the intersection, he angled his approach so that it was nearly parallel to the cross-corridor and dove onto his stomach, keeping his rifle angled upward. Four shots exploded, deafening in the enclosed area.

"Clear," he whispered.

Melanie ran forward, passing the prone Russian and the bodies of two bleeding guards. She checked where the cross-corridor bent in an L, still following the contours of the concrete outer wall. There was no one there. "Clear!"

Suddenly, Max turned to point his rifle away from them. He'd been covering the entrance to the corridor, but now pointed back the way they'd come. "We have company," he said, getting back on his feet to take cover behind a wall.

Signaling to Hermes to take her place at the continuation of the corridor, Melanie ran to the intersection and peered out. Whoever was coming was making too much noise to be planning an ambush. At least four voices were arguing among themselves.

A head came into view through the same door at the head of the stairs from which they'd emerged just moments before. She took a bead on the silhouette and let out her breath.

The man she was aiming at stepped into the lighted area. She relaxed and lowered her gun a fraction.

"It's Louembe," she said. "He has four of the Tuareg with him."

"Over here," she called, waving.

Louembe led the drivers over. They were wide-eyed and covered with blood, although they appeared to be uninjured. To her sudden relief, she realized that the third man in the group was Salah's nephew, Brahim.

"How did you get out?" she asked.

"It was the strangest thing. A monkey led us to an open door. You might not believe this, but it spoke French better than some of my troops back in Gabon." Seeing her look of incomprehension, the big soldier rolled his eyes. "French is our official language."

"Oh. Sorry. I've never been there."

A huge smile lit up Louembe's features. "You should. It's the most beautiful place in the world. Once we finish killing these scientists and their pets, I'll guide you myself."

"Thank you," she replied. "I'd love that."

Max was bent over the bodies. "These guys are in uniform, but they aren't from any army I've ever seen. They kind of remind me of North Korean uniforms, but the real ones are better than this stuff."

"Do you think they're from an African army?" Hermes asked.

"They don't look African to me. This guy looks Swedish. And that body there looks... well, it looks North Korean, and I think it's a woman."

Melanie was about to make a joke about him needing four shots to create two cadavers, but she cut short. A man had appeared in the doorway of one of the labs, hands held out in front of him, empty.

"Guys..."

But Louembe and the drivers had already seen the intruder. Every muzzle was trained on him.

The man seemed unperturbed. He was white, with pale eyes and greying hair and walked with a limp. He was dressed in a white suit, missing only the matching white hat for the perfect 'tropical gentleman' effect. He stopped and nodded to where the two dead bodies lay. "They're from Sun-Lee's personal security force," he informed them in a soft voice. "There should be at least three more of them waiting to shoot you somewhere inside."

"And the scientists?"

"About forty of them. I assume they've been confined to their quarters to keep them out of the way of the firefight."

"And who are you?"

"His name is Philippe," Brahim said. "He's one of the bosses. He's the one who designs the monsters."

"Guilty as charged," Philippe replied, with a nod and a slight smile.

"Guilty is the right word," Brahim said. He raised his gun and pointed it between Philippe's eyes. "Give me one reason why I shouldn't shoot you right now."

Philippe whistled softly and the little brown-grey creature that had led them out of the maze skittered out from inside the same lab he'd emerged from and climbed onto his shoulder. "Because I'm the one who can show you how to get around in here without getting killed, as I've already proved. And because I want Sun-Lee dead just as badly as you do."

CHAPTER 13

Max put his hand on the muzzle of Brahim's gun, still trained on Philippe, unwavering. "Not yet," he told the man in English.

For a second, the Tuareg held the gun steady despite the pressure on the barrel. Finally, he lowered it.

Hermes approached the scientist. "We can take care of ourselves."

"But if you don't hurry," Philippe replied, "you'll miss Sun-Lee."

"We have the exit covered."

"That's not the only exit."

Hermes raised an eyebrow. "Show us now."

"He's probably in the monitor room," Philippe said. "There might be guards."

Melanie spoke up. "We can take care of the guards. Or the lizards. I just want that bastard in my sights."

"All right. We need to go that way." Philippe pointed towards the exit, where the dead guards lay in a deepening pool of blood.

Max took point. He knew it was the spot most likely to get him shot at, but there were things he preferred to do for himself. It wasn't that he didn't trust any of the others to shoot straight if things got rough... but yeah, he didn't trust any of the others to shoot straight if things got rough. Mercenaries were serviceable when they had the advantage of terrain they knew really well and he was sure Louembe was quite adept if they ever got caught in a swamp. But they weren't really soldiers. Not the way he was.

Or, he was beginning to suspect, in the way that Marine sniper was.

She appeared to be laser-focused on the mission, and barely faltered when the old man was brought down in the maze. She must have figured out the dinosaurs were feeding on his body, but she didn't let that affect her. Her cold competence commanded respect.

She slotted beside him, offering to clear rooms in tandem, and he nodded. No words were exchanged.

As they stepped over the corpses, Melanie looked his way, raised an eyebrow and said: "Two bodies... Four bullets."

He chuckled, knowing that she wasn't going to let him forget it, but also that he wasn't going to modify it. Among the tribe of real soldiers, each had their own little rituals and proprietary ways of doing things. Some were downright superstitious about it. In Max's case, he liked to tap his targets twice. As a special ops soldier, he'd done so much shooting that it was a stupid waste of ammo. He could hit what he was shooting at, every single time.

He didn't care. Even though sergeants and instructors had drilled the mantra of moving on to the next target immediately, and though he could even make the single-shot method work in simulations and exercises, he immediately reverted to a two-shot burst as soon as real ammo was coming back at him—he just felt better that way, and would set the gun up that way if it was an option. The weird part was that he never had the urge to fire twice with a handgun, only with rifles.

There was no chance of him changing it, and he would not even try. It was better to shoot twice than to start thinking about what he was doing. If you stopped to think, you were dead.

Soon, he would have to explain all of this to Melanie. She would understand completely. Hell, she'd probably share some little thing she did that was unusual or just plain weird. Any real soldier would absolutely know why he did it.

And the next time he shot twice, he'd see her standing somewhere holding up two mocking fingers. That was the way things were.

They moved quickly down the hall. Unlike the straight lines they'd encountered in the complex so far, this one curved slightly, as if the tunnel had followed a seam in the natural rock. Unfortunately, that meant they couldn't see to the end, which made for a tense advance until the door on the far wall came into view. This one also had a keypad.

"Mad scientist," Max called back over his shoulder, "you're up."

Philippe punched in a four-number code and then Max pulled him away from the door and pushed him back down the hall. A moment later, before the lock could reengage, he turned the handle and opened the door a couple of centimeters.

Bullets slammed into it, not quite piercing the armored skin, and Max smiled. *Amateurs*, he thought. *Or at least one amateur*. It was always the same: someone inside got nervous and gave away the ambush.

"Louembe," he said, "do you have any flash-bangs left?"

"Just one."

"That should be enough. Hell, if we weren't in a hurry, I'd insist on doing this without them, just for practice. The people in there are not a real threat."

He motioned for Melanie, positioned on the far side of the door, to pull it open a hands-width wide, then he rolled the flash-bang through, ignoring the bullets raining on the steel. A ricochet could kill him, true, but it would have to be a really unlucky bounce.

After the canister was through, Melanie proved again that she was a true pro by closing the door far enough that nothing could get through, but without latching it.

A couple of seconds later, a deafening bang informed them that the stun grenade had gone off.

Max pulled the door open and dove through, rolling to his feet and coming up behind a coffee machine. It offered scant cover, but it was better than none at all. He ignored the dazed-looking people in the foreground and scanned the room they were in for active threats. Finding none, he shot the three green-uniformed guards. Two of them, he drilled in the head, two shots right between the eyes. The third seemed to be even more disoriented than the other two, and also seemed to have dropped his weapon, so he took a calculated risk and shot him in the thigh.

He dropped like a stone.

"Clear!" he shouted.

Louembe and Hermes charged through, trusting him and Melanie to cover them as they made their way to the far end of the room.

"No one here," Louembe reported.

"Good," Max replied. "I left one alive."

He pointed to the downed guard, and Melanie ran over. She quickly restrained the guard's hands with a cable tie.

Max approached slowly, scanning every meter of the room for further threats. The place was not another interior square like the ones they'd found in the lab area, but actually a wide concrete corridor with doors that opened into larger rooms.

"That's the monitor room," Philippe said, pointing to a door almost all the way down the hall. "Sun-Lee was in there ten minutes ago."

Hermes sprinted to the indicated door. "Well, there's no one here now," he reported. Then he peered into the room and shouted back. "Is that the labyrinth we were stuck in?"

"Yes," Philippe responded. "I knew how to help you by watching the feed."

"You should have come earlier," Louembe said. "Like before we ran into those things."

Max knelt beside the guard he'd shot. On closer inspection, she was definitely a woman. Her Asian features made him suspect she was Korean. It made sense that Sun-Lee would hire his countrymen for high-trust positions.

"How are you?" he asked.

The woman he'd shot was in a bad way. She'd bled a lot, and the jacket Melanie had pressed against the wound was black with blood. She needed better medical attention than they could get her immediately or, failing that, a tourniquet and the chance of losing a limb.

The guard said something in a language he couldn't understand, so he turned to Melanie and raised an eyebrow. She shook her head.

"Do you speak English?" he asked the bleeding woman.

"Fuck you, capitalist pig," she replied in a thick accent.

"I don't think we'll get too much from her," Melanie said with a chuckle.

"I'm not capitalist. I'm Russian," Max said.

The woman snorted, seeming to take pride in the fact that she wasn't screaming in pain and desperation. "Russians worst capitalists. Fuck you."

He turned to Melanie. "Do you know how to tie a tourniquet?"

"Yeah, but I won't. I say we let her bleed."

He was stunned, and it must have showed, because the Marine continued.

"Yeah, I know, it goes against every rule of combat. You take care of enemy prisoners and treat the wounded, yadda, yadda, yadda." She glared. "Well, I'll definitely do that when I'm back in uniform, but not for these assholes. This little piece of crap is a bodyguard for a guy who sends monsters into shopping malls to rip up little girls. I'm not here because someone is paying me, and I'm not here for some larger humanitarian purpose or to defend liberty. I'm here to kill these shitheads, every single one of them that I can get between my crosshairs. I'd kill them slowly and painfully if I could, but if not, I'll give them a bullet between the eyes." She paused, as if uncertain what to say now that the admission was out in the open. "I won't shoot her now that she's down, but if you want a tourniquet, get someone else to do it. Louembe probably knows how. It seems just the kind of thing a by-the-book guy like that would be good at."

As Max headed to where Louembe stood, a cry from the truckers brought everyone back to high alert. The strange part was that these weren't cries of alarm, but of... joy?

Max turned to see Javier Balzano, his clothes in tatters and a bleeding open cut on his face stagger into the hall. Leaning on him was another of the truckers, in even worse condition than the Argentine colonel. That was the reason for the shouts of joy.

The other three truckers quickly grabbed their injured comrade and set about tending his wounds. Brahim, Max noted, stopped to shake Balzano's hand and thank him. He nodded with approval: that was a true leader at work. Judging by Melanie's opinion of the old Tuareg chief, these men were taught well as they grew up,

Balzano refused the offered water and limped over to where Hermes stood by the monitors.

"I quit," he said. "It's one thing to survive an attack by monsters because you happen to be in the wrong place at the wrong time, but quite another to walk into a nest of the things."

"Are you going to quit now?" Hermes asked. "Just turn in your gun and sit there while we clean the rest of this place up?"

"No. I'll stick with you. But I won't shoot anyone who isn't shooting at me."

"Fair enough. How did you get out? Did the Frenchman's monkey save you, too?"

"I have no idea what you're talking about. We ran into five more of those things. We got four of them, but I also lost three men. The last one ran."

Max grunted. Nailing four of the monsters meant that Balzano must have kept his head, and kept his men disciplined, too. He might have to revise his opinion of the man. He was apparently a lot harder to kill than Max gave him credit for.

Max had seen it before. The reluctant warrior. Ask him to fight for glory or a cause and he would run as fast as he could in the other direction... but drop him into the middle of something, and he would kick ass and take names, while also trying to save everyone around him. If he was telling the truth about his dinosaur kill rate, he was currently well up on the rest of the crew.

The guard woman had lost consciousness. She wouldn't make it without help. "Balzano," he called. "Do you know how to tie a tourniquet?"

The man limped over and looked down at the guard at his feet. "So young," he said. "Have any of you got a first aid kit?"

"There's one in the monitor room," Philippe said.

As Louembe fetched it, Max approached Hermes, who had collared the Frenchman. "So where would Sun-Lee have gone?" he said.

"I assume he would go to his room. I suspect he has a bolthole there."

"Why do you think that?"

"Because it's a small room with an awkward shape. The only reason a megalomaniac like him would have chosen it instead of the biggest room in the complex is because it had some secret way out. Logical."

"And where is his room?" Max asked.

Philippe pointed. "At the end of the hall to the right, and then at the end of that hall."

Max caught Melanie's eye. She nodded.

Hermes said: "I'm coming with you."

After ordering Louembe to keep everyone secure, the trio raced in the direction Philippe had indicated.

They took risks, rushing past unexamined doors on the way, but Hermes, in the lead, seemed to think time was of the essence. Max didn't love it—every instinct screamed at him to check any spot where someone might be waiting in ambush—but he kept pace. Melanie brought up the rear.

The indicated door was locked, but not armored. Hermes slammed his shoulder into it four times before kicking it. The door's wood splintered at the jamb and they were inside.

The small room appeared to have been hit by a hurricane. Papers were strewn on the carpeted floor and the steel cot against a wall. A large flatscreen monitor and a mouse had been hastily unplugged from something—probably a laptop computer—and left on the desk. Metal shelves ran along one wall.

The room was oddly-shaped, nearly triangular, and lit only by a single incandescent light hanging from wires.

"Look for a hidden exit," Hermes said.

While Hermes tapped the walls, Max headed straight for the shelves. That was the only feature in the room that could hide a secret door. Might they be the key to opening it?

He pulled on the shelves and, to his surprise, they shifted straight towards him, revealing not a concealed opening but a bare expanse and the fact that they weren't connected to the wall in any way. He tapped on the bare concrete and concluded that it had to be solid.

"Nothing," he said.

Hermes had moved the bed out of the way. "Nothing here either."

"Do you think Philippe lied to us?"

"I doubt it. Look at this place," Max said. "Sun-lee would never have let himself get cooped up in a little closet like this one unless there was a hell of a good reason for it."

"Men!" Melanie said in that tone Max had heard so often from girlfriends over the course of his life. "You might not care for decoration but you should at least have seen the one thing this room has that none of the rest do. The carpet."

Hermes and Max grabbed the exposed edge of the carpet where it met the doorway and pulled. Sure enough, it came up easily—it wasn't glued to the floor.

"Told you," Melanie said smugly.

He wanted to tell her that the carpet was as close to being invisible as possible—it was just a cheap, thin corporate grey thing you'd never have given a second thought to if you walked over it.

But the truth was she'd spotted it and he—trained in taking complexes exactly like this one—hadn't. The chagrin grew when he saw that their effort in removing it revealed a perfectly square outline in the concrete floor.

"There has to be some kind of bar here we can use to lift this," Hermes said.

"Unless he is an idiot, he would have taken it with him," Max replied. "Then he asked the guards we shot to put the carpet back."

"And left them to die," Melanie added.

Max shrugged. "They were being paid to repel invaders. His job is to design monsters. He's not much of a shot, anyway."

"Still a dick move," Melanie retorted.

"I sense you don't like our North Korean friend."

"What gave it away?"

"Call it a sixth sense," he replied with a smile.

"Well, I'm going to give him a third eye, just as soon as I get him in my sights."

Hermes, in the meantime, had rushed out into the hallway and shouted to Philippe.

"What is it?" the flustered-looking Frenchman asked as he appeared in the hall.

"We need a crowbar or something."

"That door is a maintenance storage area," Philippe replied, pointing.

Hermes rushed in and returned a moment later with a very long and sturdy-looking screwdriver which he worked into the crack in the concrete. Soon, he'd managed to lever up the trapdoor, a ten-centimeter-thick slab.

Max helped him pull it up. A dark hole in the ground greeted them.

"Inviting," Max muttered.

"Yeah, and if there was a ladder, he pulled it down after him."

Hermes shone his flashlight into the opening to reveal another concrete space five meters below. The room under them appeared to be much larger than the one in which they stood.

"There are some cables in the storage room," Hermes said. "They should hold our weight."

Within minutes, they had Hermes tied solidly around the waist and lowered him onto the floor below.

"There's no one here," the Belgian called up. "The most recent-looking footprints lead this way. There's another door—I'm checking the next room."

An explosion tore through the room below. Flames rose up from the trapdoor and Max felt the searing heat on his face a moment before he threw himself out of the way.

The entire room shook, and then the floor let go beneath him and he fell.

* * *

"Show me the letter 'A'," Lai said.

The pig, a gigantic creature that must have weighed more than seventy kilos padded over the polished marble floor and nudged the cardboard letter with its snout.

"Amazing," Gonzalo said.

"Why?" Lai replied. "Are you surprised you know what the letter 'A' looks like?"

"I'm surprised this works at all. Try something else," Gonzalo replied.

"Fine," Lai said. "Pig, do you know which one is your chair?"

The pig walked slowly around the long, polished table and pulled back the chair in which Gonzalo sat. They'd only been using the conference room—borrowed from one of Thailand's larger outsourcing firms—for three days. And every single day, Gonzalo had sat at that very chair. He was only away from it now because standing beside Lai gave him a better view of the pig.

The man who ran the equipment, an impassive, watchful man that had come with the brain scanner, seemed amused but remained, as always, silent. He would only speak if someone asked him a direct question.

"It's your mind running the animal," Lai said. "You need to believe it."

Gonzalo seemed to be trying to process that. He turned to the crime syndicate's technician. "Is it really me in there?"

"As much as we could fit into the smaller capacity of the pig's brain, yes. What you might lose is some memory, but the pig brain can take most of the intellectual capacity of a human if we don't try anything too complicated."

"And what happens to the version of me in there? Do I have to ride the pig when it becomes bacon?"

The technician smiled, his thin slash of a mouth barely registering curvature. "Of course not. We can remove the imprint and collect the memory data, and reintegrate it with your consciousness. You will have a memory of riding the pig, but the pig won't be you anymore."

"So for a few minutes I'll have been alive in two bodies at once?"

"Exactly."

"That's pretty cool," Gonzalo said.

Lai watched without comment. He wondered if all of today's youth would react like this young man from Manila. Here he was, watching the definition of what it meant to be human change in front of him, and the only moment his façade of professionalism failed was when he realized that he would forever share fifteen minutes of memories with a pig.

Perhaps it wasn't something new. Even in his own twenties, young people had been jaded at new technology for its own sake. He'd watched Malaysia grow from a muddy jungle in the early 1970s to an industrialized nation with motorcycles, television and dozens of huge factories churning out everything from sneakers for America to cars for the local market, all before he turned thirty.

He'd never really paid much attention to the march of progress. A new car model would arrive and he'd barely give it a glance.

But when his company had made Lai wealthy enough that he was expected to show a little ostentation, all of that changed. He remembered the moment it changed.

He'd walked into a Mercedes-Benz dealership to inquire about an armored S-Class. He'd been quite jaded, as he'd just come from an inspection of the big BMW in the dealership a few blocks away. The features of the two vehicles, for the most part, were similar, or at least the ones that the salesman touted were pretty much the same to his ears.

Right until the moment the man explained that the Mercedes' driver's seat would massage his back as he drove.

He never found out if the BMW had the same feature—it was quite likely it did—because he never returned to the other dealership. He bought the S-Class on the spot.

It was only six months later, when he decided he could save a ton of time by working in the car, and therefore needed to employ a chauffer, that Lai realized he'd bought the car for all the wrong reasons.

But at least he'd learned a lesson about technology... and he had a well-massaged and limber chauffer.

Would an older and wiser Gonzalo remember how he'd bubbled about being a pig and a man at the same time for fifteen minutes? Lai could see the grey-haired version of the young executive, wearing an impeccable suit in a wood-paneled office chuckling ruefully at himself.

"All right. Enough fun. Go do the scanning and get the pig out of here before it decides to soil the carpet," Lai said.

"It's unlikely to do that with a human mind controlling it," the technician said as he herded the two Gonzalos—two- and four-legged versions of the man—out the door, to reunite them in the head of the human.

Lai hit the speaker button and dialed the front desk. "Has anyone arrived for me?"

"Yes. Two people from Elephant Human Resources," the woman at the front desk replied.

"Send them in."

The Elephant Woman arrived with a lackey in tow. The man was tiny, dressed in a cheap blue suit that showed no trace of natural fibers in its makeup. He was in his fifties, dark haired, dark-skinned and had a scraggly mustache. Had he been begging at a street corner, he would have fit right in. Ellie introduced him as Mr. Hu.

"We have ten candidates for the specialized positions," Hu said.

Lai sat back on his chair and studied the man again. The voice belied the first impression completely. It was deep, strong and cultured. Hu spoke English with a perfect Oxbridge accent.

The man continued. "I have divided them roughly into two camps, one I think of as tricky, sophisticated artists and others who are more of the blunt-object trauma school of operations."

Lai raised an eyebrow at Ellie. "Sked and Akane?" he asked.

"They want nothing to do with this. Sked only took my call to tell me to tell you not to call him anymore."

"Too bad," Lai replied. "Let's see what we have."

The men and women Hu showed him were really good at what they did. Former intelligence people, police special operations people, military personnel and talented freelancers at the top of their profession were paraded in front of him.

By session's end, they had one from each camp: a French former Sureté officer and a woman who'd spent her entire career in the Cuban military and had developed a reputation for scorched-earth campaigns when putting down insurgencies before falling afoul of Havana politics.

"Do you think she'll be interested?" Lai asked.

Hu smiled. "You would never have been shown her file if she wasn't."

"All right. Get them here. I want to meet them."

CHAPTER 14

Melanie stood. When the floor had collapsed in Sun-Lee's room, she'd instinctively thrown herself into the hall, trying to put as much concrete between herself and the explosion as possible.

Her ears rang as the dust fell from the roof. In the hallway, she saw Philippe running in her direction, Louembe hot on his heels. Their mouths were moving, but she couldn't make out the words through the ringing in her ears.

"Max!" she shouted into the room. Even her own voice sounded distant, as if it was coming from a hole in the ground. There was no way the Russian, who'd been much closer to the blast, could have heard her.

If he was alive.

She tried to see where he was, but the lightbulb hadn't survived the blast. She grabbed the flashlight clipped to Louembe's pants and shone it into the room.

It was a mess. A cracked concrete slab had half-collapsed into the space below.

Which was crazy. An explosion strong enough to knock out the columns holding the floor up should have been a lot bigger than what she felt and had a lot less flame unless they were using some explosive she hadn't seen. From her vantage it had seemed to be a gasoline bomb, though. Not high explosive.

"Max," she said again, relieved that her voice was sounding more normal.

Something dark moved in the rubble, and she sighed with unexpected relief as Max got onto his hands and knees and then climbed dazedly to his feet.

"I'm all right," he said, then pointed to his ears. "But it's going to be a while before I can hear you."

She looked for some way to climb out, but the walls were jagged and torn—she didn't want him to survive the blast only to break his neck. "Let me get some more cable and we'll pull you up."

He just shrugged and pointed to his ears again. Then he climbed down the rubble, in the direction where Hermes had gone.

"What happened?" Louembe said.

"Booby trap," she replied.

"Hermes? Is he…?"

Melanie shrugged and shook her head, indicating she had no clue. Privately, however, she knew Hermes couldn't have survived the blast. Louembe seemed to be able to read her thoughts. He hung his head somberly as she walked to the storage closet and cut a few meters of wire from a long spool.

She called down to Max. "Can you hear me?"

He turned at the sound of her voice, a good sign, but he asked: "What?"

"Have you found Hermes?" she shouted. When he didn't seem to understand, she repeated: "Hermes!"

"What's left of him is buried under that slab." He pointed to a large chunk of concrete from which, now that he'd drawn her attention to it, a single black boot protruded. "But the opening is still accessible. The bomb didn't blow it all to hell. We can still follow Sun-Lee."

"The guy who was paying you is dead. Do you still feel like working?"

She couldn't see his expression in the dim light of the sub-level, but his voice transmitted impatience. "This guy booby-trapped a hallway and nearly killed me. Now it's personal." After a pause, he continued. "Besides, I'm pretty sure Irina knows exactly how to get in touch with the actual paymaster."

Melanie handed the end of one cable to Louembe. "Don't drop me."

He nodded, and she began climbing down to Max's level.

"It's been personal for me from the beginning," she told him. "So you'd better not get between my rifle and his head. I'll shoot straight through you."

"Not if I spot him first," Max replied.

She looked around and immediately realized why the gasoline bomb had managed to knock down the floor: it had been held up by wooden columns a couple of inches wide. The blast would have been more than enough to snap them in half, which meant that this had been set up beforehand by whichever tinpot despot had built the complex. Sun-Lee had only taken advantage of a booby trap that was already there.

They headed into the dark corridor, slowly, checking for tripwires or more explosives every few steps. This corridor would concentrate a blast… and even worse, a cave-in here would trap them forever, if it didn't kill them outright. Who was going to bring a rescue team to extract them?

What felt like an eternity later… but was probably no more than a few hundred feet, the tunnel suddenly ended at a staircase. Melanie could see stars through the door at the top.

"I think we've found the exit," she said.

"Yeah. We'll need to be careful. This is a perfect place for an ambush."

They poked their heads up, and saw nothing, but they also didn't draw any fire, so they emerged into the light.

"Shit," Max said, just a few steps outside.

"What?"

"Tracks."

"I don't… wait a minute," she switched off of IR onto night vision and right there, in the enhanced light from the stars, she saw what he was talking about. The tracks of wide tires in the sand heading off into the Sahara night. "Dammit."

Her world came crashing down around her as she realized that her revenge, unless she was willing to walk back down there and butcher a bunch of scientists who were pretty much working for a paycheck, was borked. And she wasn't into shooting underlings. Not anymore. Sun-Lee, a name she hadn't even known a week before, had become the focus of her hunt.

"Let's go find Irina," Max said.

***

"All right," Irina's voice said over the radio. "Go."

The team had reunited thirty minutes after Max and Melanie had gone off in search of the North Korean. With the building reasonably pacified—and using the map Philippe had drawn for them—Louembe had led the surviving men and their prisoner to the loading dock and, leaving them there, had gone up the ramp to find Irina conversing with Max and Melanie.

They'd agreed to come back and finish securing the facility but in a more coordinated way. The hunt for the rest of the scientists would be a professional effort, not the ragtag strike they'd managed thus far. To everyone's surprise, Louembe had volunteered to take care of it.

So now, he stood beside the door to the sector of the complex that Philippe had indicated, sadness for the death of Voornacht—for some reason the South African had felt like a much worse loss to Louembe than Hermes himself—overshadowed by the indignation he felt at being in the center of the organization that wanted to turn his beloved continent into a battlefield.

Again.

He lived for the day when outside powers stopped seeing Africa as a place where they could play their power games without any regard for the lives and livelihoods of the people who lived there. Perhaps shutting down the monster builders of Mali would help appreciably. Perhaps it would only make a tiny bit of difference.

But it had to be done, which was why he had volunteered to lead the assault against the scientists barricaded in their rooms, blocking off a sector of the complex. A couple of the drivers came with him.

"Acknowledged," he said, and pressed a button.

The door to the scientists' rooms was a flimsy thing. They could probably have broken it down with their shoulders.

Louembe wasn't in the mood for shoulders.

He'd lined it with a strip of the explosive they'd brought to deal with armored spaces. The door exploded into fragments, and Louembe tossed a couple of flash-bangs after them.

"Ready or not," he shouted with a grin once the stun grenades went off. "Here we come."

Two men in lab coats lay on the ground, moaning with their hands over their ears. The truckers quickly tied their hands behind their backs with cable ties.

Louembe advanced, rifle held in front of him.

"You shouldn't have come to Africa," he shouted. "We don't want you here. We are peaceful people. You can't come to turn our lands into factories for your abominations. You can surrender quietly or I'll kill every one of you in the name of the people of the continent. Now throw down your weapons and show me your hands." He paused and grinned, trying to spot the men and women who, according to Philippe, had to be hiding in the warren of rooms and corridors. "Of course, I would like nothing more than to send you back to your colonial countries of origin in sealed plastic bags, so if you want to resist, I'd be delighted."

He heard a shuffling in one of the doors in the corridor and, as if on cue, a man appeared and fired a handgun at Louembe from about eight meters away. The man's arm was visibly shaking and the shots went well wide of their mark.

Louembe, who'd already aimed at the door when he heard the noise simply fired a short burst and the man disappeared back where he'd come from with a grunt. His pistol clattered to the floor.

"Good, good," Louembe said, grin widening. "Anyone else?"

He advanced into the corridor.

***

The loading bay held nearly two dozen scientists. Male and female, from all over the world, young and old. They had only one thing in common: they'd agreed to work for Sun-Lee, even though they knew what the creatures they designed would be used for.

Now they sat in three rows with their arms secured behind their backs with cable ties. They stared up at their captors with fear in their eyes. They did well to be afraid. The ones who'd resisted had been summarily shot by Louembe. Even the ones who had complied hadn't had an easy time of it. Brahim's men had been quick to strike them—man or woman, it made no difference—and even the surviving soldiers had been quite brutal with the researchers. Evidence shone through in their bruised and bloody countenances.

"I need to go to the bathroom," one woman who looked Japanese, said.

"Hold it in or soil your clothes," Louembe replied. "Someone will be here to pick you all up soon enough."

Max turned to Irina. The only evidence that she'd lost someone who'd been special to her—and Max knew that she and Hermes had had an on-and-off romantic attachment—were the red-rimmed eyes and how short she was with the people they'd captured. Other than that, she was all business, head held straight, jaw clenched. "Our clients will be here shortly. Each of you have been paid a bonus," she informed him, in Russian.

"Is this the same client who sent us here?"

"No. That one already knows the results of the expedition, and he wants to meet us offsite. We've been ordered five kilometers north of here," Irina said.

"Why?"

"He says he wants to discuss further operations. It's optional. You can walk."

Max shrugged. "I don't really have anywhere to go. And I want to catch that North Korean bastard, if someone will foot the bill."

"That makes two of us," she said.

"So, if it wasn't your client, who bought these pieces of crap?" Melanie, who'd been standing next to them, asked.

Max raised an eyebrow. "You speak Russian, too?"

"Not enough to hold a conversation, but enough to follow one. So don't evade my question." She stared at Irina and edged closer menacingly. "I want to know."

Max stepped between them. "Neither of you want to do this. Irina isn't as in-your-face about it as you are, but she's probably killed more people than you've ever met. Most of them at very close quarters. And Melanie is a Marine. Neither of you would enjoy getting into a fight. I admit I'd love to watch it, but only if it's in the mud and you're both unarmed and wearing bikinis." He looked at each of them. "Good, now that you're both mad at me and not at each other, let's talk. Melanie has a good point. I'm curious, too."

Irina shrugged. "I think they'll probably end up in the US, in government custody."

"What, you sold them to the CIA?"

"No. And I don't think the CIA will be involved. I sold them through an intermediary…"

"Who?" Max said.

"The Pan Pipe Cryer," Irina replied, reluctantly.

"Who?"

"She is a hacker and an online intermediary. And a revolutionary, too, but only occasionally."

"So you're giving these scientists to a nutball?" Melanie asked.

"No. I'm selling them to her client, which is the US government. They're the ones who back her revolutions."

Melanie turned to Max. "Is she full of shit?"

Max responded. "I don't think so. But I'm getting paid. Do you trust me to tell you the truth?"

Melanie recoiled as if he'd slapped her. "I suppose I deserved that. But yeah, I trust you." Then she held Irina's gaze. "And if the invitation is open, I'd like to meet your client."

Irina shrugged. "I won't try to stop you. But if he doesn't want you there…"

"I'll take my chances. And I can take care of myself."

Louembe approached. "Has anyone seen Philippe? I need to ask him something."

Max looked around, certain the French scientist had been around just a moment before. But the man was nowhere to be seen. He felt the sinking feeling in his stomach that he got whenever he'd screwed up. "We should have restrained him with the rest," he said. "I should have thought of that. Of all the people here, he's probably the person with most to fear from getting handed over to the authorities."

"You want me to try to find him?" Louembe asked.

"Yeah, but if you can't spot him fast, come back here. He probably has a dozen places to run to, and probably had an escape route figured even before we arrived. I don't think you'll find him. Take Balzano with you."

"I'll go alone. Balzano is hell-bent on keeping that guard you shot alive."

"She survived?" Max asked, surprised.

"Yeah. But only because Balzano was too stubborn to let her die. And the other trucker, the one that went through the maze with him, is helping. He also thinks he's only alive because of the Colonel."

Interesting, Max thought. He'd been right about the man: he was too stubborn to let go of things. Maybe that was the reason Hermes had recruited him in the first place.

Unfortunately, he couldn't ask now. Besides, he suspected Philippe's escape would be a more important complication in the long run.

***

The door behind the tank, the one Poupée had found before the Belgian soldiers invaded the lab, opened only after Philippe attacked it with a crowbar. An alarm went off inside the tunnel but, fortunately, this escape route—if that was what it was—wasn't booby-trapped.

It made sense. This one wasn't wired to explode because it was meant to be found. Any invaders were supposed to spend a bunch of time following this tunnel to the outside and then trying to figure out where the escaped bad guys could have wandered to.

The bad guys, of course, would have run through the tunnel under the floor of Sun-Lee's room and booby-trapped it behind them.

"Come, Poupée," he said, and the little monkey darted into the dark enclosure. Chapeau, his other pet, one that was considerably less bright, but warm and loyal, went past as well. Then he closed the door behind them.

Only when the latch clicked did Philippe turn on the flashlight.

The long corridor hadn't been deserted very long. A sleeping bag lay on the filthy ground just a few feet inside, along with a green backpack. It obviously belonged to one of the guards and Philippe wondered if the man had been posted there to keep the scientists from running away if they discovered the tunnel or if the guard had been put there to be shot full of holes if the facility was found by enemy forces, thereby selling the fake tunnel to anyone who found it.

Knowing Sun-Lee, probably both. First one, then the other, with the added benefit that an inconvenient witness would have been removed.

Which was why Philippe had essentially surrendered to Hermes' men. The risk of them shooting him—especially after he got them out of the maze alive—was much lower than the certainty of Sun-Lee murdering him once he realized the complex was as good as taken.

Philippe knew that was probably Sun-Lee's only regret as he left the complex: he couldn't afford to leave Philippe alive. Besides the fact that Philippe could easily create a competitor for the North Korean's business, there was another thing: Philippe could do math.

In this case, the math wasn't favorable to Sun-Lee. The lab's clients had bought a few hundred of the modified mega-Compsognathus dinosaurs they'd adapted from the ZooDef stock. But the incubators had been running at full speed for months, and more than a thousand were produced and shipped... somewhere.

That meant Sun-Lee had caches of monsters.

Once he'd figured that out, it had been child's play for Philippe to dig into the files and figure out where they were going.

The answer chilled the blood in his veins.

The shipments had ended up in pretty much every hotspot and revolution on the planet. Afghanistan. Iraq. Venezuela. Sudan. A couple had even been sent to the US.

If Sun-Lee had been a regular businessman, Philippe wouldn't have worried overmuch. But he wasn't. The man was basically a murderous psychopath who wouldn't hesitate in the least to advertise his wares by releasing a few dozen monsters into the middle of some of the world's least-prepared populations.

Philippe wanted to warn the correct people, but he wasn't completely certain that the men who'd stormed their facility actually were the right people. Besides, staying captured was not in his plans. Someone would probably hand him over to the French government, and then things would get unpleasant.

The little group proceeded down the tunnel for a few minutes.

"It's quite long, isn't it?" he said to Poupée.

"Breath not good," she replied.

Whether she was referring to the stuffy smell inside the corridor or the fact that the air quality wasn't the best, he didn't know, but he hoped the tunnel would begin heading upwards soon. He hadn't designed Poupée to act as a miner's canary.

Instead of heading upward, however, the tunnel spiraled down into a large open space that resembled an underground parking lot, albeit devoid of both cars and the means of getting cars inside.

However, the space did have a staircase leading up.

"Did I ever tell you how much I hate stairs?" Philippe said as he painstakingly followed the two creatures as they scampered along the steps like it was a game.

"Leg not good," Poupée replied with a chillingly human nod.

"Yes," Philippe said. "My leg is not good at all. Wait a moment. Let me rest. Do you think the men are coming for us?"

"Door not easy to find. Only Poupée find."

"You're probably right."

She was, too. This particular escape tunnel might have been designed to be found, but that was before Sun-Lee had filled the area with growth tanks and the associated electronics. It would be some time before anyone stopped staring at the growing Nothosaurs long enough to ask where a random door went.

Ten excruciating flights of stairs later, he arrived at another door. This one opened inward, which was fortunate, because a pile of sand tumbled in when he pulled. He would never have been able to get out if he'd had to push.

Dawn was about to break in the distance. So that was east.

He hefted his pack. It was full of water but, more importantly, it held a satellite phone. Not much use underground, but ideal for calling for a desert pickup.

***

"Your uncle was a good man," Melanie said, keeping her emotions in check.

Now that the immediate risk of death was gone—the monsters locked in their labyrinth and the guards and armed scientists neutralized—Brahim was visibly moved by what had happened to the chief of his tribe. He'd nearly broken down when Melanie had told him the old man's dying words.

She suspected that the only reason he hadn't started blubbering on the spot was that Melanie was a woman, and that she'd delivered the message in front of all the surviving truckers. She was gratified to see that seven of Salah's men were going to return to their families. And she also wondered whether Sun-Lee had betrayed them for real. Had the Korean actually orchestrated the leak in order to get the truckers shot at? It seemed strange, but Salah had been convinced of it at all times. She suspected the old man knew much more than he was letting on.

"And you..." Brahim swallowed. "You are a true warrior, and I am honored to have gone into battle at your side."

Now it was Melanie's turn to struggle to hold back tears. *What kind of a Marine are you?* she asked herself, *blubbering just because some guys you could beat the crap out of with one hand tied behind your back think you're worthy? Hell, your platoon back at Camp Lejeune are worth a thousand of these guys in a fight.*

Yeah, she replied to herself. *But those guys* have *to accept me. If they don't, it minimizes their own training, what they achieved to get where they are. And every one of those jarheads accepts that I can outshoot them. These guys just accepted me on the strength of what they saw, and they didn't care that it goes against thousands of years of conditioning.*

It's worth a few tears. But I'll cry them where they can't see me.

Instead, she stepped forward and embraced Brahim. At first, he stiffened, but then, with a laugh, he returned her embrace.

"This is easier if I think of you as a brother," Brahim said.

"Then I'm honored for you to consider me one," she replied. "Farewell."

Then she turned away to look for Max, because there was no way she was going to be able to keep the emotion under control.

Max surprised her again. As she approached with tears on her cheeks, he said: "War gives us a family we never imagined we could earn, doesn't it?"

She nodded, not trusting herself to speak.

"Louembe couldn't find the scientist," Max continued. "So we're giving him up as lost. The people Irina sold this place to will be here in thirty minutes, and I don't want to be present when they arrive. Tell your friends to leave, or go with them, as you prefer."

"I told you. I'm going with you."

"That makes three of us, then."

"Three?" Melanie was confused.

"Balzano and Louembe have decided they've done their part. I understand Louembe: he has helped neutralize the threat in Africa, which I think is the only part he really cared about. As for Balzano... I don't understand him at all."

"He's tired," Melanie said. "I've seen it before. Men just suddenly feel exhausted and need to step away. He seems to have reached that point."

"He was always like this. Why would he stop now?"

"Maybe he saw something he really didn't like." Melanie thought of the bleeding guard, Balzano kneeling over her. "I wouldn't be surprised if he took back his commission in the Argentine Army and asked to be sent to a jungle outpost somewhere in the north of the country. Paraguay isn't a threat to invade, so he's unlikely to see action ever again, but he won't lose the structure that goes with military life. I think that might be the one thing he really wants in his life."

Max looked at her like she'd grown an extra head. "Where did you get all that?"

"Did I ever tell you about my father?"

"No."

"Good. If I ever start, stop me. Shoot me if you need to."

"I'll keep that in mind," Max said. "Anyhow, we need to get moving."

They said goodbye to the rest of their crew and grabbed one of the assault vehicles, which Melanie had since learned were the Chinese answer to the Hummer. Max took the wheel because the driver, employed by Hermes, had decided he was out, too.

"Drive straight north," Irina said, reading off her cell phone. "The border with Algeria is just a few minutes away."

"What's so special about Algeria?" Max asked.

Irina shrugged. "I have no idea. We're just supposed to cross the border, drive a kilometer and wait. Maybe Hermes' client isn't allowed into Mali."

A couple more minutes passed in silence as the desert, more rock than sand, flew past.

"Okay, stop. This is close enough."

The assault vehicle came to a halt and Melanie immediately heard the unmistakable sound of a helicopter coming down through the Sahara haze.

She'd expected a military chopper. Something in a nice shade of desert camo, or even green. Hell, Navy grey would have been a sight for sore eyes after the days she'd been having.

But no. The thing coming to a landing and lifting half the grit in the desert was painted in a lurid shade of dayglo orange that spoke of publicity stunts and primetime TV.

"Who the hell..." she said.

"I don't have a name. Just a number," Irina replied.

"That makes me feel so much better."

The monstrosity landed and a door in the side popped open. A man in slacks, loafers and a pinstriped shirt descended looking for all the world like he made a habit of taking his helicopter to the middle of the desert to meet mercenaries. He headed their way.

"I was so sorry to hear about Hermes," he said, nodding to Irina and Max. "Ms. Olenko. Mr. Alexeyev. I was impressed by your curriculums." Then he turned to Melanie and gave her a nod. "And though we haven't met, I am delighted to make your acquaintance. You seem to know your way around a gun, and if Irina's report was accurate, you are an asset to any operation. My name is Lai." He held everyone's gaze. "And I have a proposition for you."

CHAPTER 15

The helicopter lifted off the sand.

Can it really be this easy? Melanie thought to herself as she watched the russet-streaked desert disappear below. Considering how difficult it had been to get her weapons into Ivory Coast, it seemed somehow anticlimactic to be wafted away with no questions asked.

Max grinned. "I never thought we'd be getting airlifted out," he said, speaking loudly in order to be heard over the roar of the engines.

"It wasn't my original plan," Lai responded. "But, unfortunately, I had no time to do this any other way. I received an extremely disturbing call last night." If he was still disturbed, the man showed no sign. He seemed perfectly relaxed.

Irina, Melanie and Max wordlessly waited for Lai to tell them what he wanted, refusing to be drawn into a conversation. In Melanie's case, she was way too tired to play the guessing game.

Lai seemed surprise at their silence, as if he expected his underlings to dance to his tune. Then he smiled slightly and shrugged. "The call came from a man you seem to be acquainted with. A man named Philippe."

"We should have shot him when we had the chance," Melanie said. The anger she still felt at not having been able to drill either of the men who'd run the lab was a sour taste in her mouth.

"Perhaps not," Lai replied. His mouth twisted up a little more. Melanie got the impression that the Thai businessman found the situation somehow amusing but somehow also got the feeling that he was laughing more at himself than at the rest of his passengers. "Philippe reported that Sun-Lee has caches of his genetically modified dinosaurs which he would be opening, with the objective of letting them kill a lot of people and showing the world what they're capable of. Apparently, he's been reserving some batches of them for this project for some time."

He nodded toward Melanie. "Seems that the only ones who really knew who those batches were delivered to were your friends, the truckers."

"That explains it," Melanie said.

"I'm sorry?" Lai asked. His voice was soft and refined, with slightly British enunciation. It wasn't the best voice to hold a conversation in a helicopter with.

"Salah—the leader of the truck drivers—was convinced that Sun-Lee had sold them out and that your team's appearance at the airfield was coordinated by him. I never understood why he thought that. It made no sense to me. But if Salah's men had transported several batches to handlers that even Philippe knew nothing about... then at least there's a reason to get them out of the way. It still seems a bit silly for Sun-Lee to risk giving away the location of his initial base, but seeing that he had a fallback option and an evacuation plan, maybe he felt that losing that one was inevitable, and a small price to pay if it got the witnesses out of his hair. He miscalculated badly... but then again, he is apparently an arrogant prick, so that shouldn't be a surprise." Then she gave Lai a hard stare. "But I want to know why you pulled us out of the desert."

"We've reported most of the caches Philippe informed me of to local authorities, but there's one we think we should deal with ourselves."

"Who is 'ourselves'?" Max asked.

"If you want the job, it's you, plus me, and a few specialists."

All three of the soldiers suddenly grew very serious. "What do you mean, specialists?" Irina asked.

"Most of them are soldiers, from different countries. A few of them are former special forces."

"And what are these specialists supposed to be helping us with?" Max said.

"Suppressing the creatures," Lai replied.

"No." Max shook his head angrily.

Lai's expression was a mixture of surprise and disappointment. "Do you speak for all three of you? You won't do it."

"I didn't say we wouldn't do it. But if we do, we don't want any specialists. Or even generalists," Max said. He looked around, getting a nod from both Irina and Melanie.

"But we can't—" Lai began.

Max cut him off. "How long have they trained together?"

"My people? They haven't. We just got them in the base. But—"

"But nothing. Just look at what happened with the team you sent in last time. Three dead, including the leader of the expedition."

"Considering the situation you encountered, it could have been much worse," Lai protested.

"And if we'd been well-prepared and understood our strengths and roles better, everyone probably could have made it out alive. Perhaps not, of course—war will always be war—but preparation is key. I feel comfortable working with Melanie and I think we can work out an infiltration plan that suits our strengths. Irina has valuable skills, too, so having her along is an asset, especially if we can ensure we get decent comms that actually work if we're inside." He glared at Lai. "That was a major screw up in the operation. If we'd taken the time to get Irina into the lab's systems, we might have been able to spot the labyrinth trap. Hell, all we needed to do to avoid that was to take a different route to the office areas... but we didn't know the route."

Max glared at Lai for a few heartbeats. "I'm not blaming you. Not in the least. In the field, the decisions need to be taken by the person in command, and that was Hermes, not you. And I understand why we went in the way we did: we needed to grab Sun-Lee while the grabbing was good. Hermes wanted to seize the element of surprise.

"But if the team had trained together, we would have been able to lean on each other much more to get the job done. As we tried to get in as fast as we could with as much firepower as possible, and when the shit hit the fan, we had to split our time between advancing and babysitting the truckers. It was not an ideal situation." He shrugged. "So yeah, I'd rather go in small and professional."

"The next strike will be too big for that," Lai said.

"Then split us into groups who don't depend on each other in close quarters. I don't want to have to worry about the capabilities of people I don't know. I don't mind muscle being present if it's needed for fire volume... but don't put it in our way." Max grinned. "I used to say the same thing to the regular Russian Army units who were on ops with us at times. I know my men, know what they're capable of and know their limits, even if those limits are extremely high. With regular troops, I was always afraid they'd hit a wall at some point and get us all killed."

"That could work. We're likely to be operating in a large area... and Sun-Lee will probably be far from the heavy action."

"Our job is to capture Sun-Lee?" Melanie said.

"If you accept, yes. Capture or kill. I don't actually care," Lai replied. Then he shrugged. "He'll end up dead one way or the other. I'm not planning on handing him over to one of the governments that plays nice if we happen to grab him."

Melanie grunted, then said, "In that case, I'm in. But if I get him in my crosshairs even once, it becomes a moot point."

Max also spoke. "I'll capture him only if it's absolutely safe to do so."

"Not if I see him first," Melanie said.

Lai looked at one, then the other, then smiled. "I thought I was going to have to talk you into this."

Melanie was about to say she'd do it for free, but Max seemed to sense it and spoke first. "Well, we're happy to do so, but there's the question of payment. And before we can tell you how much it's going to cost you, you should probably clue us in regarding where exactly all of this is going to happen."

"Fair enough," Lai said. "The first thing you need to know is that Philippe wasn't really certain what the location might be. All he knew was where the creatures had been delivered. With that in mind, my team has evaluated and come up with a few logical targets in the area. They're mostly military bases."

"What area is this?" Melanie asked, immediately suspicious. The fact that Lai hadn't already told them where they might be going set off all kinds of alarms. It was pretty basic information.

"The Middle East," Lai said.

"The Middle East is a big place," Melanie said. "Do you think you could be a little more precise?"

"We think the strike will be located somewhere within fifty miles of the triple border between Jordan, Syria and Iraq," Lai said.

Melanie turned to Max. "How much do you want to bet the target isn't in Jordan?"

"No bet. Do I look like an idiot to you?" Max replied.

***

Private Jonathan Stills surveyed the desert from his watchtower. With him was Mawal Masul from the New Syrian Army, a rebel group from Eastern Syria.

It was a waste of resources to have two lookouts on the same tower, but the US Army was training the rebels to be a modern fighting force, and someone up the food chain had decided that one way to make these people—who, when ISIS was finally licked, were expected to challenge the Syrian regime—better soldiers was to force them to stare out into the empty desert for hours on end.

The worst part of it was that Mawal was a woman from the west of Syria, a Christian of all things. Her family was Syrian Orthodox, and she'd explained, in her broken but ever-improving English, that they were quite traditional.

Jonathan approved of that, but it turned out that Mawal herself fell far from the tree. She had a ton of friends from Lebanon, and they'd infected her mind with ideas that were not proper for any woman, as far as Jonathan knew, but even less for a Christian woman. In quick succession, she'd been thrown out of her family's home, had a series of

European boyfriends and joined one of the rebel armies after crossing the whole of her war-torn homeland.

By all reports, she was an excellent soldier, and one of the rising stars of the rebel army—the PR value of having female fighters not wearing burqas apparently outweighed the rampant sexism of the Arab men who commanded the irregular troops.

Jonathan had said nothing as she told him her life story. In the new Army, it was best to keep such opinions confined to one's own platoon, where those who agreed would listen respectfully and those who disagreed would not-so-respectfully explain that he was a jackass—but would keep his words to themselves. Despite his circumspection, Mawal must have picked up some disapproving signal, because she'd closed up harder than an Afghan mountain bunker and they'd returned to staring out at the desert in complete silence.

Besides, what could he say? He'd never been one to disapprove—or to have a really strong opinion even—of other people's choices. Maybe the reason he was unhappy with her was that he'd found, in Syria's Muslim population, or at least in many of them, a reflection of the strict religious values he'd been brought up with. Both men and women put God before their own desires. As it should be.

He'd expected the same of Mawal, but when he'd learned of the woman's life...

...he'd been disappointed.

But not in her. He'd realized that, as the armies of the West interfered in the region's ever-present wars, Western values were seeping into the lives of the people, with all the good things that came with it.

The bad as well.

Jonathan had always believed the US did the people a service by protecting them against the privations of outmoded ways of thought. Only being on the ground and speaking to Mawal had shown him that Western morality actually wore away at some traditional values that were worth conserving.

Modern thought was colonizing people and destroying cultures just as thoroughly as the European conquest of the Americas had done. Things that were anathema to traditional values seeped in: liberalism, atheism, feminism. All those -isms that people on college campuses were constantly going on about. They were tearing up a society that had survived since the dawn of civilization and replacing it with people who would soon be going to the mall and having frank arguments about birth control methods.

The ironic part was that the same people tearing down statues of Columbus were the ones cheering the destruction of the Middle East's traditional values. It was wrong in their eyes to destroy Native American culture, but it was just fine to liberate Islamic women from the ties of their culture… because the central tenet of the progressive left was hypocrisy.

Jonathan had never understood that. It was way above his pay grade. But now that he'd spent hours staring out into the desert talking to Mawal, he finally understood, with perfect clarity, just why his people had never had any interest in anything but being part of their own community in rural Idaho. The world was broken, and had turned its back on God in the name of false idols. And no one was even sure which false idols they were supposed to be worshipping.

So Jonathan wasn't angry with Mawal.

He was disappointed with the world.

That was what he thought as he stared out into the desert. Guard duty on the southern fence was the most boring assignment Al-Tanf base had to offer. The road that linked Damascus with Baghdad crossed this Godforsaken stretch of desert north of the base. It was from there that any interesting newcomers would arrive. Trucks bearing equipment, detachments of troops entering or leaving, even high-ranking visitors… all would make their presence known at the gate, and be spotted by the sentries before that.

It was unlikely that they'd have any high-ranking visitors any time soon. The base was operating with a skeleton crew, as most of the units normally housed there had rolled out on the final push to break ISIS's back and, hopefully, install the New Syrian Army as the de facto controlling force for this region. Both the Assad régime and Russia would be really pissed if that happened, which probably accounted for the enthusiasm everyone seemed to show for the operation.

"North Tower here. We've got an unscheduled convoy headed up the driveway." The voice crackled over the radio.

"We see 'em," the gate sentry replied.

Orders came over the open frequency as the base prepared to greet their visitors. In this region, unless an approaching group was specifically expected, everything moving towards the base was treated as hostile until it could be ascertained it wasn't.

"We got them to stop," the gate sentry said.

Jonathan and Mawal listened as the orders were given for a small team—there weren't enough people on base to send out anything but a small team—to advance and check out the trucks parked a couple of hundred yards away.

Jonathan felt himself relaxing. The fact that the visitors had complied with the order to halt a prudent distance away meant they were likely on legitimate business, and the surprise had been an oversight. In Jonathan's experience, half of an army's time was spent addressing paperwork snafus.

An explosion behind him made him turn. Across the expanse of the camp, beyond the barracks, warehouses and helicopter LZ, a column of smoke wafted into the clear desert sky from the main gate house.

"Shit," Jonathan said. He rarely swore, but it looked like the war had suddenly turned dead serious. Worse, the Marines and the mechanized infantry normally based there wouldn't be around to stop it. The base had very few combat troops present while the current operation went on: mostly it was manned by support staff: cooks, drivers, helicopter mechanics.

As he watched in horror, the two northern watch towers exploded almost simultaneously. Two of his friends—accompanied by one of the Syrian rebels each—died, just like that.

The orders coming through the radio were confused and broken. The lieutenant giving them seemed to be trying to do too many things at once, apparently unable to process the fact that a simple watch assignment had suddenly gone pear-shaped.

Jonathan hoped that someone, somewhere—probably a forty-year-old sergeant, if the army worked the way it usually did—was getting their act together and organizing a defense.

But in the meantime, the camp needed every real soldier it could get, so Jonathan grabbed his rifle and opened the hatch leading to the ladder below the tower. He turned to yell to Mawal that she would have to continue the watch alone—one of the few advantages of two-person watches was that he could help out without leaving the tower unmanned.

She was staring out over the desert to the north, a shocked expression on her face.

"What?" he asked, still grappling with the trap door's tricky mechanism.

Mawal said nothing. She just pointed the way she was looking.

Jonathan stood and looked out the way she was pointing.

"What the hell is that?" he said.

***

From the passenger seat of a desert-camo Hummer—the commercial model, not the military one—Park Sun-Lee smiled. The response from the base was exactly what he'd expected. The guards at the front gate, in the absence of crack troops, had been indecisive, which had allowed his people to get their rockets off.

His own approach, towards the south side of the camp, would be riskier. The Americans already knew they were under attack and, undermanned or not, one should never underestimate the American military's response to an aggression. They tended to kill ants with jackhammers.

"Take out the fence," Sun-Lee ordered over the radio.

In the convoy of desert-equipped vehicles behind him, a dozen men and women sprang into action. Four of them stepped forward and, shouldering their rocket propelled grenade launchers, they aimed at the camp's fence.

One, two, three, four. The rockets sped away and Sun-Lee was gratified to see that three of them landed at the base of the enclosure.

Unfortunately, the base was surrounded by some kind of gigantic sand-filled bags, twice the height of a man, which didn't even seem to notice the missiles.

"Plan B," Sun-Lee said. "And take out the guard tower first."

Even as the nearest guard tower—from which a soldier was shooting a rifle ineffectually at their armored convoy—exploded in a shower of sparks, his trucks moved forward. A single transporter that looked like a car-carrier pulled ahead of the rest. About fifty yards from the wall, it reversed direction and drove toward the wall-bags backward. When it was ten yards away, the flat bed lifted and landed on top of the perimeter.

Then the truck disengaged and moved away, leaving a beautiful access ramp over the wall itself.

"Open the containers," Sun-Lee ordered.

The sides of the trucks opened and a swarm of genetically modified dinosaurs flowed out.

Ten-feet tall Compsognathus. Bulkier velociraptors. Amphibious Nothosaurs, spectacularly ill-adapted to the desert terrain, but still deadly to anyone who got in their way. All milled around for a moment, sniffing the air and trying to get their bearings.

Sun-Lee tensed. This was the moment that would make or break the operation. The ramp was impregnated with pheromones and also wired for sound. Both the scent and the aural cues were designed to herd the creatures over the ramp. They'd tested it extensively in the lab.

The Syrian desert wasn't a lab, however.

A Compsognathus cocked its head and looked towards the ramp. It considered the situation for a moment. Sun-Lee held his breath as the pause drew longer.

Finally, it sprinted forward, clanged up the metal causeway and into the camp below.

A second Compsognathus followed.

The floodgates opened and the monsters headed into the camp. Sun-Lee watched them go, a smile on his face as he contrasted the graceful lope of the Compsognathus with the slightly lumbering quadrupedal motion of the Nothosaurs. Strangest of all were the raptors. These were a far cry from the lithe and agile creatures of film and popular imagination. Sun-Lee's raptors had been modified to make them much more muscular. Bigger chests, stronger necks and, most dangerous of all, bulkier, more forceful rear legs. The legs and claws had been specifically engineered to tear through metal.

The ramp did its job, elevating the high-tech prehistoric assailants into the camp. Sun-Lee hoped his information was accurate and the camp truly was staffed by the dregs that remained when the competent troops went out on a major operation.

"Get the drones up," he ordered through the comms. "I don't want to miss any of this."

His film team rushed to get the cameras airborne and they were soon flying over the camp. Again, it was a tense moment: American bases were supposed to be interdiction zones where only exotic frequencies could be used for radio control.

Sun-Lee checked the feed on his cell phone. His creatures were spreading out, searching for prey. Sporadic gunfire showed where they were encountering soldiers, but the battle didn't yet appear to have gotten intense.

He called his team at the front gate. "Commander Hsu," he called to the mercenary captain he'd contracted for the job. "Status report?"

"They're heading in the right direction. I'd say we have about twenty of the monsters inside."

"Good. Keep herding them forward. Any resistance?"

"No. We got the tower and the gate. Apparently, they sent all their guards out to inspect us. We killed eight of them."

Sun-Lee rolled his eyes. The Americans had definitely removed anyone even remotely competent from the installation. Which made a certain amount of sense. With the enormous column and infantry divisions normally based here absent, on their way to end the civil war in Syria, the base had very little tactical value and—unless someone had actually left sensitive information behind to be guarded by laundry troops and mess officers—zero strategic worth.

Fortunately, Sun-Lee had little interest in gaining a tactical or strategic advantage against the American forces in Syria. He was just there for the publicity value: the effectiveness of his product would be unquestioned once people saw it taking on the greatest military power on the planet. He was filming the ultimate commercial.

Of course, that didn't mean the Americans wouldn't be back to hammer them if they tarried too long. They needed to be in and out in fifteen minutes. Take any longer and you invited the US Army to divert forces to slap you down.

Sun-Lee had no interest in being there when that happened.

Something whined overhead and, before his mind could process it, the truck that had carried the ramp to the wall exploded in a blinding fireball.

"Predator drone!" the mercenary driving his Hummer shouted.

"Get us out of here!" Sun-Lee replied. He didn't need to be in the area for his footage to get to him.

The driver gunned the engine and began to reverse. One of the container trucks exploded behind them. Drivers and support personnel poured out of the vehicles, knowing the equipment would be targeted first.

"Into the camp!" Sun-Lee shouted. "They won't fire missiles in there."

"There are a few dozen American troops inside. And only two of us," the driver pointed out.

Another truck exploded behind them and the man seemed to get the message. He gunned the engine and the vehicle jumped forward. They hit the ramp at sixty kilometers per hour and launched into the air.

They landed hard on their front wheels and bounced. The out-of-control Hummer slammed into a temporary building and tore a chunk off before rolling onto its side.

Sun-Lee unhooked his belt and opened the door. He turned to the driver but saw that the man wouldn't be going anywhere soon: his head was a bloody mess.

Not bothering to check if the driver was breathing—he wouldn't have time to administer any aid if he was—Sun-Lee unlatched the door and climbed out of the vehicle.

Behind them, the ramp against the wall exploded.

He jumped to the ground and lost himself in the base.

CHAPTER 16

Shots broke out in the camp, easily audible through the thin walls of the prefab barracks building that housed female support personnel.

Stephanie ignored them. The Marines and special forces based at Al-Tanf, not to mention the goons from the civilian contractors, spent half their time depleting the national budget by firing millions of rounds into targets at the range on the western end of the base. Gunfire was nothing new.

"You hear that?" Corporal Hai said.

"More shooting. So what?"

"So, the gun nuts aren't here. They went out to stomp on Saddam's toes."

"Saddam's been dead for ages, and they went west, not east," Steph responded.

"Yeah, whatever. The point is, there shouldn't be any shooting. Not that much, at least."

Stephanie sighed and pulled the curtains—crappy plastic fittings probably outsourced to a low bidder in the Belgian Congo—open. There wasn't much to see, just the walls of the next building over and a truck parked behind it.

She was about to close the curtains again when she saw movement at the spot where the alley between the two barracks met the main camp road.

"Oh, shit," Stephanie said.

"What?" Hai responded.

"Get everyone out of bed. And get your guns."

"Who has guns?"

"A few of us do. Get everyone up. The shit has just hit the fan," Stephanie said.

Moments later, eight women—and three service weapons—stood ready to hold off whatever the hell it was Stephanie had seen through the window. She wasn't exactly certain what it was—even though she'd seen it.

"It looked like one of those dinosaurs from the attacks. You know, like the one in the mall in Colorado," Steph explained.

"I don't think that was Colorado," Maria replied. "What do the ones with no guns do?"

"Grab anything that will make a dent in a skull. Most of all, don't make any noise. That thing was big."

"How the hell did it get onto the base? The gate should have stopped them."

"Maybe they got airlifted in." Stephanie pulled the curtains fractionally aside and looked out. "There's two of them now."

"We should get out of here," Hai whispered.

"No way. Those things don't know where we are, and we're better off with a wall between them and us."

The monster outside chose that moment to come crashing through the walls.

For a moment, Stephanie heard nothing but the screams of her bunkmates and a couple of gunshots at close quarters.

Then the second dinosaur came through the wall and slammed into her. Jaws closed around her neck and she heard nothing more.

***

"Where's Lai?" Melanie asked.

"With his troops," Irina replied. "He wanted to make sure they didn't do anything stupid."

Melanie laughed. "I suppose no one told him that joining a pitched battle in an American military installation is pretty much the definition of stupid."

"Even if they did, I doubt he would have listened. Mr. Lai strikes me as the kind of man who does precisely what he wants."

"What about us?" Melanie said. "Do we follow him?"

"I'd like to be paid," Irina replied. "And I would have thought you would be interested in helping your comrades."

"Not if it means getting a Hellfire missile up my ass," Melanie replied. "Besides, the troops can take care of themselves. A few dozen animals aren't going to tear up an army base in a war zone."

"From what I gather, this base was pretty nearly abandoned. There won't be many real troops inside, just support people who've probably never been anywhere close to real combat."

"Even so," Melanie said. "They'll be fine."

But she didn't believe it. She knew just how good the sharp end of the wedge was… but she also knew just how complacent camp personnel could become, especially when the base was full of really hard people trained to deliver mayhem to anyone from the PLA to rural insurgents.

She tried to think of her own camp cook faced with an angry velociraptor. It wasn't a pretty thought.

Irina seemed to understand what she was thinking but, to the woman's credit, she said nothing. Instead, she commented: "At least Lai was smart enough to equip us with Syrian Army vehicles instead of stuff the Predators will target."

It was true. The Syrian government had had dozens of vehicles staked out around Al-Tanf base ever since the installation had been put up. Damascus claimed that the base was an illegal violation of Syrian sovereignty, and that it was within its rights to place observers around the base at any time it wished. The US replied that the zone where the base was situated was a disputed area and left the base where it was. Neither side wanted the kind of international firestorm that would ensue if shots were fired, so the saber-rattling was pretty laid back.

"Yeah, that was a good call," Melanie said. "I just wish we weren't going to be driving into a war zone in nothing but a bunch of tan pickup trucks."

"I have a feeling the troops at the base will be otherwise occupied."

Max jogged back to the truck. "It's a go. Lai thinks one of the camera drones spotted Sun-Lee climbing out of a wrecked vehicle in the base. If it's him, he's on foot."

"Might be a little hard to pick the guy up," Melanie remarked.

"No-one said it would be easy. That's why we get paid the big bucks."

"That's why *you* get paid the big bucks," Melanie replied. "I'm on the payroll of the US Marine Corps." She'd refused Lai's offer of payment and a job. It was one thing to go off on a vendetta on her downtime. That alone would be enough to get her dropped in Leavenworth if anyone found out... but if they caught her on the payroll of what amounted to a mercenary army during her leave, things would ramp up exponentially. Firing squads would not be out of the question.

Max climbed in and Irina gunned the engine. On their way through the desert, Melanie had come to suspect that the Russian woman—was she a spy? A field operative? Something else?—had a death wish, and the run towards the main gate confirmed her suspicions.

They bounced across the dirt road, catching about three feet of air and, even before the truck had stopped bouncing, Irina had it fishtailing toward the ruins of the armored gate. The jagged metal on either side of the road made Melanie wonder what the hell Sun-Lee had hit it with; she knew those gates were designed to hold off a regular RPG. They must have brought big explosives to the party.

The radio was alive with chatter. Lai was radioing to anyone who would listen that an international team of specialists was descending on the base to assist with the monster problem. A too-young-and-too-scared-sounding American voice insisted that they should stay clear of the area, and that anyone entering the base without authorization would be treated as hostile.

"Authorize me, then," Lai said.

"I… I can't do that," the voice replied.

"Of course he can't," Melanie said to Max and Irina. "He's probably the lieutenant in charge of towel sorting. Anyone with either experience or brains is probably trying to rally the troops—or whatever passes for troops at an empty base—to fight off the monsters. They won't be wasting time on the radio."

Lai had apparently come to the same conclusion. "We're coming in," the Thai man said. "Look for people wearing yellow armbands and shooting at monsters. Those guys are on your side. I'd appreciate it if you could at least tell your men. I promise you can arrest the lot of us when it's done."

Irina accelerated around one of the monster delivery trucks. The trailer was spewing flames from a drone strike, but the tractor was heading straight for the entrance. Whether someone was actually driving it was anyone's guess. Melanie was too busy holding on to check as they drove by.

"And what happens if the troops in there shoot at Lai's men?" Melanie said.

Max looked grim. "Lai has fifty ex-special forces people with him. They are going in hot, knowing exactly what they're up against. If the forces in the base are as hopeless as you've led us to believe…"

"Let's hope it doesn't come to that, then," Melanie said. For the first time since leaving the States, she wished she'd packed a uniform. A combat-ready Marine barking orders might make the difference between most of the skeleton crew surviving and taking unnecessary casualties.

The pickup truck caught air again as Irina drove over something on the ground, probably a piece of metal fence.

"We're in," Max reported. "And no one's shooting at us. In fact, there's no one in the immediate vicinity."

"Can you see where they are?" Lai replied.

"Not immediately. They're probably on the other side of the group of dinosaurs right in front of us." He got off the radio. "Irina, they've seen us. We'd better avoid them."

"If they're not around, we'll go in through the front door. Let me know when you spot the Americans. There has to be a few of them around. I can hear shooting."

"Yeah. I'll call you back," Max said.

Like Melanie, he was grabbing onto the windowsills, the dashboard and anything else he could grasp, trying to avoid being thrown out of the seat by Irina's evasive maneuvers.

The last thing on anyone's mind was to locate a battalion of laundry wranglers and potato peelers.

***

Sergeant Brian Fernandez hadn't wanted to get his ass sent to the sandy wastes of Eastern Syria, but then, Uncle Sam had never been in the habit of asking his opinion. Not after he went into the Army, anyway.

And though he might have been packed up onto the worst tour ever and then friggin' left behind to babysit a bunch of assholes completely unworthy of the uniform, also against his will, he was damned if he was going to let any more of these bedwetters get killed on his watch.

Not by a bunch of friggin' lizards, at least. A couple of divisions of Chinese tanks? Yeah, there was honor in that. But lizards? No way.

"Shoot for the body, you moron," he shouted at some dude who'd probably never fired a rifle at anything more dangerous than a paper target. "Do you really think you'll be able to hit the head on the run? And take it off full auto. If you run out of ammo shooting at the sky and dirt, you're dino food!"

He'd quickly realized that there was no immediate need to take cover, since the monsters heading towards them weren't shooting back.

Tactically, the creatures' most dangerous feature appeared to be the fact that they simply didn't fall over when you shot them. His troops had managed to down a few through the sheer expedient of pumping tons of lead into them while staying just out of range.

That last part was the hardest. The monsters—all but the four-legged ones, at least—were faster than humans. Much faster. That meant that you couldn't just fire as you ran.

Fortunately, the creatures weren't the brightest bulbs on the tree, and they were easy to confuse. Brian had split his team in two: the more distant would keep up a steady stream of fire; the team closer to the danger zone would run for a new position.

It worked beautifully. The dinos were confused and angry—they might not die as soon as you shot them, but the bullets appeared to cause them considerable pain.

Good, Brian thought. *I hope you pieces of shit are suffering.*

The main problem was that, though the tactic they were employing would eventually wear down the monsters in front of them, Brian's team was doing very little to help the rest of the people in camp. He could hear the screams and occasional shots from soldiers pinned down by another group of monsters.

"All right," he shouted. "Hold your ground. We need to try to move north. We're no good to anyone up here."

The four soldiers with him looked up, but none said anything. Maybe they weren't useless: a soldier who knew enough to fear an army sergeant more than enemy monsters could never be completely stupid.

He watched the phalanx of monsters and considered how to get on the other side of them. There were eight of the things left, six a mottled greenish-grey and bipedal, the others quadrupedal and uniformly dark. All of them had blood streaking down their flanks, turning the dust into black mud.

At least we've managed to hit them a few times.

The creatures advanced in a rough line, heading straight towards the troops firing at them. Only occasionally would one break away, usually to snatch up some poor dazed bastard who wandered too close, or to worry at a carcass—human or reptilian—already on the floor. Brian marveled at the discipline they showed: most human troops would have broken ranks and run instead of advancing that way. How had they been trained? It couldn't have been easy to get them to ignore the pain and move like that.

Or maybe it was. Maybe the fact that they had brains the size of a walnut worked in their favor. Was it actually possible the creatures were too dumb to realize that the pain was somehow linked to the humans running away from them?

Of course. How would dumb lizards understand that suffering could be delivered at long range?

"Circle around them," Brian shouted. "Don't keep running south. Go that way."

His troops nodded.

"Follow me!" He led the way, cutting across their original line of advance. The other team fired to cover them, but he realized they'd cut it too close. The nearest dinosaur, one of the two-legged ones taller than a man, hurtled in their direction.

"Run!" he said, and turned to face the threat. His team might lose its leader, but he was the only one with a chance to drop the thing. He aimed between the creature's eyes and fired off a quick burst. He could hit a much smaller target at that range with his eyes closed. He hit this one.

The monster kept coming.

"Come and get me, you motherfucker!" he shouted.

It cocked its head in a surprisingly human gesture and charged.

Brian tensed to jump out of the way, but before that, he calmly emptied most of the clip at the thing.

It didn't stop, so he jumped away.

A line of fire crossed his chest and he looked down to see that the raking claws, which had moved too fast for him to see, had gotten him on the left pec. A deep cut ran across it. A couple of inches higher, and the thing would have gotten his neck. Not a fun way to die, bleeding out from the neck.

"Dammit," he muttered as he scrambled to his feet and trained his rifle on the creature which was scuffling to turn back in his direction. "What a bad day to forget my flak jacket."

He squeezed the trigger and two shots emerged. Then nothing. Out of ammo.

He tried jumping to one side, but even as he did it, Brian knew he was too late. This was it.

Two deafening, low-pitched thumps shattered the air, but he had no chance to see what the hell it was all about. Five hundred pounds of reptilian flesh slammed into him and bore him to the ground. He hit hard, but even with the wind knocked out of him he clawed at the monster about to tear him to pieces, trying to keep the jaws away.

His arms were pinned, though, and the creature wouldn't budge.

He braced for the killing blow… but it didn't come.

Instead, he felt the monster shifting, not as if it was moving to strike him but as if someone was pulling on a dead weight. When it moved a foot, strong hands grabbed him under the armpit and pulled hard.

Brian opened his eyes to find himself being pulled to his feet by a black man a head taller than he was and built like a brick shithouse.

"That was ballsy," the man said in, of all things, a deep Texas drawl. "Glad you made it."

The guy was dressed in a uniform Brian didn't recognize, with a yellow armband on his left arm. It certainly wasn't one of the services or any of the rebel armies around. Not the Syrians or the UN Peacekeepers either. And the gun he was holding looked like a cross between a standard European FAL and a grenade launcher. Not issued by the US Army.

The dinosaur was very dead. Two entry wounds the size of beer cans adorned its flank.

The rest of them were also down. Nothing was moving in this particular sector except Brian's team, who were now running in his direction

"You do that?" Brian said, nodding to the creatures.

"Yeah." The big guy held out his hand. "I'm Jocko Avery."

"Sergeant Brian Fernandez. You got a rank? I assume you're part of some special forces unit too secret for me to have heard of?" The rest of the guys pouring out of the pickup trucks that had materialized were, if anything, even scarier-looking than Avery. Not as big, but they looked like they could end the Syrian Civil War without help from anyone else, by the simple expedient of kicking everyone's ass.

"Not quite. For now, just be happy we're here to pull your ass out of this. You'll get all the news later."

"That sounds like I should be throwing you off the base," Brian said.

The big guy shrugged. "You could try. Or you could let us clean up the monsters and get out of your hair. Your call."

Brian wordlessly watched Avery walk away. His troops reached him as the man climbed into a pickup truck and sped towards the sound of shooting coming from the south.

He ignored the backslapping and the compliments and glared at his men. "That guy thinks he can do a better job of defending this base than the US Army," he told them. "Are we going to stand here like idiots and prove him right? No fucking way. Get moving."

"Uh, Sarge…" one of the soldiers, a slip of a girl who had to be too thin to survive basic, said.

"What?" Brian snapped.

"There's a truck we use. For laundry. We'll get there a bit faster, and maybe we can run over a few of those things."

"Good thinking, soldier," Brian said. "Just for that, you get to ride up front."

The truck was parked behind a ravaged barracks. Brian took a look inside the building and looked away. There was no one left alive in that charnel house, and the monsters who'd done it hadn't even bothered to use the door. The thin walls of the barracks looked like they'd been chewed through.

The truck was a basic model standard truck, with two axles at the back, designed to never get stuck no matter the terrain… It wouldn't be fast, but it would be faster than running.

"All aboard," he shouted, swinging into the driver's seat. He confidently fluffed down the sun visor expecting to find the keys there and was stunned when they didn't drop into his hands.

"They're in the ignition, Sarge," the laundry lady said.

"Thanks," he replied, looking over at her as he turned the engine on and put the truck in gear. There was a tightness around her eyes.

"You okay?" Brian said as he accelerated towards the south of the camp.

"That was my barracks," the woman said. "I had friends in there."

"Let's mess up some dinosaurs," Brian replied.

***

Even as he huddled behind a parked assault vehicle, Park Sun-Lee smiled. His mix of Compsognathus, raptors and Nothosaurs was tearing through the camp like the defenders were a bunch of kindergartners. The footage of modified creatures killing troops in American uniforms, in an American base no less, would bring him orders by the hundreds. He wouldn't just be rich: he'd be famous, too.

He'd also be on the run from the Americans for the rest of his life, but that didn't matter. By the time they pieced together who'd done what to whom, he'd be safe and sound under the protection of the one government the Americans would never cross: the Chinese Communist Party. He'd negotiated a lab and everything else he might require, just outside Beijing.

He'd be the most wanted man in the world. And he'd be untouchable.

As a group of men firing automatic weapons passed without paying him any heed other than to assure themselves he wasn't some befanged and hungry monstrosity, Sun-Lee stood and surveyed the scene.

A Compsognathus appeared to his right, peering around a barracks that appeared to have been hit by a tornado. It cocked its head, peered at Sun-Lee for some moments and then headed off in a different direction.

He pulled out his phone and hit the voice recording function. "Ultrasound on frequency five effective on Compsognathus even in field conditions," he said.

Then he ambled after the monster to see what it would do.

The genetically modified dinosaur looked magnificent in the battlefield. Even though Philippe was a treacherous bastard, Sun-Lee had to hand it to the man: he'd turned the inconsequential little creature, a dinosaur that needed to hunt in packs to be dangerous to any reasonably strong human into a true battlefield predator, lithe and strong and well-armored. It was his greatest triumph.

And now it belonged to Sun-Lee. He could build as many as he needed, anywhere in the world. The equipment was not even all that complicated to obtain. The incubators that worked so well—despite Philippe's paranoid misgivings—was produced in China in the first place. He could have unlimited access.

Since no one challenged his presence, Sun-Lee watched and observed. He also used his phone to get some footage. The drones should have been able to film everything very well, but ground-level film could be a nice touch to add to the edit. That would be his first task when he got back to civilization.

He strode along behind the Compsognathus, hoping it would do something worthy of recording. Ideally, he wished it would come upon some unarmed soldier in a US uniform. The world usually associated the US Army with the invincible force that would invade your country if you happened to display a tendency not to side with them on any issue. Watching his dinosaur tear one of them a new asshole in a straight fight, would be an impressive sales tool.

Unfortunately, this dinosaur appeared to have wandered into an empty area of the camp and was just walking cautiously, occasionally sniffing the ground or one of the structures.

A hot breeze picked up and the Compsognathus froze, sniffing the air, or perhaps listening.

The wind subsided and the creature started moving again. Now, however, its earlier amble was replaced by a purposeful stride. This was no longer a monster on a stroll through the desert; this was a monster going places.

Park followed, taking care to stay far enough away to avoid disturbing the creature: he really wanted to see what it was doing.

The Compsognathus walked into a narrow passage between two squat structures, probably barracks or perhaps a utility area. These had been spared the brunt of the initial monster charge. They were intact, with their tan finish unmarred and looking as if they'd been painted yesterday.

The monster sniffed a door and stopped. It cocked its head one way, then the other. Finally, it leaned back on its haunches and, with a movement almost too quick for Park to follow, it lashed out with a hind leg.

The door exploded into splinters, leaving a jagged hole in the wood.

The creature didn't bother to pull away the rest of the door. It simply squeezed through the opening, widening the hole as it went.

Sun-Lee followed, hoping his monster repellent would work in close quarters. It had never really been tested under these conditions, but he didn't care. His heart raced. He was excited to see what the monster had found. Would it be ripping through trapped soldiers?

That would make incredible viewing. He held up his phone and stepped across the broken threshold.

And stopped, stumbled once and laughed at himself.

The monster had found what appeared to be the base recycling center. Green bags were open along several tables with an assortment of cans and paper on one end and some disgusting-looking sludge on the other end.

That was what had caught the Compsognathus's attention. There were no humans in the building.

Sun-Lee laughed at himself and backed out of the room. He felt perfectly safe... but why push his luck?

CHAPTER 17

Rhianna Brown tried to keep her rifle steady. When she enlisted, she thought she'd get base duty Stateside, some boring assignment designed to teach her the Army ropes before letting her do anything relevant.

Instead, they'd shipped her out—at age nineteen—to one of the most godforsaken outposts in the US military.

It had made her feel...

Incredible. For the first time in her life, she believed she was doing something important, and that people felt she would amount to something, and that, if they told her what to do and left her alone to do it, she would get it done.

No one back home had ever treated her this way. Not in her house. Not in her neighborhood. Not even at school. The attitude seemed to be that she would turn out like everyone else around her: a dead-ender who never moved farther than the city limits, and who would not climb a single rung on the social ladder. Born poor to die poor.

Yet here she was, in Syria, with actual responsibilities. And when it had hit the fan, they hadn't told her to run or hide. Some blond guy from Tennessee had glanced at her uniform and handed her a rifle.

It felt incredible.

Unfortunately, the monster she was shooting at hadn't gotten the memo about how cool Rhianna was. It appeared determined to run her—and the three guys with her—down, and have them for breakfast. Her breathing was ragged from sprinting in the intense desert sun.

She fired another burst. The monster looked like a taller, bulkier version of a lizard, walking on all four legs. It stared in their direction as if it knew that the pain from the weapons came from them, and didn't care. Then it charged.

Rhianna dove to her left as the empty fuel barrels they'd been crouched behind scattered through the air like building blocks kicked by an angry toddler. Having had to roll the empty drums into position earlier, she was impressed. Those things were heavy... and the monster was strong.

Fortunately, it didn't seem too smart. It spent the next several seconds chasing rolling drums, which allowed Rhianna and her companions to regroup behind a trailer. "You see it?" she asked the blond guy.

"Yeah, it's coming this way." He stepped out from the cover of the trailer and opened up on the thing. Rhianna joined him without even stopping to think about it. It felt like the right thing to do.

The monster approached cautiously, as if it had finally decided that the bullets were enough of a nuisance that it should proceed slowly. Rhianna's companion hit it with a burst to the chest. It stumbled, blood pouring freely from the wound.

"I think we got it!" Rhianna yelled.

A huge sand-colored truck appeared around a corner and slammed into the monster. The creature collapsed in a heap and lay completely still as the truck stopped. Locked wheels gouged the packed dirt of the camp road.

A dark-haired guy wearing sergeant's stripes called out of the window, "You guys okay?"

"Yeah. We're good. We had him without your help," Rhianna replied.

That gained her a grin. "Yeah. I know you did. You guys are badass. But I wasn't going to risk losing anyone else today. So I'm jumping in even when people have stuff under control. You guys want to kill some more? Hop in."

This time, Rhianna didn't follow the blond guy. She was aboard the truck before any of her companions even managed to move.

A few bemused soldiers sat upon the bags of laundry and looked up at her as she climbed into the bed of the truck. "Brian get you, too?" one of them said as she sat beside him.

"Brian the guy driving the truck?" she asked.

"Yeah."

"He got me, too."

"He's crazy. Seems to think the monster attack is a personal insult to the US Army, and he's going to do something about it, and no one had better get in his way."

"Sounds like a guy who knows what he wants," Rhianna replied. She grinned. "Knows what I want, too."

That earned her a set of comprehensively rolled eyes as the guy turned to another guy next to him and muttered, just loud enough for her to hear, "Oh, no. God made *two* of them." Then he said: "You better sit. It's gonna get bumpy again."

Rhianna sat beside them and the truck started with a loud roar and gear whine.

Whoever this Brian was, he wasn't screwing around. He gunned the engine like the hounds of hell were after him.

**

From atop one of the barracks buildings—a perch that had been reasonably easy to reach by the simple expedient of climbing onto the roof of their pickup truck and then, using a high ventilation tube as a handhold, onto the roof of the building—Max and Melanie watched a gigantic truck slither as it turned onto the main road in the camp.

"Someone's in a hurry," Max said.

Melanie grunted. She had her eye on her rifle scope, panning slowly across the camp.

"You see him yet?" Max asked.

"No."

"You think he's here?"

"He came in. He wrecked his car. He didn't leave on foot. I'll find him."

"You really loved that girl, didn't you?"

"My niece? Yeah. And I got a text. She's going to be fine. She might get home before I do."

"But you still want to kill Sun-Lee."

"Of course. Don't you?"

Max shrugged, knowing she couldn't see him. Then he wondered at that: why did he even care what this Marine thought? A woman he'd never seen before, and that he'd probably never see again. Why would he care? He'd already learned his lesson about American women. Marianne had taught him all he needed to know about just how hard they were to get along with... and just how hard it was to make a relationship work when you were based on different continents.

"I'd love to get that bonus," he replied.

She actually snorted, which surprised him. Not because she reacted that way—he wasn't expecting her to act like a society lady—but because he knew it would throw off her aim if she happened to spot their target. But she hadn't spotted him yet, so maybe she was still not in that strange sniper's trance he'd seen so often on missions. "You're so full of shit," she said.

"Huh," he said, and then chided himself for sounding exactly like Homer Simpson.

"You pretend you don't care. Like when Balzano said he wasn't coming with us. You acted he didn't matter, but I was watching you. You wanted him around." She actually looked away from the scope. "I thought it was weird. You really didn't care about Louembe, who'd been kicking ass since the first time we went into the field. He saved you from making total fools of yourselves on the airfield, from what you told me. And yet the guy you regret not having is Balzano. I don't get it. He doesn't seem like much."

"He's a quiet warrior," Max explained. "A guy who doesn't look for a fight, but if you bring it to him, he'll win. Against anything. And he'll save everyone around him while he does it. He'll never brag, never bluster, never ask to be the leader of the team. He probably won't want to be there when the shooting starts. But he'll get the job done. He's the perfect guy to have on a team."

It was Melanie's turn to shrug. "Didn't seem that way to me. Seemed a bit of a wallflower."

"That's because you're a true warrior, not a quiet one. An alpha in all situations."

"You sure have a lot of types of warriors," she said. But she sounded pleased.

"I mean it. You were always my first choice from the group. You are the kind who doesn't shirk the battle. You don't walk away. Hell, you're avenging a girl who didn't even die."

"It's not just about my niece," Melanie whispered. "There's also Cora."

"Cora?"

"A mentor. No. More than that. A real friend. The woman who taught me that girls could kick ass, even when everyone around you is a Marine. She's the woman I always wished I could be."

Max let out a low whistle. "She must really have been something. What happened to her?"

"She was killed. Remember that island? The one where the monsters appeared and attacked a tourist spot? She was the security chief for some billionaire."

Max gasped. Suddenly it all made sense. And he even knew who the billionaire was. He wondered if he should tell her, and decided she wasn't the kind of person you kept important information from. "Yeah. She worked for Lai."

"Lai? The guy with the pink helicopter?"

"The same guy. He was the billionaire who nearly got killed on the island. He's pissed, and has decided to rid the world of genetically modified monsters."

She stayed silent for a moment. Finally, she spoke again. "Do you mean it? Would I really always be your first choice to go into battle with?"

"Yes. You're an impressive woman."

"That can mean a lot of things," she replied, half-teasingly, but also half-accusingly.

He was about to respond that she could interpret it any way she wanted, when Melanie spoke again.

"What the fuck is that?" she said.

***

Lai smiled. Beside him, Gonzalo squirmed a bit, while the captain of his professional soldiers, an ex-Sureté Colonel, looked on impassively. Lai got the sense that the Frenchman disapproved of his latest idea, of the mission in general and of everything on the planet that wasn't French. But that impression was unconfirmed by any word or gesture or even expression. The man himself could have been carved from a block of ice.

The fourth person in their van was the Russian woman, Irina, who'd returned after dropping off Max and Melanie. If the Frenchman could have been carved of ice, she was a slab of diamond, harder and deadlier than even a man who'd spent forty years dealing with the worst French criminals and chasing the Islamist extremists that had been such a thorn in Paris's side the past few years.

She appeared to be concentrating on ensuring that Max and Melanie had their bases covered while also checking for any kind of electronic evidence that the Americans might have seen through their disguise as just another pair of Syrian support vehicles unrelated to the new threat inside the base. He knew she had to be concentrating on anything her sensors could detect; any interest from the Predator drones circling above them would give them only seconds to evacuate before a missile tore their vehicle to pieces.

Nevertheless, he felt it would be unwise to assume that Irina wasn't acutely aware of everything going on inside the truck. He suspected she wasn't missing a thing.

Suddenly, Irina spoke into her comm, giving instructions to Max and Melanie: "Don't shoot the pink dinosaur. I repeat—mainly because I'm having trouble with it myself—don't shoot the pink dinosaur."

A pause.

"Because it's on our side," Irina said.

Another pause as Max or Melanie responded.

"Apparently, they have some kind of tech that allows Lai to download a human mind into the dinosaur brain, and wear it like some kind of meat suit."

Lai wished he could have heard what the other side was saying. It would probably have been quite interesting. Unfortunately, he could only catch Irina's half of the conversation.

"Of course it's gross," she said. "But it seems like a good idea: infiltrate the enemy with a soldier they can't identify."

Pause.

"I guess they won't care if it's pink."

Lai was quite pleased to realize that Irina not only knew what they'd been doing, but had managed to communicate with the soldiers at the sharp edge of the wedge without losing concentration. The satisfaction came both from the fact that he'd been right about Irina knowing exactly what was going on but also because he liked the way she worked. Regardless of what might happen with Max and Melanie, Irina was a talent he really wanted to keep on the payroll.

He turned to Gonzalo, a copy of whose mind inhabited the pink monster in question. "How do you think you'll hold up under combat conditions?" Lai said.

Gonzalo didn't appear fazed in the least, and Lai couldn't tell whether it was a genuine lack of concern or simply the macho façade expected of men from his culture.

"How can I fail?" he asked. "Installed in the body of a predator the likes of which no one has seen for millions of years and backed up by the boys with the biggest guns? I'll dominate."

Lai grunted. Bravado, then. And something else, maybe. Relief? The version of Gonzalo sitting beside him hadn't been the copy that suddenly woke in a tiny brain, almost unable to think, heading out to face hundreds of guns.

That one must be terrified.

The big question, however, was whether it would be too terrified to do its job.

That was what they'd really come here to find out.

Saving the American base—with the publicity value that entailed— was secondary.

He watched the screens intently. The feed from the cameras strapped to the dinosaur would be very informative.

***

I feel drunk, Gonzalo thought. Or tried to think. The words weren't quite there, and the concept... it was brought in from memory, not real thought. Thinking was nearly impossible.

This isn't me. He thought it again, because it was hard to hold onto a thought from one moment to the next. He couldn't concentrate because.

Because…

Because his mind seemed to be pulling him in several directions at once. His senses were different somehow. He tried to concentrate on what he was seeing.

That was easy enough: the desert was the same one he'd been traveling across with… people whose names he couldn't quite remember… before. It was full of soldiers. There were small buildings and fences. He knew what they were, remembered their purpose. That was good at least.

The soldiers were running and shooting at… monsters. There was something about those monsters he thought he should remember, but he couldn't think what it might be.

It must not be too important, or at least his mind didn't seem to feel the need to think about it too hard.

There were other things calling for his attention.

It took him a long time to realize that these were his other senses. Smell. Hearing.

Gonzalo found it difficult to understand how the call of those two senses could be so strong. It would have been impossible to explain. It wasn't that the senses of smell and hearing blotted out the sense of sight. It wasn't diminished in any way.

It's just that the other senses called to him, demanding his attention more strongly than he'd ever felt before.

The smell of… frightened food? How did he even know what frightened food smelled like?

And the sounds of footsteps skittering across the sand, half the desert away… since when was that something he could make out easily?

It was distracting, too much to take in all at once, especially on a day when he seemed unable to concentrate, and when his body appeared to be acting funny.

Even his hands looked strange, short, thin fingers, too pink to be familiar.

At least he remembered what he was supposed to be doing there.

Lai…

He felt triumph at remembering the name.

Lai had asked him to obey Kino.

Another name!

Kino was the big man who smelled like lavender and sweat.

That was weird. Shouldn't he have known what the man looked like? He couldn't really tell, and it didn't really matter.

The important thing is that Kino would tell him what to do.

"Finish off that Compsognathus," Kino told him.

Compo… Comp…

The bad monster that smelled like gunpowder and blood. A lot of blood.

Gonzalo heard a whimper from the wounded creature and felt his body respond without any conscious instruction on his part. It was the sound of an enemy in distress. He knew what had to be done.

Gonzalo jumped forward, instinctively positioning his powerful body for maximum velocity, allowing his tail to counterbalance the movement of his neck.

Tail. Fleetingly, he realized that he shouldn't have a tail. But with so many thoughts crowding into him, it didn't seem important. Even if it was, he wouldn't have been able to concentrate on it.

The smell of blood was too strong.

It pulled him toward it, and his body obeyed. His careful, balanced steps turned into a lope, the lope into a flat out run.

As he ran, he wondered how he was going to get to the blood and the warm flesh around it. His arms, stunted and short, didn't seem up to the task. No matter, he would deal with the problem when he got there.

The bad monster was dying. Even his addled brain could tell that it was too weak to defend itself. He salivated in anticipation of the meal.

And when he arrived, the question of weak arms never came up. He simply lunged forward and drove his teeth into the enemy's neck, savoring the flow of warm, juicy blood into his mouth. Pure bliss.

Gonzalo reveled in the sense of teeth—his own, enormous, powerful teeth—breaking down the flesh, scraping the bone and exerting their will on the prone enemy.

He felt as if he was waking from a dream. *This* was life.

***

Gonzalo, sitting next to Lai in the pickup truck, stared in fascination at the dinosaur some reduced version of his mind was controlling.

Lai chuckled. "You seem a little more aggressive than normal."

It was true. Gonzalo was a typical example of a corporate middle manager—thirty-three, efficient, smart and willing to do nearly anything to advance his career.

He wasn't the kind of person you'd expect to go full savage and bite into a dinosaur's neck.

Nevertheless, that was precisely what the creature he was controlling was doing. He seemed to be enjoying the process, too: the monster was tossing gobbets of food everywhere as it tore its victim to pieces. Lai's troops—the ones he could see on camera, at least—ducked for cover as the gore spattered them.

"I…" Gonzalo shrugged, obviously at a loss for words. "Maybe the mind copy didn't work?"

"I'm not so sure," Lai replied. "If it hadn't worked, I think the monster would have gone after my troops. That isn't happening. It's following orders, which means you're in there somewhere."

Gonzalo watched, pale and wordless.

***

"No." Melanie felt the fury course through her as she pulled her eye away from the scope. She suddenly wanted nothing more than to drop everything and go home. Only the thought that that would mean accepting the most abject of failures stopped her. "How can he do this? Didn't he learn anything on that damned island?"

Max turned to face her. "What?"

"Lai. He should know better. We need to destroy those things, or at least lock them up in a nature preserve somewhere where they can't hurt people."

"You mean like Jurassic Park."

"Don't be a dick. I mean we're supposed to be shutting this crap down, not creating new uses for deadly monsters. Once people figure out that we can control monsters with human minds, no one will ever be able to put the genie back into the bottle."

"I think it's already too late for that. Too many people have the tech to build monsters. You saw the tanks back in those labs. Those weren't produced on a shoestring for a tiny operation. Someone is mass-producing them, which means someone is buying them. Sun-Lee might have been the most advanced user, but he certainly isn't the only one out there."

"Then why the hell are we even bothering with this? What use is it?"

Max's expression spoke volumes. Melanie saw the temptation to give a glib reply, probably something along the lines of 'because I'm getting paid very well to do it,' flitter across his face. But either his sense of tact or his sense of self-preservation nixed that avenue and he turned serious. "Because if we destroy Sun-Lee's operation, it will set back the tech a few months or a year or whatever. We're buying time to prepare for the next wave."

"I don't want to prepare for the next wave. I want to stop this."

"I don't think we can," he replied, his voice surprisingly gentle. "I wish we could. And not for the world. For you."

"Thanks," she murmured. Her anger almost subsided at his words.

Almost. He might be worth thinking about, but that would come later. Right now, she was too mad. "But if we're the ones propagating—and even improving—the tech, then we're part of the problem."

"You should probably take that up with Lai," Max said.

"Maybe I will. Or maybe I'll just put him on my list of people whose aesthetics would be greatly improved by adding a third eye to the front of their head and fist-sized exit wound to the back."

She turned angrily back to her scope and, without a thought for the fact that doing so would give away her position, she took a bead on one of the four-legged dinosaurs in the mix. Lai had called them Nothosaurs and explained that they were reptiles, not dinosaurs, and that their DNA was probably the base for all the other creatures that had been released into the wild. Fuck Lai. It looked like a dinosaur, so it was a dinosaur.

She aimed carefully, released her breath and fired.

Lai had also explained something she already knew: headshots were the worst way to deal with these creatures because the brain was tiny and it was hidden behind a thick skull.

She really didn't give a damn about any of that. Sometimes, you just had to shoot something in the head. So that was precisely what Melanie did.

The surge of satisfaction she felt when it dropped like a stone was childish. After all, the dumb animals weren't to blame.

"That's called a 7.62×51mm NATO round, you bastard. Your little bony skull is no match for it," she explained to the carcass.

Then she put another round in the rifle, pulled back the bolt and looked into her scope, already searching for her next target.

CHAPTER 18

Interesting, Park Sun-Lee thought as he watched the brightly-colored dinosaur attack one of his own creations. *I wonder if they painted it or bred it.*

He shook his head. *They must have painted it*, he concluded. *We had no whispers of anyone playing with skin coloration to that degree. It would be quite simple compared to the kind of stuff other groups are doing, but also quite useless. Especially since this particular mod has made the thing stick out like... well, nothing sticks out quite as much as a pink dinosaur in the middle of a desert.*

More interesting than the way it looked was the way it was acting.

As Sun-Lee watched, the creature actually walked away from a free meal, apparently at the command of one of the men with guns.

That meant it not only had more intelligence than the average creature on the field, but also that it was being directed by the other team.

He watched the pink dinosaur advance alongside the team that appeared to have come out of nowhere specifically armed and prepared to do battle with genetically modified dinosaurs and concluded that the control they were using was much more sophisticated than his own method of pheromones and sound.

He thought he knew how it had been done: mind transfer.

Damn.

He'd run afoul of that before. In fact, it seemed that everyone had access to that tech but Sun-Lee himself. He'd seen it in Russia before deserting the government-backed lab he worked for there, and now this team—which looked decidedly non-Russian—was using it. He made a note to track down the sellers and buy it, regardless of cost. It would make his product even more effective.

Then he'd copy the tech and stop wasting his money.

Sun-Lee knew his objective in the American base was more than achieved. The footage from drones and dino-cams was nothing short of spectacular.

Nevertheless, anger coursed through him. What the hell were these people doing here? Were they related to the team that had struck at his labs? If they weren't, it meant there were two separate groups out to get him, or at least working at counter-purposes to him.

He plunged a hand into his pocket and pulled out a canister of scent spray. He checked the label and smiled. This one would turn whatever he sprayed it on into a target, it combined the scent of fear with the scent of blood. Every carnivore in the vicinity would be attracted to the smell.

Sun-Lee walked towards the group of soldiers around the pink dinosaur. No one paid him any attention. Ignored by men because he wasn't a monster, and by the creatures because of the scent and sound markers he wore, Sun-Lee felt the power of invisibility.

The dirt of the camp road was peppered with drops of blood. He stepped over a fallen soldier, throat ripped away and eyes staring up at nothing. A dozen yards further on, he encountered the unidentified force managing the pink monster.

Unlike the American troops, who'd been caught—sometimes literally—with their pants down, the new players were impeccably uniformed in unidentified markings reminiscent of jungle commando wear: much too green to be suitable for desert operations. They were also well-armed, with rifles that looked like they packed quite a punch, supplemented by what looked like personal artillery pieces. Sun-Lee was no expert on guns, but whatever flew from the wide mouths of those weapons would be large caliber indeed.

In the parlance of big game hunters, these troops had arrived loaded for elephant... which meant they likely knew exactly what they would encounter.

They were here to kill his dinosaurs.

None of them paid him any heed. To them, he was just another man in dusty civilian clothes in a camp where others were also out of uniform. His Asian heritage likely also helped him pass unnoticed: in this base in a desert in the Middle East, most people of Asian descent would be American troops.

The man who appeared to be the leader of the interlopers was actually talking to the pink dinosaur, which proved Park's suspicions. Once done, the enormous soldier walked away.

Sun-Lee approached it from behind and, taking care not to step on its tail, he let the hand holding the spray drop to his side. He depressed the button as he walked by without slowing, catching the entire side of the creature's body as he passed.

Job done, he walked away with a grin, making certain to discard the can without getting any of the spray on himself. He trusted his current protection, but would it hold against the kind of temptation the new spray represented? He didn't want to trust his life to it.

He also preferred not to be around when the Americans started asking questions. He checked his watch: ten minutes had passed since he launched the strike, more than long enough for the owners of the base to react and send people here to reinforce it.

He pulled out a satellite phone and hit the first preset on the dial. He hadn't expected to end up inside the base, isolated from his scattered people... but he had planned for the contingency just in case.

"Come and get me. Use the base LZ," he told the voice on the other end.

"Please confirm pickup."

"Confirmed," he replied calmly. He sidestepped a confused-looking Nothosaurus with blood pouring from several head wounds, and walked towards the landing zone.

***

The truck hit something and, out of control, slammed into the side of a building.

The impact threw Rhianna from the pile of clothes she was sitting on into the bulkhead that separated the cargo area from the cab of the truck.

"Fuck, that hurt," she said. "Is everyone all right?"

A chorus of groans brought confirmation, except for one guy, the wag who'd welcomed her to the truck in the first place, who said: "I think my arm is broken."

"Do we have a doctor here?" she asked.

"Are you kidding?" another guy replied. "They all went with the combat troops. I heard there was a medic to dispense Aspirin left at the base, but I have no clue who he is. He sure as hell ain't here.

"You're gonna have to sit tight for a bit," she told the injured man.

"It hurts."

"I can imagine, but I've got no choice. We need to see what happened, why we stopped and what's going on out there. I'll be back in a bit."

"Don't leave me here."

She squeezed his good arm. "I said I'll be back. That's a promise."

Rhianna got to her feet and pulled the canvas out of the way to check the situation. Whatever had hit them wasn't behind, so she climbed onto the dirt path. She waited for the other three guys who were still in decent shape to join her and then peered around the side of the truck.

"That's not good," she said.

"What?"

"Come on," she replied and charged.

The Sergeant—the guys in the back had said his name was Brian—was trapped in the cab of the truck, unable to get the door open. One of the two-legged monsters stood on the hood and was trying to spear him with the claw on its leg, right through the windshield.

On the floor just behind the left front wheel was the body of one of the four-legged creatures, bloodied and crushed. That must have been what they hit.

She fumbled with her rifle—she hadn't even held one away from a range since basic—and managed to get a burst off in the general direction of the monster.

"Try not to hit me," Brian yelled.

"Don't worry," she called back. She stopped a few yards from the front of the truck and circled to get a better angle of fire.

The thing on the hood looked down at her with eyes that were orange and yellow and green, depending on the light. It opened its mouth and a sound like a high-pitched roar emerged.

"You don't scare me," Rhianna said. She raised her rifle and shot another burst. This time, she scored some hits. At least one, possibly two or even three.

The monster screeched.

"Hurt, didn't it?"

Scuffling noises on the sand made her look up. Four more dinosaurs like the one she was shooting were sprinting in her direction, tails raised. "Guys, we're gonna have company!" she told her companions.

The men raised their weapons and opened fire in a ragged display that sent lead everywhere. Fortunately, there didn't appear to be anyone behind the dinosaurs.

One of the creatures faltered, took two more steps and fell, blood pouring from its mouth, but the other three didn't notice their injuries, if any, and kept coming.

"Run!" Rhianna shouted. It came out as a half-shout, half-scream, but she didn't care. She wasn't used to being in combat against ravening monsters, and she would worry about sounding less scared once the monsters were dealt with.

Three steps later, she realized she wasn't going to make it to any meaningful cover, so she dove to her right, trying to get as far out of the way as possible.

Something clamped onto her foot and she turned to see the monster's teeth biting into the leather of her boot. Pain coursed through her as they hit her skin.

A sudden flash—could she have seen correctly? Was it actually pink?—slammed into the monster from the side. The wrench against her foot felt like it would tear away everything below the ankle.

Luckily, the pain only lasted a moment. The monster let go of her foot to engage the lurid thing that had attacked it.

***

Before the creature turned his way, Gonzalo had a fleeting moment of relief that the monster had let go of the woman in its jaws. It was a strange, unaccustomed sensation. Why should he care about some human when there were more important things to focus on?

Like fighting the dinosaur facing him.

It was slightly bigger than he was, but it was also bleeding from several injuries to its flanks. The smell of the blood drove him into a frenzy.

He lashed out at the creature's neck with his jaws before it could regain its balance.

Nothing could ever be quite as satisfying as the sense of grasping another creature's neck and feeling your teeth slice through its skin before they caught on the muscles below. The blood dripping through the puncture wounds became a torrent as the injury tore open. Perfection.

Unfortunately, the heavenly sensation was only his for a moment. His ears and his nose told him that more enemies had circled around him. Two more creatures remained.

His diminished intellect struggled with the situation. Why were they focusing on him instead of attacking the weaker animals, the humans? It made no sense.

Gonzalo circled around the monsters facing him. One darted closer, feinting an attack, and he jumped back, not allowing the monster's companion access to his flank.

Movement from the corner of his eye caught his attention. More monsters were approaching from the downwind direction.

He assumed they'd go after the humans… but the charge didn't change direction. They came straight towards him.

It makes no sense, he thought, as the wall of dinosaur flesh, mixed species even, carried the creatures facing him straight into Gonzalo himself. He tumbled backwards, the sheer mass of the attack making defense impossible.

Mouths and talons and claws tore at him as he scrambled to get back on his feet. Why the savagery of the attack? He couldn't understand it.

As his body was twisted back on itself, Gonzalo suddenly felt an overpowering smell—the scent of fear and blood. He'd smelled it before, as a background thing, and ignored it... but now that he was bent over onto his own flank, it threatened to overwhelm him. He wanted to rip, and tear and rend... and his target was his own side.

That must be what the other creatures were attacking.

"Stop," he tried to say. "This is a mistake!"

His throat emitted a confused gurgle.

In his panic, Gonzalo realized his true nature had come through. He suddenly remembered he was a human, and the knowledge he was about to die overwhelmed him. Every fiber of the body he wore fought for its life, to fend off his attackers long enough to flee.

But the human in him froze, a huddled mass of fear and confusion. Gonzalo's life as a corporate functionary hadn't prepared him for the realities of nature, red in fang and claw.

A razor-sharp claw tore at his belly. Teeth closed around his weak foreleg and bit it off.

Pain filled his world. He tried to scream, but the creatures around him showed no mercy.

A mouthful of teeth attempted to tear his throat out, and Gonzalo lowered his head to block it, and bent his neck to attempt to move it out of the way.

His antagonist insisted and pinned him down. Then the creature, a bulky-looking monster that smelled of dominance, managed to clamp his neck.

Blood was everywhere. His own, that of his earlier victim, the little he'd managed to draw from the new monsters attacking him. Its scent filled his consciousness, overwhelmed any attempt at thought. It was maddening, at once a call to attack and a message to flee.

The primeval instincts of the body he occupied overthrew the terrified human and tried to reassert themselves. Gonzalo thrashed, he kicked, he tore himself loose.

He—or at least that part of him that was the animal—immediately realized the damage was too severe. He realized it immediately and lay on his side, to die peacefully as animals did.

Only the human part of his mind, the part that had never quite integrated itself to the body, screamed silently to itself.

No! Don't let me die! Somebody do something. Help!

But the encroaching darkness wasn't listening, and soon he knew no more.

***

"Did I just die?" Gonzalo asked as they watched the feed from the dinosaur.

"The version of you riding that monster did. Yes," Lai replied, trying to remain calm. It wasn't easy to watch a creature—not even one of these genetically modified monstrosities—die when you knew it could understand what was happening to it. There was a person inside, Lai knew, and that person must have understood what was going on.

"Fuck," Gonzalo said, shaking his head. "I... I'm not sure how I feel about that."

"Would a large bonus help?" Lai asked. Gonzalo knew he would be generous.

"I..." he looked up suddenly, as if he was surprised by something that had occurred to him. "I'm not sure. This is heavy stuff. I'll need to think about it."

Interesting, Lai thought. *And here I thought he was an unimaginative office climber whose only emotion was ambition. Live and learn.*

***

On his way to the helicopter LZ, Sun-Lee emerged from behind a barracks to see two people, a man and a woman, perched on the roof of the next building over. Their green—but not US-Army-issue—uniforms marked them as members of the opposing forces. Further proof was that they weren't doing battle with the dinosaurs, but lying on their stomach on the highest point of the curved roof, observing the proceedings.

The woman, he noted, was watching through the scope of a long black rifle, while the man used binoculars.

Then Sun-Lee smiled. He recognized these two.

Keeping his head down to avoid notice—if he recognized them, then they would surely recognize him—Park approached the building they occupied. Once the walls concealed him from discovery, he rummaged inside his pockets. A second canister like the one that he'd sprayed on the pink dinosaur was the only thing remaining.

He pulled it out and checked the label: it was the same formula he'd applied earlier. He thanked the inspired luck that had nudged him to grab these two canisters instead of more protective solutions. He hadn't had time to think in the overturned Jeep, so he'd reacted.

His choice was about to evolve from useful to inspired.

Canister in hand, he waited for the shooting to start again and cover his motions. Gunfire erupted in the distance, and he sprayed the side of the wall opposite the shooting, making sure to leave a trail on the wall, and also spraying upward to get some of the mist on the roof. *There, that should make any of the monsters think that something afraid and hurt waited on top of the building*, he thought, satisfied.

Then, being careful to keep away from lines of sight that might reveal him to the people on the roof, he walked to the landing zone to await his ride.

***

"He's not fucking here," Melanie said.

"He can't have disappeared into thin air," Max replied. "Maybe he's in one of the buildings."

"Yeah. Well, we need to find him pronto, because if we're not out of here soon, we're going to be up to our asses in reinforcements. They'll lock you up in Gitmo for being Russian and, when they find out I'm actually a Marine, they'll shoot me on general principles. AWOL with intent to commit treason or something."

Max chuckled. "You knew the risks when you took the uniform."

"I wasn't banking on having my own people put me in front of the firing squad," she replied.

He held up a hand. "Wait. Do you hear that?"

"What?"

"The scratching sound."

"All I hear is someone shooting over there," she gestured vaguely in the direction everyone seemed to have disappeared in.

"This is much closer," Max said. He jumped to his feet and, moving in a crouch, approached the back of the barracks. "Dammit. There's one of the fat raptors here. It's trying to climb the wall."

He pointed his rifle down, and Melanie heard him fire a burst.

A moment later, he fired another burst. "Got him." Pause. "Oh crap, here come three more. Compsognathuses, this time."

"Coming here?"

"Sure looks that way."

"Why?"

"Do you really expect me to know what a dinosaur is thinking?"

Melanie grinned. "Male brains are much closer in size to dinosaur brains than mine is, you know." She joined him looking down over the side. "It doesn't look like anything is chasing them."

The dinosaurs stood by the wall, and Max and Melanie took a step back. "They're definitely here because they want to be here," she said.

"Like the two-hundred-kilo gorilla."

"Yeah, if the five-hundred-pound gorilla had teeth the length of my fingers. Watch out!"

One of the Compsognathus, slightly bigger than the rest, had sniffed the wall for some moments and taken five steps back to stare at Melanie and Max. Then, never taking its eyes from them, it ran straight towards the wall.

Instead of crashing into it, however, it stepped on the body of the raptor Max had shot and, using it as a springboard, launched itself upward. Its rear legs scrabbled for purchase, tearing deep gouges in the wall.

They stumbled back, out of reach as the jaws appeared in front of them. Max tried to bring his rifle to bear, but tripped on the roof and fell onto his back.

The monster was on him instantly.

Max managed to get his rifle up, and slammed it butt-first into the creature's mouth. It attempted to maneuver its head to get its jaws free, but Max managed to stay a step ahead of it, twisting the FAL with all his strength.

He wouldn't last long.

Melanie did something she would never dream of doing. She brought the stock of her Remington to her shoulder and fired off a snap shot.

Blood and bone sprayed, and one of the creature's eyes disappeared.

The Compsognathus screamed, an almost human sound. It reared back in pained rage.

Melanie scrambled with the bolt-action, wanting to reload before it redoubled its attack on Max.

She needn't have bothered. In the instant of respite, Max re-angled his gun and opened fire at close range, center-mass shots that disappeared into the creature's torso. This time, when it reared back to scream, it gurgled and spluttered.

And collapsed on top of Max.

Melanie ran over to help him push the unwieldy mass away.

Scratches from the wall told her that more monsters were coming.

Melanie turned to see another Compsognathus a foot from her face.

She froze.

She saw every muscle under the leathery skin tense as the creature prepared the leap that would remove her head from her shoulders, to be consumed by the dinosaur at its leisure. Evil eyes, yellow with vertical slits, reflected her slack features.

She'd trained for years to respond instantly in situations of danger, to act when others couldn't. She commanded her body to obey, to throw herself out of the way, to teach that overgrown lizard a lesson.

Nothing worked.

The creature leaped.

Gunfire tore through the air. Blood splattered against her face as Max's burst opened a line of crimson on the monster's neck.

The shots snapped her out of her trance; bullets, she could deal with.

Melanie threw herself backward, just far enough that the creature's snapping jaws couldn't tear her open, but not far enough to avoid the monster altogether. She needed to get some distance.

The thing's chest slammed into her, and knocked her ass over appetite down the curved slope of the roof.

Melanie tried to get a hold, to arrest her progress, but the violence of the impact and the smoothness of the roof conspired to keep her moving right to the edge. Her head hung over a twelve-foot fall.

A Compsognathus jumped up at her from the ground, its jaws snapping shut mere inches from her face.

"Fuck off," Melanie said. Ignoring the Remington, which had fallen a yard from where she lay, she pulled her service revolver out of its holster, aimed down at where the creature was preparing for another jump, and shot it in the face. She knew it was unlikely to do much damage, but sometimes you just had to shoot an asshole monster in its ugly maw.

She rolled away from the edge and got back to her feet just as the monster Max had shot charged her again.

This time, she was quicker and the monster was slower. She dove out of the way and watched it lose its footing on the roof as it tried to turn her way. The creature disappeared over the side.

Max had managed to extricate himself from under the carcass of the raptor pinning him. He was covered in gore from head to foot, but didn't seem the worse for wear.

Melanie caught his eye. "Thanks," she said.

He shrugged. "We're even now." He looked past her shoulder. "But I think we need to get out of here."

She followed his gaze and saw not one but two of the dinosaurs pulling themselves onto the roof. "What the hell? There weren't that many down there."

"I don't think they received that particular memo," Max replied. "Another one coming up."

They backed away, keeping their guns trained on the monsters until they reached the other side of the roof.

"Uh-oh," Max said. "There's more down here."

These were of the four-legged persuasion, and there were three of them. Had every surviving dinosaur suddenly decided to come visit?

"There's something going on here," Melanie said.

"Yeah. Any ideas on how to get ourselves to a place where we can think about what that might be?"

"No. We'll have to shoot our way out," Melanie replied.

"Yeah, that's the only thing I could think of, too. Follow me."

They ran along the length of the roof, away from where the concentration of creatures was highest, all the way to one end of the long barracks.

Two Compsognathus appeared just as they reached the edge.

Max opened fire on the nearest, shooting it in the neck and head.

Then he kept running and bowled straight into it. The creature lost its balance and fell to the ground with a sickening thud.

"You are a crazy son of a bitch," Melanie said.

Max smiled at her. He looked like the murderer from a low-budget slasher flick, all covered with blackening blood and grinning like a madman. "I bet you say the same to all the guys," he replied. "Now come on. That one's not going to be a threat."

He jumped off the roof.

Melanie looked down. It was a twelve-foot drop, with only a dinosaur stomach to break it. All in a day's work.

She aimed for the fallen monster and jumped.

The impact jarred her bones, and she felt like something got wrenched in her back... but she was functional and nothing hurt too much to move.

Before the second monster on the roof could jump back down and follow them, Max sprinted across the dirt camp road and took cover behind a truck. Melanie joined him a second later.

"So what's the plan?" she asked.

"Last stand, I think," the Russian replied grimly. "We're not going to take down that many of them. And they're faster than we are. And they climb better, too."

He pointed back the way they'd come. She saw eight dinosaurs coming their way slowly but surely. They fanned out along the dirt road.

"I don't think much of your plan. Give me a minute."

She jumped into the truck's cab and lowered the visor. The key fell out, as it invariably did. Soldiers hated looking all over for the keys.

"Wanna ram them?" she said, once the engine was running.

Max swung himself in. "Sounds better than my idea. We're still going to die, of course, but this has more style."

"Like hell we will," she said, and graunched the truck into gear. "Hold on."

She gunned the engine harder than she probably should have, and the truck lurched forward. Sand sprayed upward as the double rear wheels struggled for purchase, and then they started moving towards the creatures.

The nearest, one of the lithe Compsognathus, jumped clear, but two of the more ponderous Nothosaurs weren't fast enough, and the truck slammed into them.

"We'll make it!" Melanie shouted, pumping her fist.

She spoke too soon. The second of the Nothosaurs must have gotten tangled in one of the front wheels as the truck went over it. The wheel ground to a halt, pulling the steering to the left.

The truck came to a halt against the barracks.

"Here they come," Max said. "I wish I had some vodka."

"Will you stop that? Climb into the back. They're coming through the glass."

Shards of windshield sprayed into the cab as they climbed through the narrow opening in the bulkhead that separated the cab from the cargo bed.

The back of the truck was filled with crates.

"Tableware," Melanie said, as she read the stencils.

"Oh, good. The monsters can eat us at properly laid tables. Do they have those little salad forks, too?"

A creature tried to get in through the hatch between the cab and the cargo area. It was too large to fit, which gave her a little time to think.

Unfortunately, the clock ticked by, and nothing whatsoever came to her.

They're going to figure out this truck has canvas sides pretty soon, she thought.

As if the monsters had read her mind, a claw punctured the wall of the truck beside her.

Using the claw as a marker, Melanie estimated where the monster's head might be and fired her Remington at that spot at point-blank range. Not even a skull a foot thick was going to survive that.

Unfortunately, the noise infuriated the monsters. They began tearing at the cloth with redoubled force.

Max, meanwhile, appeared to be fiddling with something on the floor of the cargo area.

"A little help here," she said. "There are tons of monsters coming through the walls."

"If this works, you'll have a lot of help," he replied.

"Why? What are you doing?"

"I managed to get a fuel line cut through an access panel in the floor." He held up a wicked, serrated knife. "I'm thinking we set these things on fire."

"How?"

"I'm soaking tablecloths…"

"Ooh," Melanie said. "Nice."

"Indeed. I just need another minute."

Melanie tried to judge which one of the monsters tearing through their shelter was likely to reach them first. The decision was made for her when one of the Nothosaurs poked its head through and bit a chunk out of a crate.

She fired and the monster pulled away with a ferocious roar.

"Hurry," she said as she reloaded.

In answer, the interior of the cargo bay lit up. She turned to see Max pressing a flaming tablecloth against the canvas side of the truck.

"What the hell?" she yelled.

"Animals don't like fire."

"Neither do I, when it's about to cook me."

"We need to get them away from the truck," he replied.

The heat burned her skin, but Max seemed to be right. As the flames spread, the monsters stopped trying to enter.

Out of the gaps in the canvas, she suddenly realized they could escape out the back of the truck without running into any of the creatures.

"It worked," she shouted. "Let's go!"

They jumped out of the truck and sprinted across the dirt street. Behind them, the blaze grew ever larger until, with a wave of heat, the entire truck exploded.

Melanie looked back. Burning monsters, screaming in agony, were the only enemy still visible.

"I think we're okay," she said.

"Just in time, too," Max replied. "We need to get out of here."

He was looking into the sky. A helicopter was circling the LZ.

Melanie stared at it for a long moment. It should have been a Blackhawk, or some kind of gunship. Instead, it was a bloated, overweight bird with a red cross painted on the side. It looked to be forty years old.

"Not yet," she replied. "I want to get on a roof."

"I thought we'd done that already. It didn't go well for us."

***

"You've heard of the Geneva Conventions, right?" Max asked. "Hell, even Spetsnaz troops are supposed to obey those. Well, unless we have orders to the contrary."

"I know about the Conventions," Melanie replied tersely. Her eye was pressed to the scope of her rifle, which was aimed at the landing zone and the helicopter which was just setting down. Desert dust swirled into the air, obscuring her view of the airfield, and she cursed. She needed to see what was happening down there.

"It's just that they're very specific about attacking Red Cross vehicles."

"Will you shut up?" she replied. "I need to make this shot."

***

Sun-Lee waited until the helicopter set down. It was quite convincing: sand-colored, with red cross emblems on the side and, very prominently, on the belly. The Americans weren't going to shoot at that.

He scooted across the airfield, head down. He didn't trust helicopter rotor blades.

At the door, he met the man he'd hired to fly him out, a Turk who worked closely with the Chinese.

"Are you alone?" the man asked in English.

"My driver didn't survive," Park replied, neither knowing nor caring whether that was true.

"Get in."

The man handed Sun-Lee a headset, waited until he was strapped in and then said, "We're going up."

Park nodded and they lifted off.

"Where to?" the pilot said over the intercom.

Now that they were out of the swirling dust cloud that was the landing zone, Sun-Lee got a good look at the camp. Smoke wafted lazily from several sectors. A truck had caught fire, and the nearest barracks was ablaze. Bodies lay everywhere. The destruction was more than he'd ever imagined possible.

"Take me around the camp one more time. I need to get this on camera."

"You're the boss, but I'd suggest making it quick."

"Understood. Just a pass. Try to make it look natural, then we'll leave in whatever direction you deem best."

Park pulled out his cell phone and began to film the carnage.

***

"Fuck!" Melanie screamed.

"What? They're probably just flying out some officer needing medevac. They wouldn't have called in a chopper for an enlisted man," Max said.

"That's not an American helicopter," Melanie said. "I think it's French, and it looks like something from the seventies. No one on the base called that thing in."

Max shrugged. "I'll take your word for it. I always thought all helicopters that aren't Russian are crap, so it's not like I could tell."

Melanie glared at the aircraft as it lifted. Then to her utter shock, it began to head in their direction.

"Wait," she said.

"It's not as if—"

"I said *shut up*."

She looked into her scope. A man holding a cell phone was pressed against the window.

It's him. It has to be.

She hesitated. Was she willing to risk shooting an innocent bystander because she needed the man she'd been chasing to die? Could she live with herself if she was wrong? Did she even want to live with herself under those conditions?

She stared through the scope, feeling the seconds ticking away.

The man moved his hand.

She saw his face.

And acted. She pulled the rifle into a position that would account for the helicopter's movement, breathed out, held for a second and squeezed the trigger.

A moment later she got a visual on the impact. The man's face pulled back in a spray of blood and the helicopter turned away from its gentle curve and flew at full speed in the opposite direction.

Melanie pulled her eye away from the scope to find Max staring down at her, mouth agape.

"Scratch Park Sun-Lee from the list of active players," she said.

"Are you sure?"

"One bullet, one body. Man, you special forces guys are dense, aren't you?"

"I meant, are you sure it was him."

"Positive," she replied. "No doubt or I wouldn't have pulled the trigger."

"Then we need to get out of here." He called Irina for pickup. She might have been a crazy driver, but she'd heard their plan to observe from a rooftop and decided it was too insane even for her. She'd buggered out.

"Says to give her ninety seconds," Max said.

"Sounds good. I will be so happy to get the hell out of here," Melanie replied. She felt tired for the first time since reaching Africa. The ordeal had taken a lot out of her, and she'd been living on adrenalin and pure hatred the past few days. "I might be able to squeeze in a couple of days at the beach before my leave runs out."

Max smiled. "That sounds awesome. Mind if I join you?"

"I hadn't really thought about it. How about this: come along, and if I don't tell you to leave at any point, you can consider it an invitation to stick around."

"I've never felt so welcome," he replied.

"Take it or leave it," Melanie said.

CHAPTER 19

Lai looked out across the well-appointed boardroom. It felt right—fitting—that he should be standing there, in front of a roomful of men and women in business suits, discussing strategy moving forward.

Except the business suits didn't contain chain-smoking, overweight, middle-aged men. Most were worn by men and women in their thirties. The oldest person in that particular grouping was a trim and fit forty-three. Those were Lai's people.

The older members of his audience were representatives of several major governments. The Americans had sent a retired general who consulted on matters of national security. The Russians had sent a man Max had assured him was a spy. The French, English and Germans had sent women from their defense ministries.

The Chinese had sent their regrets. No one was particularly surprised at that.

Invited as a courtesy, Gabon had sent a newly-minted general, rewarded for his part in destroying the genetic monster production capacity in the Sahara.

Louembe didn't look comfortable in his new uniform with the star on his shoulder. He looked like he wanted to sit with Lai's troops and plan an incursion into Thailand's jungle interior, maybe round up some smugglers or, better still, some poachers working for the exotic animals trade.

But Louembe was a man who respected his superiors and understood the honor given to his country by his mere presence in this company. He sat with the foreign dignitaries.

"Thank you for coming," Lai said with the smile he'd practiced for hours, the same one he'd used when he was building up his former company. "I suppose no one here needs me to recap the unfortunate events in Syria of three weeks ago."

"We know why we're here," the American said. "And we probably know more about what happened in Al-Tanf than you do. So how about you give us your pitch?"

Lai chuckled. "Very well," he said. "I'd like to create an international consortium tasked with the control of genetically modified weapons systems."

"Run by you, of course," the American consultant said.

"With oversight from the participating countries, of course," Lai replied.

"But you'd be in charge of the day-to-day operations," the German delegate said.

"I would. The structure I'm proposing is based around the current operational capacity of the company I've put together. You've already seen how effective we are."

"Yeah," the American said sourly. "If you'd just let us know beforehand, we could have taken care of things. My government isn't happy with you."

Lai nodded. "As I explained to Ambassador Terry when he spoke to me, we weren't one hundred percent certain of the time and place of the strike. We took our chances and happened to guess right, but it could have easily been a false alarm. There was nothing to tell until the trucks carrying the monsters arrived. And when we offered our help, it was rebuffed anyway." He looked around the room. "It would have been much better for everyone if we'd coordinated the defense of the base instead of arguing amongst ourselves. That's what I want to talk about."

"So what are you offering here, concretely? A solution? Or are you just going to ask us to pay for your little folly while you make millions?" the representative from Great Britain asked, her voice telegraphing the sneer her face was too well-trained to express.

"I'm offering two things. The first is pretty obvious: the service, a quick-response, well-trained force that can deal with genetically-modified threats anywhere in the world. The officers are chosen from the best of the best. Military forces, police and even private contractors are represented, experts in all kinds of terrain and urban environments. We have biologists on the team and links to a dozen research institutions for technical support."

"All of which can be duplicated by everyone here except maybe Gabon, in a matter of months," the American drawled.

"But we already have it up and running. There's no need to duplicate efforts." He looked around the room, meeting the eye of the representatives of the democratic countries present. "All of you, each of your governments, is already under pressure to minimize defense spending. The press will have a field day if they realize you've decided to recreate a service someone else offered for a fraction of the price, particularly if that organization, with a few months head start, hired the best available experts in the field... meaning you'll have to settle for second-best."

To take the sting off of the implied threat of going public, Lai continued: "Which brings us to the real advantage of using our services: neutrality. By having an international organization in charge of this, in which every country that wants to be protected has a stake and a seat on the steering committee, we can ensure that help reaches the places it needs to be without all the mucking about with national borders. We can get in quickly, pre-approved. Unlike the fiasco in Syria, everyone will be on the same page. Quick. Surgical." He let his smile widen and pointed it at the woman from Britain. "Press friendly."

The Russian smiled slightly. Russian forces had never been too picky about national borders. Lai assumed the Russian Federation, like China, would choose its own path. But he had to try to get them. If Russia or China came, the western powers would have zero choice in the matter.

He continued: "The best way to ensure this works is to pool our intelligence resources. Our organization has contacts in the clandestine networks that create and distribute the creatures. We should be one step ahead of them."

"In China?" the Russian asked, openly amused now. "I hear they're gearing up to flood the world with the creatures."

Lai nodded, acknowledging that points had been scored against him. "We can't reach into China," he said. Then he turned to the American. "That is where shared assets would be a real advantage. But as soon as the creatures go into transit, we can have a line on many of the movements. All of them? No." He looked everyone in the eye. "But then again, none of the vaunted intelligence services in any of your countries has been able to predict when terrorists will attack, have they? We can work together to stop this new technology from playing into terrorist hands."

"I'm still not convinced we need to let you manage everything," the American said.

"I'm not surprised. But you need to know that this is actually a courtesy meeting. The Consortium, as such, is," he smiled at the French woman in a tacit acknowledgement that he was about to mangle her language, "a fait accompli. Seventeen countries, including most of South America and a number of Arab nations are already on board. Oh, and Israel, of course. They offered to give us an operating base even if everyone else pulled out and the UN declared us a terrorist organization. Fifteen more will be signing soon, with twenty others interested. That includes countries in Asia, Africa and even most of Europe. We're funded for the foreseeable future.

"I invited you here because your governments are the ones who can turn the Consortium from a controversial organization which will exist despite the outcries of the press into one that everyone considers legitimate." He grinned at the American. "As for what's in it for you, it's the existence of that very same press. When you're getting hit with monster attack after monster attack—after all you are the fattest targets—journalists are going to ask some really hard questions... like why is it that so many developing nations seem to be protected against the strikes while your own people are becoming dino munchies every other week?" He grinned. "And you can be certain our communications department will be very active in shouting about every single operation we ever run, and telling people why the attack in Uruguay was stopped without loss of human life the week before Paris or New York was savaged."

There was silence in the room, which lasted a few moments as the delegates thought about what they'd tell their superiors. Finally, the American broke the silence. "Is that it?"

"Yes. The rest of the allotted time is so that you can meet our team leaders and talk to them."

"Very clear, thanks. I don't need to meet them. I have their files... there's stuff in there they probably don't know about themselves." The retired general got up and left.

His decision seemed to make the choice for the rest of the Western powers, as the Euros filed out behind him like chicks after a mother duck.

Only the Russian stopped to exchange a few pleasantries with Max and Irina before waving Lai over.

His grin was wide and genuine. "I wanted to thank you for letting me watch," he said. "It's wonderful to see the Americans and Europeans squirm like that." Then the Russian nodded his head. "And I think you might have maneuvered them into a corner. Who knows, a few of them might even sign up for your little project. Good for you."

"And Russia?" Lai asked.

This time it was a guffaw. "Oh, no. We will continue to deal with our internal issues the way we always have."

"Violently?"

"When necessary. But I prefer the word 'effectively'." He walked out.

Louembe was the last to approach. "I've just confirmed with my president that Gabon will be a part of this. We are honored you invited us to this meeting."

"The honor is mine," Lai replied. "Will you be a part of the team?"

"I'm afraid not," Louembe replied. "My field days are past. But I have a couple of excellent trackers to recommend to you. Excellent trackers and even better men."

"They will be welcome," Lai replied. "But we will miss you."

Louembe looked around the room. "It's kind of you to say so, but I really think you will be fine without me."

He turned around and walked over to speak to Max and Irina.

Lai found himself alone again in a luxurious corporate setting. Apparently, being at the head of an international Consortium built to fight terrorists using large-scale bioweapons wasn't that different from being at the head of his family's company.

Lonely.

CHAPTER 20

Melanie sweated in the mild Virginia heat and cursed her extended leave. You'd think going on a dinosaur hunt in the Sahara Desert and the Middle East would have allowed her to keep up her physical condition and be able to enjoy a run in the woods... but no. She'd lost a step and the training sergeant here at the Quantico Marine Base was delighting in making her pay for it.

She refused to drop back or ask for mercy, but everything was going to hurt tomorrow. And it had been hurting for a full month now, ever since she'd returned to base. The sergeant knew it, too. That man could smell weakness.

This, too, shall pass, she told herself. No matter how much pain the sergeant decided to dish out, it was nothing compared to Basic. That had been intense, with the constant fear that she would prove inadequate lurking constantly. This was just getting back to a level she already knew she could attain. Child's play.

"All right," the sergeant said, dismissing the platoon. "You guys seem to be back at full strength. Good work." He nodded to Melanie once and walked away.

She nodded back, pride heating her face, and followed her team toward the showers.

Once changed, she started tossing some stuff into a duffel bag. A couple of t-shirts. Panties. A bra. An extra pair of jeans. Deodorant. Socks.

"Going somewhere, Viña?" Morales asked when he saw her packing.

"Yeah. Got the weekend off. I'm gonna go see my niece."

"How's she doing?"

"Better. She's back in school and everything," Melanie said.

"That's very cool," Morales replied. "And I hate to do this to you, but CO wants to see you."

"Major Appins?"

"The Colonel, actually."

"On my way," she replied.

She left the open duffel on her bunk. If the meeting went the way she feared it might go, she would not need any of the stuff inside. The good folks at Leavenworth would be supplying her clothes and toiletries for the foreseeable future.

But she still had to go. Trying to run would only make things worse.

Besides, maybe her promotion had come through.

Yeah, right, she thought. *Who are you trying to kid?*

The answer, depressingly, was: only herself.

She walked as slowly as she dared, taking in the sunshine, feeling the cool breeze against her skin, trying to catch every glimpse of greenery she could. It would be these memories of the outside that would sustain her in the years to come, with only cell walls to look at.

The office door was open, so she walked in. Corporal Kine at the desk waved her through.

The first thing she noticed about Colonel Osella's office was that the carpet was a deep blue color that at once made the place seem more intimate and more imposing. A large desk dominated the space, decorated with two small, framed photographs.

The Colonel himself was seated at the round meeting table to the right of the desk with a man she'd never seen.

She snapped off a salute.

"Sit down, Corporal," the Colonel said. He looked tired.

"Yes, sir," she replied. Then she sat, despite every second of her years in the military screaming at her that it was wrong to sit when the base CO could see you.

"You've got a visitor," the Colonel continued. "A visitor with one of the strangest stories I've ever heard. I told him he must be out of his mind, but he insists in discussing this story with you."

Melanie realized a manila folder was open on the Colonel's desk. It had her name on the front.

For a second, the sight caught her off guard. Did people actually still use those things? She thought everything was on computers, backed up in the cloud or something. Paper was bad for the environment.

She concentrated on the matter at hand. She was in enough trouble without going off on a tangent.

"Miss Viña," the man began. No rank, just 'Miss Viña'. "I have reason to believe you've been a... let's say a witness... to some remarkable events, and that you might have a certain amount of insight into a developing situation."

"I'm not sure what you mean," she replied.

He was a short guy, with pale blue eyes and greying hair. He wore a suit, but held himself straight, like a soldier. She estimated he must have been around fifty.

The man raised an eyebrow. "This can go two ways. The hard way and the easy way. You won't like the hard way, but the easy way might allow you to keep serving your country. You want that, right?"

Patronizing bastard, she thought. "Yes, sir," she said.

"Glad to hear it. So, the easy way or the hard way? Saying 'I don't know what you're talking about' automatically takes us down the hard way."

She sighed. "The easy way."

"Good choice." He opened the file. Instead of the expected reams of performance evaluations, a bunch of photos emerged. He flipped through them quickly and she saw that they were a combination of aerial drone shots and security camera pics. One of them was in color and looked like it had been shot with a cell phone.

They showed a woman with short dark hair doing various things: climbing out of a pickup truck and onto a barracks roof, aiming a sniper rifle at a distant target and even in hand-to-hand combat with a dinosaur.

"We know the guy next to that woman is a Russian Spetsnaz soldier named Max Alexeyev. He admits to having been there, and was part of the team that briefed our people about what happened, a couple of weeks after the event. The problem is that the woman in these pictures isn't one of the base personnel, and our facial recognition software thinks she's a Marine who shouldn't have been on that base." He gave her a hard look. "Is this you, Miss Viña?"

"Yes, sir."

The Colonel raised an eyebrow and sat back in his chair with an "oof," but the man in the suit seemed pleased.

"I need the whole story. For starters, is that your government-issue rifle?"

"Of course not," Melanie replied. "My rifle was here all the time, in the armory."

"Good. Were any of the weapons you used government-issued?"

"No."

"Good. That will make everything easier. Now tell me the story, from the beginning. Don't leave anything out, because it will come up later and anything we negotiate under false pretenses is null. Meaning if you lie to us now, we can still dump your butt in Leavenworth, even if we promise we won't. Colonel, you might want to step outside for a bit."

"Are you ordering me around on my own base?" the Colonel asked.

"Wouldn't dream of it. I'm authorized to conduct this debriefing in your presence if that's the way you prefer it. But there are some things it's better not to know, especially if Congress decides it wants to ask questions about why this woman wasn't summarily sent to federal prison. And if she cooperates, under certain conditions, I'm going to keep her out of prison."

The Colonel looked at Melanie and raised an eyebrow, as if to ask: 'How bad is this going to get?'

She looked down and mumbled. "You'd better go, sir."

He nodded and left.

"All right," the man replied. "The first thing you need to know is that you're no longer a member of the United States Marine Corps. What you are after we're done will depend on how useful I deem you to be."

"Judge, jury and executioner?" she asked.

"I don't execute people. I have specialists for that," the man replied. "Tell me your story."

"It started with the dinosaur attack on the mall in…"

***

"You're sure you got Sun-Lee?" he asked when she finished telling him about returning to the US after two days in Greece with Max.

"Absolutely."

The man sat in silence for several moments. A minute passed before he looked up at her. "All our intelligence suggests you're right about that. The Chinese are livid. They think the CIA sent an assassin after him."

"If they did, I didn't see him around."

That made the man chuckle. It was the first sign of anything but professionalism from him since she'd walked into the room. "Between you and me, I think they did… but they lost the trail in Ivory Coast." He pulled a final sheaf of papers out of the folder. "I don't have time for you to read this whole thing, but in essence, it says that if you repeat any of what you've told me to anyone outside certain sectors of the US government, you will be shot for treason. Sign here, here and initial here and here."

She signed without question.

"Good. Here are your discharge papers."

He handed her a DD214. She scanned it and found her name. Then… "Honorable?"

"We can't hire you otherwise," the man said. "My name is Stephens, by the way. I have a job offer for you. You will still be serving your country, but you'll be working on a less official basis. Your official position will be as Liaison between the Pentagon and the Lai Consortium."

"I read we weren't working with them."

Stephens grimaced. "That was the original plan, except it turns out Lai has become a bigger pain in the ass than we expected. So we're meeting him halfway. No funding, but we'll help with intelligence and coordination. Hence the Liaison position. Which is only part of what you'll really be doing."

"I can imagine. Snipers aren't great liaisons. When do I start?"

"I believe you have a big weekend planned. You can start after that." He handed her a business card with a Virginia address on it. "It's not far from here. Be there first thing Monday morning. No... not first thing. We don't work Marine hours. Get there at nine."

"I don't have a big weekend planned," she said. "I'm just going to see my niece and visit a grave."

He smiled enigmatically. "You never know what might turn up."

Then he got up and left, leaving her with the paper that had put an immediate end to a decade and a half of her life.

CHAPTER 21

Melanie knelt on the dark grass, as the skies wept gently. The tombstone was a marble marker, grey as the clouds above. It read

Cora Gimenez
Marine. Beloved Daughter. Much-Missed Friend
1981-2020
Semper Fi

"You should have a real grave," Melanie said. "Your body should be inside it. You shouldn't be decomposing in the belly of some sea monster somewhere. And your cross should be in Arlington, not out here in Nowhere, Ohio. You're a three-hour drive from the nearest airport, for God's sake. You. You never even wanted to take days off in town because you insisted the base was more civilized than any of the hick places we could go to.

"Crap. If you were here, you'd kick my ass for this. You'd know that I'm not actually worried about you—you're dead, right, how would you even know what I'm saying?—but actually feeling sorry for myself. You'd tell me to pull myself together. That Marines don't wallow, or something like that.

"Well, it's hard. I just came back from seeing Stephanie's scars. She looks like one of those surfers who got chomped by a great white. She'll have the marks for the rest of her life. When I saw them, all I could do was cry, thanking every power that the monster hadn't chomped off her hand or her foot. It could have done it, no problem. She was lucky it grabbed her by the torso and shook. Left a terrible serious scar, but her ribs saved her from worse.

"She seemed all right, I guess. Maybe a little more spooked and serious than the happy kid I remembered. But then that's natural, isn't it? I'd be spooked, too, if that had happened to me. Or maybe it's so natural I'm imagining it. Seeing stuff that isn't there.

"But, you know what? It made the whole thing seem worthwhile. Those marks, still a bit red and swollen, the marks of the stitches around the scars and everything, made me believe that I did the right thing in going after that bastard. I'm glad I did it. A man who can do something like that to little girls deserves to get a bullet between the eyes.

"They tell me we can't put the genie back in the bottle. The best they can do is offer me a job keeping things contained. And you know who's in charge? Your old friend Lai. I wish you could tell me about the guy. He seems completely obsessed with tearing up the monster industry. I wish I knew whether that was real or if he just wants a part of the defense budget. He's a business guy, after all. Profit is his only reason to live, right?"

She paused, remembering Cora's easy laugh, the casual profanity with which she would have dismissed a whiny rant like this one if they'd been in a barracks.

They weren't in a barracks, though. They were in a cemetery. The grave she was talking to was empty.

And she'd spent a plane ticket to come here.

Dumb? Possibly.

Unfortunately, Melanie knew she would never have closure without this little ritual.

"Man. You'd kick my ass if you saw me, wouldn't you? Talking to a piece of grass. Or maybe not. You always said I should do what I needed to move past things, to take the next step forward. Well, this is what I needed for that. Is it wrong? I don't think so."

She lowered her head. Emotions welled up, and tears threatened to spill from her eyes.

The weird thing about crying in the rain was that you couldn't tell if the water around your eyes was tears or precipitation. She wiped it away with the back of her hand and stood.

"Thank you. Again. It always seems to be you I tell these things to."

She was about to turn away, to head to her rental car and then to the airport. It was still 10 AM, but she had a long drive to Virginia.

She stopped midmotion. She suddenly realized that she would never come back here. This was her last visit to Cora's grave. The chapter of her life that contained Cora was coming to an end. She would carry her friend around in her memory and use her as an example… but she would never again talk to her directly.

This time, the tears were definitely hers.

Eventually, she turned away.

A man stood behind her. He was dressed in slacks and a button-down shirt, both soaked. He stood straight, with his hands respectfully at his sides.

His blond hair was matted down against his head and she immediately understood that he'd been there for some time but hadn't wanted to interrupt her. And he'd been far enough away that he wouldn't have heard a word she said. He'd done that on purpose, out of respect.

She walked right up to him and hugged him for a long time before stepping back and looking into the blue eyes.

"Two questions: how the hell did you know where to find me? And who was the irresponsible lunatic who approved a visa for you to enter the country?"

Max grinned at her.

"A man named Stephens told me you would probably be here. He said you had a plane into Columbus, and this was the only connection to Columbus you had. He was also the one who got me my visa. I'm a respectable citizen now, hadn't you heard? I work for Lai's consortium. My job is to coordinate with the US military."

"Isn't that a coincidence," she said. "I just got named Liaison."

"Stephens told me. He also told me he wouldn't let you work with me directly."

"Why not?"

Max grinned. "I can only assume he must have heard about Greece."

"That was just two days. I would never compromise my professional reputation for a guy I barely spent time with." She returned his grin, however. "And now the big question. What are you doing here?"

His grin widened. "I enjoyed my time in Greece and wanted to offer you an escort as you drive to your new job."

"And if I say no?"

"I'll have to hike back to the nearest town and figure out what to do from there. I let my Uber go as soon as I saw you were here."

She laughed. "You're kidding." She studied him. "You're not."

"Nope."

"Were you so confident I would say yes?"

"Nope."

She laughed again. "All right. I'll let you come. But if you offer to drive, you're hitchhiking back."

"Why wouldn't you let me drive?"

"You're from the same country as Irina," Melanie replied.

EPILOGUE

It was forty degrees in the shade. Sweat poured down his face, around the hat band as he sat at a table surrounded by jungle and waited for the woman to arrive with his drinks. The air felt like it would stick to his skin.

Philippe gloried in the sensation. After a year in the desert—spent mostly in air-conditioned labs and offices—his skin sucked up the moisture.

The woman, a rotund, middle-aged matron whose smile revealed sparkling white teeth, popped a sweating jug and a large pink plastic cup on the table. "Best pombé for monsieur," she said.

He tasted it. It was terrible, even by the extremely variable standards of Gabonese pombé. Astronauts could probably do better in a still on Mars. He smiled at her.

"This is wonderful," he said.

She hovered around his table, and Philippe smiled. He knew the ritual: any stranger was a source of entertainment in secluded African villages, a foreign visitor doubly so. And Sette Cama was tiny even by bush-community standards. The name meant seven beds... which might have been an exaggeration or an anachronism... but it didn't miss the reality by much. There were maybe twenty clapboard houses in the village.

"What kind of monkey is that?" she asked, nodding at Poupée, who was under strict instructions to pretend to be mute.

"This? It's a Gibraltar Ape," he lied, knowing that the internet access in this part of the world precluded her going off and googling it.

Poupée cocked her head at him. She still wasn't quite sure what to make of the concept of lying. Philippe preferred to keep it that way. He'd explain the situation later.

"And are you going to be here long?"

That, of course was the question she'd been waiting to ask. Would he be a source of entertainment for months to come, to be dissected deliciously at leisure, or was he a fleeting morsel who needed to be picked clean immediately? His response would define how she continued her interrogation.

"I'm thinking of exploring the Park. Do you know anyone who has a boat with sleeping accommodations? Something I can rent to explore the mangroves?"

"There's a man called Samo, out by the bay. He has a boat for the sea and a boat for the swamp."

"I'll go see him."

The woman moved off. He heard her bustling around inside her house as Poupée jumped onto the table and lowered her head into his cup.

He let her sniff and then watched as she reluctantly sipped.

She spat it out and he laughed.

"Why you drink this?" she asked, forgetting his instruction not to speak when people were near.

The woman was still in her house, some distance away, so he answered. "It reminds me of the last time I was here."

"When you created me... but before?"

Philippe nodded. "Not you. You are perfect. The one I made before... she was not perfect."

"Are you going to kill the old Poupée?"

That caught Philippe off guard. He hadn't come to Gabon with that particular purpose in mind. He'd come to Gabon to disappear, to lie low for a while in a country where he knew the rules and where some of the people knew him and remembered him fondly. This was a place that could work to his advantage. His years in the country would serve him well.

Besides, there truly was no need to hunt down his earlier failure. Rumors told him that the creature had run off into the interior of the country with her ally, a genetically modified dragon named Harold. Both had human genes and high intelligence, and they could be dangerous if one went after them on their own turf.

"Not immediately," he replied. "Even if we find her, I think I want to talk to her before we kill her. What do you think?"

Poupée said nothing. She just looked into his pombé, an expression of deep thought on her face.

He shuddered.

Then he shook his head. He was just letting his imagination run wild. It would be all right.

This version of Poupée was under control.

THE END

CHECK OUT OTHER GREAT DINOSAUR BOOKS

FLIPSIDE
by JAKE BIBLE

The year is 2046 and dinosaurs are real.

Time bubbles across the world, many as large as one hundred square miles, turn like clockwork, revealing prehistoric landscapes from the Cretaceous Period.

They reveal the Flipside.

Now, thirty years after the first Turn, the clockwork is breaking down as one of the world's powers has decided to exploit the phenomenon for their own gain, possibly destroying everything then and now in the process.

A MAN OUT OF TIME
by Christopher Laflan

Five years after the Chinese Axis detonated an unknown weapon of mass destruction off the southern coast of the United States, Special Ops Sergeant John Crider and the members of Shadow Company have finally captured what they all hope will lead to the end of the war. Unfortunately, the population within the United States is no longer sustainable. In an effort to stabilize the economy, the government enacts the Cryonics Act. One hundred years in suspended animation, all debt forgiven, and a chance at a less crowded future are too good to pass up for John and his young daughter.

Except not everything always goes as planned as Sergeant John Crider finds himself pitted against a land of prehistoric monsters genetically resurrected from the fossil record, murderous inhabitants, and a future he never wanted.

CHECK OUT OTHER GREAT DINOSAUR BOOKS

PRIMORDIA
by **Greig Beck**

Ben Cartwright, former soldier, home to mourn the loss of his father stumbles upon cryptic letters from the past between the author, Arthur Conan Doyle and his great, great grandfather who vanished while exploring the Amazon jungle in 1908.

Amazingly, these letters lead Ben to believe that his ancestor's expedition was the basis for Doyle's fantastical tale of a lost world inhabited by long extinct creatures. As Ben digs some more he finds clues to the whereabouts of a lost notebook that might contain a map to a place that is home to creatures that would rewrite everything known about history, biology and evolution.

But other parties now know about the notebook, and will do anything to obtain it. For Ben and his friends, it becomes a race against time and against ruthless rivals.

In the remotest corners of Venezuela, along winding river trails known only to lost tribes, and through near impenetrable jungle, Ben and his novice team find a forbidden place more terrifying and dangerous than anything they could ever have imagined.

PANGAEA EXILES
by **Jeff Brackett**

Tried and convicted for his crimes, Sean Barrow is sent into temporal exile—banished to a time so far before recorded history that there is no chance that he, or any other criminal sent back, has any chance of altering history.

Now Sean must find a way to survive more than 200 million years in the past, in a world populated by monstrous creatures that would rend him limb from limb if they got the chance. And that's just his fellow prisoners.

The dinosaurs are almost as bad.

CHECK OUT OTHER GREAT DINOSAUR BOOKS

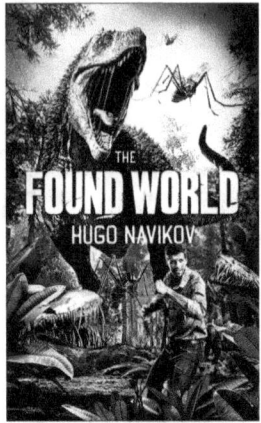

THE FOUND WORLD
by Hugo Navikov

A powerful global cabal wants adventurer Brett Russell to retrieve a superweapon stolen by the scientist who built it. To entice him to travel underneath one of the most dangerous volcanoes on Earth to find the scientist, this shadowy organization will pay him the only thing he cares about: information that will allow him to avenge his family's murder.

But before he can get paid, he and his team must enter an underground hellscape of killer plants, giant insects, terrifying dinosaurs, and an army of other predators never previously seen by man.

At the end of this journey awaits a revelation that could alter the fate of mankind ... if they can make it back from this horrifying found world.

HOUSE OF THE GODS
by Davide Mana

High above the steamy jungle of the Amazon basin, rise the flat plateaus known as the Tepui, the House of the Gods. Lost worlds of unknown beauty, a naturalistic wonder, each an ecology onto itself, shunned by the local tribes for centuries. The House of the Gods was not made for men.

But now, the crew and passengers of a small charter plane are about to find what was hidden for sixty million years.

Lost on an island in the clouds 10.000 feet above the jungle, surrounded by dinosaurs, hunted by mysterious mercenaries, the survivors of Sligo Air flight 001 will quickly learn the only rule of life on Earth: Extinction.

www.ingramcontent.com/pod-product-compliance
Lightning Source LLC
Chambersburg PA
CBHW071507170626
46811CB00007B/2764